CHAIN WORLD

QUANTUM ASSASSIN BOOK ONE

MATT
LANGLEY
PAUL
EBBS

AETHON
BOOKS

CHAIN WORLD

©2019 Matt Langley & Paul Ebbs

Print and eBook formatting, and cover design by Steve Beaulieu. Artwork provided by Maxim Kostin

Published by Aethon Books LLC. 2019

THE CREATION MYTH

Creation Myth

When the Gods created this universe, they built the anvil of creation upon which all species of this universe were forged. Some called it magic, but it was far from that. It was crafted, shaped, refined. It was constructed. The only magic lay in the fact that its creation lay beyond the understanding of smaller minds. That made it seem more wondrous than it was. But that was the way with such incredibly advanced technology.

When the God-King was happy with what he had made, he left creation to populate the new universe itself.

It was his way.

The energies this universe transmitted would go towards feeding him, his God-Queen, and his children for many millennia.

Satisfied, the Gods travelled to create another universe. And another. And another.

It was their way.

As is the way with beings of ultimate power, when you can create anything, when you can do anything, all that is left to you are petty jealousies, imagined slights and an immense and paranoid sense of betrayal.

The God-Queen became unhappy with the God-King. The reasons for this are lost.

They fought.

They parted.

The God-Queen wanted to kill the God-King—but it was a ludicrous notion. Gods can never die.

So, if you cannot kill your enemy, what can you do?

Well you could break something he loved.

The God-Queen could certainly do that...

PROLOGUE

"Forgive me Mother for I have sinned."

"How long has it been since your last confession?"

"Thirty-five thousand, four hundred and ninety-six years," he said. There were days and months in there, but he thought such accuracy was irrelevant.

"This is going to take some time, I assume?"

"I have much to confess," he agreed.

"Start at the beginning."

"Difficult."

"Start where you are comfortable starting then."

"Thank you. I'll start *before* the beginning."

The horse died before Shryke reached the line of clouds shrouding the top of the sacred peak.

There were better beginnings, and better endings. He felt no pity for the beast. It had served its purpose. Its death merely slowed him on his journey out beyond the links of Chainworld up to the Sun-Machine.

Shryke imagined his Familiar anxiously waiting for word of his success. He had sacrificed much to protect the Dreaming

Armies from the ravages of the God-Queen, but sacrifice and failure were different creatures. Shryke did not fail. It was not in his DNA. He imagined his Familiar with her head in her hands. It was as close to mourning him as she would come. She was practical. She would already be looking for someone else to carry out the mission she'd given to him, assuming failure on his part.

Shryke took a breath and reset the codespells in his mind.

The lines of code would mask his thoughts from all but the most savage enquiry. They were a thin defence, but his head was filled with thoughts that were too dangerous to think, so any trick he could employ was better than leaving himself open. That way lay death and madness. Or worse.

Shryke should have anticipated the horse's death; the animal had struggled with the unrelenting rise up through the mountain range. Even Shryke, a hardened veteran of the Thalladon Climbs, felt the hollow rasp beneath his breath that marked the onset of mountain sickness. It would be nothing short of a miracle if he made it all the way to journey's end: The Sky-Shrine.

The mere thought of the place caused a tingle in the codespells as they moved quickly to erase the image from his mind and suppressed any further thoughts of the mission.

The scrubland stretched all the way to the solid cloud line up ahead. Behind him lay the tan line of the trail cutting through the rocks and tangled undergrowth—a scar that ran all the way back down into the valley where the river, fat with autumn storm water rushed and sparkled in the smoky dusk.

There was too much cloud to see clearly an Overchain stretching across this section of mountain-halved sky.

The loopmoon was fast approaching, and with it wolves and mountain cats who would be drawn to his horse's carcass. Firstsun dropped below the far rim, meaning Shryke could look forward to five hours of Quarternight. The cloud line thickened as the temperature dropped.

Heaving his pack across his back, hanging a gourd from his thick leather belt, and holding his sheath of steels under his arm,

Shryke struck out for the cloud line, knowing there were five more miles of mountain ahead of him.

The forest was hidden in a permanent fog.

As the Firstsun waned the heat it provided chilled away quickly, the mist-shrouded forest became a cold place.

For the first half-hour he could still see his feet, dim shadows in the mist, working mindlessly like the clockwork automata he'd seen on hawker stalls in Saint Juffour, the walled town at the neck of Lake Tarsh. Willing the darkness away, he walked on, keeping a hand outstretched, to feel for the trunks of pines and other thick undergrowth.

He listened for any signs of predatory animals …or worse, tracking him, as the darkness descended around him. His ears were filled with his own muffled footfalls and the heavy silence of the fogged wood. He couldn't smell anything beyond the rank dampness of the air. Even the delicate aroma of endless pines was engulfed by the fog. But if Shryke couldn't smell so much as the rich resins and perfumed fronds of the trees then he had to believe the predators out there would have the same difficulties picking his scent out on the foul air. It was a small mercy.

Shryke stalked on in the damp darkness.

The temptation was to throw up a couple of the seedlights he carried in his kit, but they would betray his position to anything watching. So, better darkness.

His Familiar had briefed him in terms of what to expect: after a few miles the forest would thin out, and the he would break the cloud line. He was to find the stream, which when crossed at a narrow pinch-point, would lead to a track hidden by two levels of security magic that he would need to circumvent.

If he could have risked the use of magic, getting through the hidespells and other alarums would be relatively simple. Shryke had more than enough codespells of his own to side-step even the most elaborate defences, but the screaming vengeance that would befall him should he risk even the pettiest of his codespells made that choice suicidal. No, he would need all of guile and none of his magic to continue his journey.

Which was why the horse dying had fucked up everything.

It slowed him down.

He should have reached the pinch-point before Firstsundown. Instead he was going to have to find the path in the dark, without the aid of his codespells.

Shryke spat a curse as his luck drained away. He heard the howl in the near-distance. It could be a wolf, but it could equally be something considerably bigger.

The crunching of his feet in the damp brush had taken the guts out of the howl, but the beast was on him, a fat-pawed, snarling monstrosity crashed into him, lunging out of the dark. Its rank breath stank, making his eyes water as the gnashing jaws bit and tore at his protective synthskin armour.

Shryke fought desperately, forced to defend himself with his bare hands as he fell back. The beast snapped and snarled at his face. Instead of recoiling from those wicked-sharp teeth, Shryke went for them, thrusting his elbow between the jaws to rob them of their bite. With his other hand Shryke punched up into the animal's rib-cage, with such brutal strength behind the blow he felt the snap of bone on impact. The wolf howled and tried to withdraw, tearing at him with its front paws, but Shryke was not about to let the animal off so easily.

He curled his arm around its neck, prepared to deliver a vicious final snap as a voice in the darkness barked, "Hold!"

The wolf relaxed in Shryke's grip as the single word cut through the Quarternight. The word had power. It sizzled on the air. Shryke relinquished his hold on the animal through no conscious act of his own.

A myriad of seedlights floated before Shryke, coalescing into a ring of light around a woman. She wore the red habit of a nun and held a staff in gnarled hands. The wolf lay at her feet, licking at the fur above its broken ribs and eyed Shryke warily.

"Mother Superior?" Shryke asked, knowing it had to be.

She nodded, the seedlights keeping the fog at bay.

Her dark eyes glittered with long experience and acute intelligence.

"Shryke, I presume?"

He nodded, his codespells reeling. How could she know? Had she dug into his mind already from a distance? Was he exposed?

"We had word you were on your way," she said in answer to his unasked question.

Shryke faced the old woman. "I told no one."

"Words are not always spoken Warrior Shryke. Sometimes words find us by other routes. Shall we?"

And in that moment, he knew that he was vulnerable. He felt the emptiness around his mind but couldn't understand how his codespells had failed.

The Mother Superior offered a hissing signal and the wolf's ears pricked up. The animal looked at her, then loped off ahead into the fog and the dark.

The sphere of clarity and light moved with them as they walked.

Shryke wasn't about to give voice to his reason for travelling to the Sky-Shrine, and the Mother Superior seemed happy enough with the silence, so they walked on without unnecessary words.

The Order of the Sky-Shrine of Thalladon was not a silent order but such was their remoteness, living high up on the rimwall near a lonely cloudbridge that stretched the miles up to the Overchain, meant they did not see many visitors.

Shryke was almost certainly the first in a dozen years or more.

This Order's needs were humble, their devotions non-taxing and their lives simple.

There was a good argument to be made that the Order was mainly forgotten on this Link.

In many of the towns and villages between here and Port Rain there were few mentions of their existence let alone their magnificent spired eyrie in the clouds.

And that was as he needed it to be.

Very soon, the seedlights dispersed.

Shryke and the Mother Superior climbed higher, beyond the fogbound pines towards the thin stream curling amongst the rocks. The air was clear now but thin, and each breath bit with ever-increasing razor-sharpness into Shryke's lungs.

The Mother Superior, for all her years and seeming frailty, was fully acclimatized to this rarefied altitude. She moved easily as Shryke took step after stumbling step. His muscles burned. His ears sang. He was grateful that the Mother Superior's wolf hadn't waited to attack him. He would not have been able to fight it off. He wasn't even sure he could muster the strength to fight off the Mother Superior, never mind her hellish hound.

They crossed the stream.

The Mother Superior waved her hand to unlock the security spells hiding the track up to the Sky-Shrine and its attendant cloudbridge. It was a dizzying sight. He had reached the end of his journey.

"Please, Mother Superior," he said, struggling to catch his breath. "A moment."

The old woman looked at the tall, brown-muscled warrior, with his heaving chest and the raven, sweat-lank, hair plastered to his brick-like forehead and shook her head as though she was so incredibly disappointed by his all too human frailty. She curled her wrist and muttered an incantation.

Almost immediately, Shryke felt his lungs fill with cool, nourishing air.

He could breathe.

"All you had to do was ask," she muttered with a chuckle that rustled like ashes falling into a grave plot. She took pity then, taking his huge hand into her tiny, bird-like claw, with its cracked and yellowed nails. The skin stretched across the bones in dry whispered skeins of flesh. "Not far now. The shrine is but a mile along the track. Once there you can rest and eat. And when recovered, we can get down to finding out why you're really here…"

Shryke said nothing, but his codespells buzzed and sparked

behind his eyes, trying desperately to protect his thoughts from her invasion.

The Sky-Shrine of Thalladon rested upon the lip of mountain that hung out over nothing.

A two-mile drop into the valley from the rimwall made it look like it was floating in space. Black night enveloped it and the two vivid loopmoons arced through their otherwise empty horoscopes. Behind it, lit faintly by a third loopmoon, the cloud bridge curled up towards a smudge of Overchain, like a wisp of hair blown from a giant's forehead.

The first smears of Secondsun were unfurling on the horizon of the far rimwall and a cool breeze dried the last of Shryke's sweat sodden curls, as they made their way towards the edge of night and the impossible Shrine.

Even though he had seen the stone spires and gilded minarets of the Sky-Shrine once before, a churning sense of awe rushed through his veins, not unlike the first time he'd seen the Guild Nest on Pantonyle. Such were the manmade wonders of the Chainworlds.

Ivy coursed up the thick stone walls in a green tide. Windows shone with a yellow, welcoming, warming light. In the walled gardens below the battlements, Shryke saw novices, marked out by their yellow habits, marching from the iron-doored entrance, holding their hoes and shovels, ready to tend the vegetable beds. Shryke knew good loam-rich farm-magic when he saw it. The low levels of personal energy needed to maintain those tiny spells were easily recouped from the abundance they produced.

Shryke did not sense many Wielders behind the walls as they approached.

Almost certainly the sheer force of the Mother Superior's raw energies swamped the others, drowning them out.

But there were at least three Wielders amongst the order.

Shryke remembered them from before.

Perhaps they had persuaded more to join the Order in the interim? Regardless, the shrine wasn't awash with codeweavers. The Mother Superior's breath-salve was beginning to lose its vitality, but his lungs were adjusting to the altitude now.

Shryke allowed himself a wry smile as they walked through the shadowed portcullis into the courtyard beyond.

Secondsun reflected like white fire in the windows of the highest turrets.

Quarternight was firmly at an end.

Rested and fed, his trail-dirty clothes had been replaced by rough-hewn shirt and britches stitched, he assumed, out of a nun's habit. Dressed, Shryke made his way across the Secondsunlit courtyard to the Sacristy, where the Mother Superior waited to hear his confession.

He had his story prepared, and ringed in his head with two more codespells, doubling his mental defences for all the good it would do him. If he had been a religious man, he would have prayed that in doing so he hadn't betrayed himself to the Assassins, lighting up his location in the Quantum Aether.

He was not optimistic.

The sacristy was a hollow stone chamber with a large, clear-glassed window. Through it, he saw the whole, endless blue void of sky between rims.

The cloudbridge, a sharp and definite slice in the air, flew up towards and past Overchain on invisible ramparts. It cast a thin shadow through the sacristy window as the white Secondsun moved behind it.

The Mother Superior sat on a simple wooden pew near an even simpler altar, her head bowed as if in prayer.

The continual buzzing itch of the codespells occupied Shryke's attention as he reached the Mother Superior. She didn't look up but said: "Ah, Shryke, there you are at last. I trust you are refreshed?"

"Yes, Mother Superior. I am. Thank you."

"I sense your turmoil, Quantum Assassin." He did not deny it. "No one comes here when they are at peace. One like you, a soul with no need for God, or faith, one who has seen so much, but understood so little, needs to reach the very edge of their despairs to come to me for assistance."

Shryke felt the edges of his codespells begin to crumble.

He knew that before long he would have to return... if the Assassins didn't separate didn't separate his head from his body first.

"Tell me Shryke. Why are you here?"

Shryke fought the hollowness in his chest, the ache in his head and the sudden dryness of his mouth. "Forgive me Mother Superior, for I have sinned."

"How long since your last confession?" The cloudbridge shadow chose that moment to fall across the Mother Superior's face—or perhaps it was some other phenomena, Shryke could not be sure.

"Thirty-seven thousand, four hundred and ninety-six years," he said truthfully, even though his physical body was only nineteen summers old.

The Mother Superior's face was in deep darkness now. It shivered around her head. A cloud of flies on carrion. Her lips were a yellow rind around an infected wound of mouth. "This is going to take some time then?"

Her voice cracked like wet bones in fire.

"I have much to confess," the words struggled from Shryke's mouth. He tried to keep the trembling from his tone, but tears came unbidden from his eyes.

The Mother Superior reached a hand towards his chest. In the flickering dark surrounding her tiny body he could not tell if there was any skin at all left on it or if the cogs and gears beneath were exposed like bones for all to see.

"Start at the beginning," the thing that used to be the Mother Superior said.

"Difficult," he said. And it was. Oh, so difficult. Almost impossible.

"Start where you are comfortable starting then," the thin metallic joints of her fingers drilled easily through his sternum with little resistance, getting almost to the jagged-edged cubes of her wrist joints before he was able to answer.

"Thank you," he gasped. His words continued the charade played out between the twin pillars of *magic* and *murder*. "I'll start *before* the beginning."

The Mother Superior's fingers curled around Shryke's quivering heart. The gears and servos hissing and rasping, rasping and venting as she smiled a wound at him. Wet and slithering. Her eyes were alive with flies laying fat larvae in the folds of her lids. There was no skin. There was no woman here.

The codespells crumbled, the lines of code streaming away into the processors of the void, filling the universe with his soul. Because what was a soul if it was not mathematics, biochemistry and luminal energy?

There was nothing he could do.

This thing never had been the Mother Superior of the Sky-Shrine of Thalladon.

The God-Queen hissed and began to squeeze the lifeblood from of his heart and it was all he could do to die and die again.

And die again.

Again.

Death became him.

And he became death.

CHAPTER 1

The wood and rope bridge was slung between the two rock faces above a deep granite-splintered ravine.

The drop beneath was a mile if it were an inch, and the driving rain stinging through the ravine made the heaving, swinging slats of wood deathly dangerous.

Unhindered, Shryke might have covered it in seconds.

The girl, unconscious in his arms, a deep and ragged-lipped gash across her forehead, wasn't a heavy burden but she was limp and awkward, and carrying her was going to slow him down. The straps of his pack bit into his shoulders. The slanting rain hacked with savage gusts into his body; drenching the material and making it weigh on his bones.

Going back wasn't an option. The Raiders did not need to pick up his trail. They would know that the only way across the range of mountains was to cross at the Riven Bridge. The storm howled and boiled overhead. They were a good three hours from Quarternight and the cover of dark. Lances of lightning pierced the clouds. The boom of almost immediate thunder swelled all around them.

The bridge was his only option.

Unless he left the girl.

Which he couldn't do.

Shryke spat an oath.

Why could he never just walk on by?

He shook his head. He refused to regret of his humanity. It was not weakness. It was what made him who he was. He put his foot on the first slat of the bridge.

He wished that he could remember why he was here in the first place.

Galdar knew something was wrong the second she woke.

She rubbed her eyes to clear the sleep from them and wiped a hand across her mouth. The hollow where she'd slept the night was sheltered and still dry, but as she looked up into the sky, the barrelling thunderheads, doom grey, coalesced into an oncoming storm.

She heard hooves and voices.

The harsh, guttural dialects of Saint Juffour were not welcoming sounds. There was bitterness and anger in them. These were not the murmurings of prayers or the welcome sounds of the Congregation of the Moveable Church.

She was in trouble.

Galdar hugged herself and wished she hadn't argued with Carlow last night.

Hell, if only the pig-headed half-man hadn't laughed in her face when she suggested a slightly different interpretation of the Holy Text in verse 906 things might have been so different. She wished, too, that she'd not flushed with embarrassment as Carlow and the other Curates had laughed at the "silly girl with her silly girlish ideas." She wished that she hadn't punched Carlow or ruptured his nose in a rush of blood—but most of all she wished she hadn't run blindly from the camp, into the night, angry and tearful. That had been her worst sin. She had run so blindly, so recklessly, that she hadn't been able to find her way back to camp, through the dark rocks and ravines of the Thalladon Climbs even as she regretted running and the blow and all the rest of it.

Galdar had stumbled into the hollow at full dark, cold, sad and thirsty, determined, come first light, to find her way back to The Movable Church and apologise.

"Fool," she muttered, and she knew she wasn't just thinking of Carlow when she said it.

Galdar made the Firstsun prayer, working off memory to guess the rough location of the East Rim.

As she finished the whispered prayer, she picked a few grains of earth from between the rocks, popped them in her mouth and swallowed the gritty powder down without water to complete her Devotion of the Land.

Then she leaned against the rock and listened again for the voices.

The wind whipped up, the distant storm making its way towards the range, and bringing a rough blanket of clouds with it.

The distant rumble of thunder forced Galdar to make a silent Prayer of the Air. If she listened below the wind, she could just make out the voices but no actual words.

The slang of Saint Juffour was difficult to penetrate at the best of times, but these were no native speakers. They were the defectors and the banished, the robbers and the criminals, the embezzlers, spies and the rapists who had escaped capture. In other words, Raiders of the western Thalladon Climbs. Dirty fighters. Murderers, land pirates and cutthroats. Lawless and itinerant, Raiders roamed the lands stealing and agitating for the highest bidders, or for the hell of it. They scavenged the land of the Climbs and beyond. They were the scourge of the Third Link.

Although sheltered, the hollow where she took refuge got plenty of First and Secondsun. Lichen and mosses stained its surfaces, making a decent enough mattress for Galdar to sleep on, but was close enough she felt trapped. There was single path in and out of her hiding place; if she just stayed put maybe the Raiders would pass her by? Anyone walking past would be able to see her if they happened to look up, and the hollow meant there was no escape.

Better to run, she thought, knowing that to run first she had to crawl.

Galdar crept along the south face of the hollow.

There were five Raiders.

Short and stocky, their black leather armour filthy.

Five helms, rusty and stained, rested in a pile near their unsaddled horses. The animals tugged at rough grasses with yellow teeth.

The Raiders had their backs to Galdar's hollow.

It was a blessing for which she immediately thanked The God of Safehome.

Galdar was about to turn, intending to make her way across to the other face of the hollow and slip away, when the chilling scream stopped her dead.

She couldn't help herself.

She had to look.

Between the ring of five men, she could just make out a small thin figure lying in the dirt.

One of the Raiders stepped away intent to retrieve something from his pack, and as her view cleared Galdar saw who was screaming. A boy. He was young, considerably younger than Galdar. Perhaps ten or twelve. He was dressed in a simple goat-pelt jerkin. He was terrified. One of the Raider's knelt, pressing a knife at the boy's throat. The point dug in with a broken smile, drawing a small prick of blood which swelled around the blade. It would take nothing to force it all the way in and end his screams.

The Raider said something to him that was whipped away on the wind.

The boy cried, his body convulsing, and for a moment she thought he had been butchered, then she heard the Raider's questions:

"Where is your *skelling* farm boy? Is there *buldous* grain? Are there *hunfery* women?" And knew the man wouldn't waste his words on a corpse.

The boy, even if he knew the answers to their questions, was too terrified to speak. Fresh tears squeezed from the corners of his eyes; they were lashed from his cheeks in the killing wind.

Another Raider lifted an axe in preparation to dispatch the petrified child.

She couldn't help herself.

She should have stayed silent.

But she couldn't. Silence was murder. Plain and simple.

"No!"

It almost didn't feel like Galdar's voice.

It was though someone else spoke for her. Someone else took control of her limbs, forcing her to scramble out from the safety of the hollow and run headlong at the Raiders.

Every sinew in her body was screaming for her to run the *other* way, but she wasn't in control of her body. The God of Safehome wouldn't allow the boy to be murdered like this, and she was his divine instrument. It was His courage coursing through her now. All she could hope to do was take the killing blow for the boy and give him the chance to run.

The fight lasted two seconds and was no fight at all.

Galdar crashed into one of the Raiders, spinning as she stumbled into the boy, whose screams had turned into a low sobbing.

The Raider Galdar had bounced off reached down, his breath as foul as his grizzled face. As he came close to Galdar, dazed as she was, she was sure she could see things moving around in the crusts clinging to his beard. But that wasn't the most frightening thing about the Raider; that was the glint of lust in his rheumy, bloodshot eyes. He smiled a mouth full of ruin and yellow spit. "Well, what do we have here then?"

The Raider reached for Galdar's throat.

She recoiled instinctively.

"Don't touch me! I am a Follower of the God of Safehome!"

The other Raiders laughed at her, their mocking laugher every bit as vile as Carlow's. He hooked his index finger into the neck-line of Galdar's linen cotte. He leaned in for a look at the flesh he'd exposed.

"You have three seconds to save your own life."

The Raider's face was confused.

The voice didn't belong to the woman at his feet, or the boy.

"Two."

All five Raiders stiffened and stood, reaching for the black-steel weapons at their sides as the voice mocked, "You should have run. Boy, go."

The boy next to Galdar did not need telling twice; he scrambled to his feet and ran.

"Girl. Run."

The Raiders moved instinctively into battle formation. The nearest Raider, the one with the fell interest in Galdar, was their lead, his sword point wavered in her face.

"You move, girl, and you die," he rasped at Galdar. His eyes were fixed on whoever was behind her.

Two storms hit. One storm with a fizz of lightning across the sky, the boom of thunder almost above their heads, and the lash of wild rain. The other storm was presaged by a boot in Galdar's back that sent her sprawling forward, slicing her forehead open on the Raider's blade. She'd been kicked so hard she crunched into his chest, her loose and whirling elbow smashing out two more of the fool's rotten teeth. He wouldn't need them where he was going.

Galdar fell hard, smashing her bloodied head against a rock.

The blissful silence of unconsciousness descended like the shroud of night.

It felt like death.

Shryke killed all five men without mercy.

His blade slick with blood and rain worked its magic. He had given them a chance. They should have run. Instead they died. The Quantum Assassin was beyond anything they could stand against. Stabbing and slicing, the tall warrior felled all five with ruthless efficiency. It took five strokes to open their bodies to the rain and expose their secret innards to the lightning.

He didn't linger. He had no time.

He knelt to tend to the girl, checking the open wound on her forehead, the drumming of hooves announcing the arrival of fifty more Raider's horses as they crested the rise on the plateau above him.

He couldn't leave the girl.

With her cradled in his arms, the assassin ran through the sheeting rain, surefooted as he drove himself on, up, up, up, only thinking to escape, and that meant reaching the Riven Bridge. If he could reach it first and cut the crossing behind him, they would live. But survival depended on getting there first.

As he ran, he heard the shrill shouts of the war-party and knew they had found their slaughtered kin.

They raged.

They howled.

They spurred their horses into wild chase up the mountain.

Shryke ran on, his long legs moving fast and true, the girl's head bouncing bloodily in the crook of his arm.

The third slat of the Riven Bridge was slippier than the first.

The soles of Shryke's leather boots slipped more than once, making his stomach lurch, as the mile-deep drop into the ravine swung beneath him. The confusion was only exacerbated by his presence in the Thalladon Climbs. He had no recollection of making the journey, or how he came to be carrying an unconscious woman in his arms.

The girl stirred.

Waking up over the drop wasn't ideal but knocking her out again wasn't much better.

"There he is!" The shout came from behind, too close for comfort.

Shryke risked a glance back.

A dozen Raiders scrambling up the Climbs on foot. They were maybe thirty yards from the first steps of the Riven Bridge.

Shryke cursed. He had no choice but to risk everything and run. Slat after slat skidded beneath his feet. The rain swirled and gusted. The bridge lurched wildly, and then a second shout,

"There he is!"

Only this time it came from up ahead. He made out five more Raiders scrambling down the ridge at the far end of the bridge, black steel drawn, fifty-crowns worth of murder in their eyes. He didn't have a prayer. But he wasn't a religious soul.

Shryke stopped.

The only sound above the wild swirl of wind and the rush of the driving rain was his own ragged breathing. The rain streamed down his body. His hair lashed his face. He was the eye of the storm. The heart.

He couldn't go back.

He couldn't go forward.

So, with no choice, Shryke did the only thing he could. He pitched the girl over the side, shrugged out of his pack and threw himself over the rope barrier behind her, welcoming the mile-long fall to the rocks below.

CHAPTER 2

Barl dragged the barrel of beer through the corn.

Bringing the first beer of the day was an honour he didn't feel like he'd earned.

The sky was a bowl of blue, the sun a hot hand caressing his back and shoulders as he approached the circle. He heard men laughing. Women singing. Above it all, he heard his father, Garn, bellowing orders to the gangs of men as they toiled, raising the festival tents.

Garn was a powerful man in all the ways that mattered and respected by his people. As Headman's son, Barl knew well the pride that came with being at the centre of all things. He belonged. He was tall for his age—eleven summers—and wiry, with a keen eye and a sharp tongue. He was unlike the others, too, in that he had a wanderer's soul. His gaze was always fixed on the horizon, looking into the far distance and the limitless upward curve of *God's Heart* imagining the adventure it promised.

The barrel stuck fast in a plough-line. Barl pulled several times on the fraying cord to free it from the sucking mud. It was too heavy for him to carry on his shoulder, and already tapped, it was impossible to simply roll it out to the circle without destroying the brewer's tap. So, the fat-bellied keg had been placed on a small sled, the runners of which mostly slid easily over the harrows in the field.

Mostly.

With a crunch and a skitter of small stones, both sled and barrel came free.

Now, the workers in the field were downing tools. The women were stopping their songs, and Garn, big, wide, glorious Garn was beckoning Barl over with a grin that spoke of love, pride and satisfaction.

Garn had already prepared a trestle and easily lifted the barrel onto it, breaking the wax seal on the tap with his thumb and holding the first flagon beneath the amber stream.

Barl watched with fascination as the flagon filled with foamy liquid, and a thirsty crew of men and womenfolk lined up behind his father, each with their own leather cup or pewter flagon.

Garn's pint drawn, he raised his hand. "Before we drink my fellows, I wish to give first sup to my own son, Barl, who has made a fine job of bringing sustenance to us this day!"

Among the half-raised tents, and the quarter-constructed stalls, the line of workers raised a cheer as Garn placed his flagon against Barl's lips.

Barl had never tasted beer before, but the smell of it was inviting and the foam popped pleasingly against his nose as he dipped forward to drink.

Unfortunately, that was where the fun stopped.

The first rush of bitter liquid across his tongue caused him to retch almost immediately. His eyes bulged and his stomach heaved. His flailing hands pushed the flagon away from his mouth and he fell back, retching up not only this morning's breakfast, but—or so it felt—every breakfast he'd ever eaten, in a long stream of bile and watery food.

It wasn't until he'd stopped puking his guts up that Barl was able to look up at his father and realised many of the village workers were chuckling at his predicament. Barl sank down heavily on the crushed stalks and looked up at his father with wounded eyes.

Garn smiled and reached down for the boy, pulling him up smoothly and settling him on his wide and welcoming shoulder.

"I am sorry, father. I have shamed you."

"Nonsense boy," Garn boomed with amusement. "You could never shame me. Everyone's first taste of beer is a rite of passage. It's an acquired taste and let's just say that some, like our master brewer, acquire it quicker than others."

"Were you sick, father? The first time?"

Garn shook his head. "No, boy, I was not, but believe me, I feel sick when I see the workings with numbers and words you learn every day with Shaj. I can forgive you a little queasiness, if you can forgive mine!"

"Of course, father."

Garn squeezed the boy's shoulder, then set him down on the table of one of the half-completed festival stalls. "I trust this will be the only time either of us has to forgive the other."

"I do too," Barl said with all seriousness, and Garn was off again, laughing fit to shake the whole of *God's Heart*.

Festival night began with a torch procession along a narrow pathway that had been cleared through the corn. From inside it looked endless as it curved all the way back to the village.

Villagers walked arm in arm. Some carried instruments, others dragged more beer kegs through the night. Barl walked with his parents, Shaj and Garn. He grinned sheepishly as Garn promised water was being transported as well as ale. Earnestly, the lad swore he would never drink again, first swallow from a keg or last. He was done with the stuff. That earned an even broader grin from his old man.

Up ahead, the villagers formed a circle, each holding a torch in one hand, their arms linking through the elbows of the person next to them. The guttering torches transformed the circle into the ceremonial heart of the village, and as Headman it was Garn's privilege to get the festivities underway. His father loved this time of year more than any other. So many of his duties included sadness, like only last week when he'd been forced to preside over the funeral of one of his oldest friends. Nights like this, where everyone came together in joy, were a delight.

Barl looked beyond the circle at the stalls set with so many challenges and games just waiting to be played. Barkers were ready at each one, eager to entice the villagers into trying their luck and parting with their coin.

The canvas tent in the centre of the flattened corn circle was already alive with the grunts of wrestlers psyching themselves up for their bouts. Barl heard the slapping of flesh and the stamping of feet. What happened in that tent was as much a dance as the arm-in-arm twirls and swirls to the music that happened outside the tent.

A second wide oval had been stamped flat in the field, large enough to allow for the horse and dog races that, as far as Barl was concerned, were the high point of the festival. He'd spent too much of the year begging and pestering his parents to buy him a dog from one of the trainers who travelled through the village, bartering them for lodging, food and beer. The promise was always the same, "Maybe next year, son. When you're a little older and can look after the mutt yourself." The thing about next year was it never came.

Garn stepped into the centre of the circle, raising his own torch high. The light danced shadows across his face. "I am a simple man," he said, earning a hoot of laugher from someone nearer the back. His grin spread. "I enjoy simple pleasures. The land, the air," he found a familiar face in the crowd. "Even you, Hojek…" which was greeted by uproarious laughter from everyone apart from Hojek, Garn's younger brother, who just shook his head and called back, "It would be my honour to beat you in the ring later, old man."

"Maybe you'll get lucky this year," Garn chuckled. It was a ritual. Everyone loved the back-and-forth of the brothers. "Believe me, friends, when I promise you this: it is the simple things which are the best things. The *Song*, The *Story* and The *Game*." There were nods around the ring. "Who doesn't enjoy the thrill of competition, the honour of the victory when hard won? Who hasn't drawn on the sadness of defeat to spur them on through the next challenge? I know I have."

"You'd think you'd be used to losing by now, old man," Hojek chimed in, much to the amusement of the others.

"It is this struggle, this glorious struggle, which sets us apart from the beasts of *God's Heart*, brother. It's these games which make us richer...not in terms of coin, but if anyone wants to wager on my win against Hojek later, I'll give you ten to one... Make that twenty. I'm feeling good this year."

Another cheer went up as Hojek ripped off his shirt with a yell of triumph and cast it at his brother's feet in challenge. "Get on with it, man, there's people here who'll die of age before we get to the fighting at this rate," Hojek mocked.

Barl clapped and cheered and hooted along with everyone else, beer sickness completely forgotten. He looked to the dark horizon. The sheer upward curve of *God's Heart* arching away and up into the night was an awe-inspiring sight. It was impossible to believe something so fundamental to life could have been imagined never mind constructed by mere mortals. It was proof of divinity if ever there was proof to be found. The Shadewalls were across the suns now, producing the night they were about to enjoy. The Shadewalls were more than regulators to divide day from night, when coupled to their nearness or distance to the endless surface they created and controlled the seasons. Nothing would grow in the fields without them, and likewise no animals would flourish.

God had thought of everything inside his *Heart*.

Barl's people along with the billion other tribes who lived their lives on the inner surface of this boundless sphere were happy, settled, and above all, safe.

"Let the games begin!" Garn bellowed, and the villagers responded with their most raucous cheer yet.

This was the very stuff of life and a life worth living, at that. Barl's heart swelled with love, for his father, for his clan, for his home, for the arch above them, and the trampled corn beneath them. Such was the joy in his soul he could have climbed the miles of the arch to the keystone and floated safely back down on it. He could only imagine what it must be like to stand in front of the torchbearers, their Headman, leading them with wisdom and love.

Gran stripped off his shirt and clasped forearms with his smiling brother. Both men lit in torchlight, their eyes alive to the moment and the thrill of the wrestling bout to come.

Barl was half way across the circle when the first scream came.

In that first half-second it was easy to mistake it for a caw, the shriek of savage fighting birds, but Barl recognised the screamer.

It was Shaj.

He turned as his mother screamed again.

This time there was no mistaking the sheer terror driving it.

Barl ran towards his mother—or tried to. His feet wouldn't work. He wasn't moving. A chill rush of wind swarmed all around him. He felt the rapid frost burn across his skin, which made no sense. It was the height of summer. There was barely a breeze.

But before he could isolate the cause of the sudden cold burn, more people screamed. Once voice rose above them all. Garn yelling, "Noooooooooooooo…"

Silence sliced through the yell, cutting it dead.

Barl didn't understand.

The world had been robbed of sound.

All around him there was nothing beyond the emptiness where it should have been. And it was truly deafening.

He looked down and tried to make sense of what he saw: the

ground beneath his feet—the trodden down stalks of corn and scuffed dirt—had hinged away onto a freezing blackness filled with a billion diamond points of light. It was as though he stared into the very core of *God's Heart* and the sucking void where the long dead deity had rotted away to nothing.

Barl fell.

It was gradual—sickeningly so—a collapse down through the hole in the world, and even as he clawed out desperately trying to find anything to hold onto, he could only fall faster, his mother and father's faces sick with terror as they silently screamed his name.

Barl spun and flailed and fell, ice forming on his skin, eyes frozen in their sockets as his ears filled with the desperate drum of his last heartbeat as it froze solidly in his chest.

CHAPTER 3

The Riven Bridge lurched alarmingly as the Raiders ran across it, several instinctively moving to follow Shryke even as their fifty-crowns fell into the grey rain clouds glutted between the peaks below them.

Shryke, in free-fall, back first, arms spread-eagled, savoured their rage as he, the pack and the girl, were swallowed by the rain.

The feeling in his guts, that hollowness, that chill shiver, wasn't unfamiliar but he would never get used to it, no matter how many times in his endless life he fell.

The drop from the Riven Bridge was by far the highest drop he had thrown himself from.

Shryke stole a glance at the girl beside him, falling headfirst, like a rag doll, limp and unconscious as the winds buffeted and bullied her. It was a blessing that he didn't have to calm her. He needed all his wits to concentrate saving them both.

The jagged edges of the granite slopes rushed, vague dark-nesses barely visible through the mist of rain. Below, now less than half a mile down, boulders and broken rock formations waited to crush Shryke and the girl into blood and bone.

There was barely enough time to perform the incantation before they reached the ground, but that little technicality was the least of his worries. Using the codespell magic would be a terrible drain on his physical powers, but he could live with that. What he didn't know if he would get to 'live with' was what happened when the ripples the codespell sent out into the Quantum Aether reached the Guild Assassins. Every trigger had its own signature, and that would burn brightly across the Aether for anyone with the ability to see, pinpointing him, not just where but when. And that was considerably worse than being shattered on the rocks below.

Shryke was not ready to die. Not today, at least.

He closed his eyes. He drew one, two, three calming breaths, slowing his pulse, and stilling the blood in his veins as his heart froze within the icy hand of a deity he had long ceased to believe in. Because there was nothing magic in the world. Nothing.

Shryke prepared to walk upon The Plain.

Smoke. Fire. The screams of the damned.

Shryke stood on a rocky promontory above the battle. The Dreaming Armies of the Plain met once more in the eternal clash of the forever battle. The crucible of war boiled beneath him. The conflict had begun before time, and it would continue long after time ceased to matter. Blood ran thick as a silted river beneath the combatant's feet. Carcasses rotted. The stench of death, the burning of flesh and the screams of the souls being extinguished battered Shryke's senses in a brutal barrage of stimuli.

He stumbled forward a single step, then dropped down on one knee. He needed his hand to steady himself against the heaving ground.

The red and black of the battle reflected cruelly in his eyes.

He took a deep, acrid breath from the corrupt air. He had no choice but to descend into the maelstrom of eternal war.

Shryke drew his sword. He felt nothing. Not the thrill of the blade's hunger for fresh souls, not the ache of emptiness that the end promised. None of it. He was disconnected. Distanced despite the fact he was wading into the heat of the battle's rage. All around him things that might once have been human hacked at things that might evolve into humanity if they survived long enough—faces streaked with spit and blood, skin slathered with a black-rain which fell mercilessly from swollen skies all around them. The clash of steel, the soft hiss of metal separating flesh from bone. The rush of bodies plunging recklessly through the blood and mud, and everywhere the dank stink of sweat.

Battle beasts looming over the throng, huge furies in the air slamming down and ripping a trail of heads from lines of combatants. Dragons wheeled in the grey air overhead, burning and scorching through the dead and dying, their huge black wings flapping slowly through the ragged plumes of smoke.

Shryke waded into the thick of it, knowing his doom waited in this world, as it had in the last and would in the next if he made it that far. The sickness of the free-fall still clenched in his guts, his body remembering what should have been its death as he plunged from the Riven Bridge. In both worlds, he knew he was rushing willingly to his death. But here, that death would damn him in this world and rescue him in the other. That was the secret nature of this place.

Black armoured Wraiths, their jaws just slack bones hanging over hollow throats, came at Shryke from all sides, howling. He took the first blow on the flat of the blade and rolled it away from his body with ease. The Wraiths offered no thought behind their assaults; they were mindless. Shryke took seconds to turn the blades of the second and third on their wielders, and seconds more to cleave jawbones and skulls, ending the threat. He moved forward, hacking at bone-legs, disarticulating spines and scything open the bone cages that once upon a time had been living bodies as though nothing could touch him. He moved with ruthless efficiency through the fringes of the battle, pausing momentarily before a blasted mound of bones that climbed steeply up to a bleak, battle swept platform of skulls and ribs that towered over him. The bone mound was surrounded by a moat of blood.

Shryke waded into the cold, iron-red liquid.

Clots and coagulations floated around his legs. The stuff of life clung to his armour like leeches. His feet slipped and slid over unknown things beneath the surface—things he did not want to imagine—as he forced himself to wade on deeper into the blood until it was waist deep.

Through the worst of it, Shryke began to rise, climbing up the lower skirt of the bone mound while the conflagration of battle raged all around. He ignored the screams, the roars and rage, the weapons clashing, and the dying being done. His focus was on the bone hill, and what he knew he would find at the summit.

A snarling cat-beast, hide tiger-striped and protected by rusting armour, leapt at him from its place of concealment between two immense bone cairns, dislodging a crushed skull that skittered down over tibias and fibulas and other bones. Shryke didn't flinch. His breathing didn't so much as quicken. He merely reacted and a heartbeat later a viscous line of blood ran down his forearm, the beast dispatched with a strike through the heart. The cat's claws lost purchase on the bone slope and the dead beast rolled down the slope into the blood moat, where it sank below the surface.

Shryke walked on.

He closed his eyes, savouring a single heartbeat's dislocation, and in that moment, he was still falling from the Riven Bridge, the woman at his side, the pack slipping out of his grasp.

"*Raaaaaaaaaaaaaaaaaaahhhhhhh!*" The shriek tore through the moment, bringing him back to the endless battle. A Fornian Warrior of the Seventh Legion leapt upon that heartbeat of dislocation and hacked at Shryke with its wicked double-headed axe. The blade, each wing of the iron butterfly bigger than his head, slammed into Shryke's breastplate, splitting through treated leather like the carapace of a bug. The axe head dug deep into his sternum with a sudden shock of pain. It blossomed black agonies within Shryke's chest, blood, muscle and bone tearing apart as if they were his soul rather than his meat.

Shryke grabbed at the thick leather-wrapped haft of the axe, making it impossible for the Fornian to yank it free from the gaping cavity at his heart, and with his free hand severed the enemy's throat with one fierce slash of his blade. The creature fell away, axe forgotten as he clawed desperately at his neck, trying to stem the flow of blood with his fingers.

Shryke cared nothing for the Fornian's death. He trudged on, pulling the axe from his chest and throwing it aside. He ignored the blood and exposed bone. He would heal. He always did.

Unless he died on the rocks in that other place.

Vultures and crows circled in a cloud of slow feathers on lazy wings.

He followed them, trusting that they would lead him to where he needed to be.

Shryke crested the bone rise. The whole battle was laid out before him, but now it was so much nearer and more immediate. The tang of blood sprays from vicious and unrelenting hand-to-hand combat turned flesh into the flimsy fabric of war banners, lashing about in the fierce winds. The moans and screams of death became a vibrating symphony of horror and of despair that swarmed his senses.

Shryke closed his eyes again.

The ground was almost upon him.

The girl and the pack would hit the rocks first, the impact exploding their flesh in the silence between the last heartbeat he'd ever feel and the first heartbeat he'd never experience as Shryke was unmade.

"Shryke?"

A sliver of ice far colder than the free-fall ran through Shryke's body in response to hearing his name.

He opened his eyes.

He stared at the bloated belly of an armoured gargantuan.

He looked up, and up and up.

The armour was stained and rusted with blood and seemed to go on forever.

He had to retreat a step to see the whole creature.

"Shryke?" she boomed again, hefting an enormous axe that was easily the size—and weight—of Shryke's body from mailed fist to mailed fist.

Shryke knelt at the huge figure's steel-plated feet, "I come looking for power my Familiar."

"Do you now?"

"I have a spell to cast but lack the energy to shape it."

"You are dying?" The double-headed axe, ragged-edged from the eternal battle, still glinted between the stains. Shryke felt the glints against his eyes like physical manifestations of light. He ignored them and nodded.

"I am moments from death," he admitted, his mouth parched. Death was close. "I have walked here, across the fields of endless warfare, to offer myself to you. I will use the powers exchanged to save myself and one other."

She looked down on him. "You are aware of the risk? Of who will see?"

"I am."

"And still you would make such a powerful casting?"

"I am not ready to die. Will you feed me?"

The huge helm bowed in a single nod. She raised the axe high into the blood red sky as Shryke knelt and made his peace with his conscience.

The axe came down.

Shryke opened his eyes.

Rain fell across his face, blurring his vision as all around him the storm continued to rage. High above him, the Riven Bridge was drawn like an eyelash from the lid of the dead god's eye.

Shryke sat up, every bone in his body hurting. His right arm was crusted with scabs from the cat-beast's attack. His chest burned with the slow-healing wound from the Fornian's axe. But he was alive, and had settled on the rocks at Ravine's base, as if he'd just laid down there the night before to sleep.

The girl beside him murmured in her unconsciousness, bliss-fully ignorant of the miracle that kept her alive. Her hand brushed at the now healed but livid scar on her forehead. To his other side, the pack lay precisely where Shryke would have put it if he'd left it there himself.

Shryke took one breath and savoured the moment's stillness as he prepared to meet the screaming death rushing towards him through the Quantum Aether.

Death came at him then, dressed in Assassin's blacks, with a face constructed entirely from the determination to prosecute a righteous execution.

CHAPTER 4

B arl awoke in blackness.
Not the ordinary night-time dark of the Shadewalls as they moved across the Suns burning at the centre of *God's Heart*, but blackness as an absolute. Blackness as the absence of light. The cold bit bone-deep. Every breath burned in his lungs. On his hands and knees, Barl reached out desperately, trying to feel *anything*. He was on some sort of flat, polished-smooth surface that stretched on beyond his reach.

He didn't dare move.

Not at first.

The darkness was utterly disorientating.

His heart thumped in his chest, quickening with anxiety as he remembered how his heart had seized in his chest as he fell through the yawning hole that had opened beneath him, and with the recollection came the memory of ice forming across every inch of his skin.

The memory was tactile.

What else did he remember?

Think.

Think…

There was something. An image. He tried to focus on it. Bring it back. What had he seen? A hinged section of corn and soil spilling into darkness from the inner silvery skin of *God's Heart*, those grains of dirt shimmering in the reflected light of a million pinpricks of light?

Had he really seen inside *God's Heart*?

The sense of awe at seeing inside *God's Heart* for the first time swept through him again in a rush of wonder and fear.

Barl swallowed. His throat burned raw. He had to swallow again, and when he did, he started a fit of coughing that hawked up saliva and phlegm. An incredible thirst took root. He managed one word:

"Hello?"

Barl's voice was dead in the space. No echo or reverberation, but there was an undeniable sense of vastness that engulfed the word. This place was bigger than any room he'd ever imagined.

"Where am I?"

Nothing.

"What is this place?"

The blackness itself wasn't scary. At least not at first. Barl wasn't afraid of the dark, not like some of the kids in the village who still believed imaginary creatures lived in the dark.

The sharp thought of his father's despairing face, at the pain and sadness where there should have been fear, brought tears to Barl's eyes. He hadn't called out like a child for his father to save him. He had been strong. But it was hard to stay strong in the darkness.

Barl rubbed his eyes as much to clear the memory as to wipe away the tears. He wasn't going to learn anything by sitting in the darkness waiting for something to happen *to* him.

He got to his feet.

Barl clenched his fists. He steadied himself against the heaving thumps of his heartbeat which felt so much more intense than they had before the organ had frozen. He mustered all his strength of will and determination and took a step, then another. Edging forward he reached out like a blind man, feeling for a wall. He needed something to give him an idea about his surroundings.

But there was *nothing*.

He didn't want to think about what that meant.

He concentrated on what had become his reality. No walls, no change in the level of the ground as he continued to shuffle in what he hoped was a straight line. Forward, always forward. All he could hear was the beating in his chest and the scuff of his boots against whatever the ground beneath his feet.

Barl walked on, no sense of time. It could have been hours. It could just as easily have been minutes. One foot in front of the other. His heart calmed eventually. The only sounds he heard, his footfalls.

He stopped.

Looked around, trying to divine any kind of detail in the blackness.

It was a formless void.

Time stood still here.

He walked on, now it could have been an hour or a day.

He couldn't see any part of his body, and his mind began to whisper that he had ceased to be. This was death. He had left his body. He was a soul wandering in the eternal dark, inventing the sound of footsteps and the beats of his heart as a familiar trick to pretend he was still alive.

Barl pinched the back of his hand.

It hurt.

But did it?

Was he inventing that feeling too, simply because it was meant to hurt?

He had no way of knowing. Not for sure.

He began to feel uncomfortable with the possibility that he was nothing, a cloud of thoughts travelling in a nowhere place, thinking nothing things.

Barl imagined himself shrinking into a point in the air, maybe just one of a billion points in the deadened atmosphere, like one of those grains of soil he'd seen pinprick bright. And imagined a billion other boys like him who were nothing more than a collection of thoughts in a cloud of other clouds.

Barl had to stop walking then.

His imagined heart was threatening to burst out of his made-up chest.

He might be an idea floating through a blackened dream, but he'd succeeded in terrifying himself to the point of paralysis.

"*Where am I?*" he screamed at the void.

"You can travel," the darkness replied.

The voice, a female voice, seemed to come from all around him. It was at once distant and right up close, whispering in his ear so intimately, surely he felt her breath on the nape of his neck? Barl clawed at the blackness either side of his head, expecting his fingers to find flesh.

But there was no one.

He spun on the spot, reaching out now, fingers clawing, hoping somehow to snag whoever had spoken.

Nothing.

No one.

"Who are you?"

"You can *travel*." That wasn't an answer. It made no sense.

"I don't know what you mean! Please! I just want to go home."

"It's not within my gift to do that, but in time perhaps you will be able to achieve the great distance needed to go home."

"Great distance…" the words hit him like hammers. "Please… I… don't know not what to call you… Please, tell me, how far am I from my home?"

"As far as it is possible to be."

The sobs wracked his thin frame. Barl fell to his knees, the rush of fear enveloping him in a crashing wave. It washed through him. He was flotsam on the tide, curled and drowned. His breath stuck in his throat as if his lungs were filled with water and then…

Barl really *was* drowning.

Suddenly he was beneath water. Still in the blackness, but *underwater.*

Barl could swim, he'd been to the nearby coast with his father in *God's Heart* many times to catch fish and boil water for salt. He'd enjoyed swimming in the gentle waves and the deep blue waters that ran onto the wide white beaches of the estuary. But this was nothing like that. He was deep beneath any waves; water was thick in his throat and his lungs were bursting.

He looked up and saw sparkling through a glitter of wavelets a tiny light. It hung in blackness, so it wasn't a faraway sun… *unless this place had no Shadewalls to produce night.* The impossible thought came unbidden.

Barl put his arms to his side and kicked up for all he was worth.

The light grew brighter fast, and immediately felt nearer, spurring him on.

The pain in his chest was immense. Crushing. But the light was so near, he kicked on and on and on until…

He burst through the surface with a roar, taking a shatteringly deep yet wholly restoring breath from the cold air. The light was a round, yellow-lit ball that didn't seem to shine with its own light, but rather reflected a light from a more distant source.

Barl's back bumped into something solid and cold.

Something floating on the water behind him.

He twisted around in the dark water to see what he had come up against.

It was a small black hulled skiff, big enough for perhaps three or four adults. There was a woman, tall and beautiful, in a black robe that was secured at her throat with a silver chain rowing the small boat. She reached an ebony-skinned hand down to him.

Barl hesitated, but what else could he do but take her hand?

It was warm.

The woman smiled.

"See?" she told him. "You travelled."

He felt the codespell end and his essence flood back into his system.

It was something.

A change in the balance of the fight, though not enough to unmake all the mistakes he had made thus far. Surely?

Sensing the sudden surge of power in her enemy, the Assassin retreated a cautious step. The ground betrayed her. She stumbled. Only half a step, but it was enough. It was her first mistake in the combat. She didn't trust herself. In her place he would have gone in for the kill. He needed to make it her undoing, with or without his sword.

The Assassin took a moment to catch her breath and to transmit a vampiric smile through the black pools of her eyes. The smile died on that masked face as Shryke pulled a fist-sized lump of granite from a crevice by his feet and hurled it with all his might. She instinctively brought her hands up to shield her face. It was instinct. And it was that instinct Shryke had counted on.

As the rock crunched into her wrist, he heard the satisfying crack of a bone taking the full impact and breaking.

The sword fell from her hand. There was nothing she could do to stop it.

The Assassin stood, holding her broken hand to her side.

Shryke rose up.

There were no more suitably sized boulders nearby for him to use as impromptu weapons, and the Assassin still held the dagger, so she was far from helpless. She was trained by the Guild Masters. She was every bit as lethal with the small blade as with the sword, and quite capable of hitting the mark if she threw it. It wouldn't matter which way he hurled his body, the black blade would fly easily to pierce his heart or skull, offering whichever death she preferred.

The Assassin moved the knife around in her practiced fingers.

Holding the blade, she lifted it ready to let fly.

There was nothing Shryke could do.

There was no cover. No chance to escape.

He was dead.

So, he tried the only thing he could think of to disarm her. "Will you give me kneeler's privilege?" Shryke asked. They were the first words he had spoken to the Assassin and he had no right to ask, and less to expect her to say yes.

The woman took a moment to consider and then nodded her Red Guild Star. Resigned, Shryke fell to his knees. If he was going to die, he was going to do it at peace with himself and his deeds.

He looked up, ripped open his jerkin and exposed the breast above his heart— sternum raw and livid from the healing Plains-wound.

There wasn't even a chance of retreating inside his head for Magic. More dream-wounds inflicted on the Quantum Aether would kill him as effectively as the Assassin's blade. And the ripple such a tactic would send out across the Quantum Aether would only serve to draw yet more black-clad killers intent on ending his existence.

"Make your peace," the Assassin said. "You fought with honour and pride. And no little skill, Shryke. Go into the long night with my respect."

"Thank you," Shryke bowed his head.

He waited for the blow that never came.

He waited. And waited.

Until, frustrated at being played for a fool, he said, "There's no honour in this kind of pisstake, woman, just be done with it, I'm ready."

But she wasn't.

The Assassin fell face first hitting the ground hard. Shryke's sword was buried almost to the hilt. It went deep into her spine and then out through her heart.

Galdar stood frozen.

Her face was a mask of shock and regret.

She looked down at her hands as if they'd betrayed her.

And in so many ways they had.

There were dots of blood spattered up the bare skin to her forearms. The blood wasn't hers. It came from the wound in the back of the dead woman. Galdar took a step back in the rain, watching the speckles of red mix with the rain, sluicing away from her skin in rivulets turned pink.

Her foot slipped, not because the ground was dangerous or uneven, but because the strength drained from her legs and that single act of violence. She collapsed, looking from her hands to the body skewered on the sword and then back to her hands as a hollow of regret opened in her heart. Her eyes filled with tears made invisible by the rain.

What would Yane think of her when she made her confession?

How would the other members of the Movable Church treat her after this heinous transgression of Safehome doctrine?

She had committed murder.

Her soul was forever tainted.

She didn't even know the man who had saved her from the Raiders, but she had killed for him.

How had she become this person?

She looked up from her hands to see him watching her across the corpse.

The man got to his feet, blood was running from the open slice in the back of his hand where the tendons had been exposed, and the raw wound across his chest which looked barely healed. It would need treating if his life wasn't to bleed away. As though reading her mind, the man put his hand under his arm to apply pressure to the wound and walked to the body.

The body of the woman Galdar had… *murdered*.

She'd come around, not sure where she was or how she was even alive to see her saviour fighting for his life. Her forehead hurt, but the wound she remembered receiving from the Raider's sword point was already scar tissue. How long had she been unconscious? Surely not *that* long?

The fight was vicious. The pair went at each other with brutal ferocity. Two souls raised in war, determined to injure, maim and then kill the other.

And then the woman raised the dagger to throw at her saviour, and Galdar acted without thought.

She got up, retrieved the man's sword from where it had fallen between the cracks in the rock while the man asked for the kneeler's privilege and did the only thing she could: she rushed at the Assassin's back and plunged the sword between the bones.

There were no screams.

The woman stood rooted to the spot, transfixed by the blade emerging from her chest, and then collapsed. She didn't hold her hands out to break her fall. She hit the ground face first, blood radiating rapidly from around the steel like the petals of a deadly flower.

The man approached the dead woman.

He knelt by her side and began unwinding the turban from her head—not to get a look at her face, he was far more pragmatic than that. When he had a length of the black material, he held the end of it in his mouth and reaching for the woman's fallen dagger, cut the material. And used it to bandage his wounded hand.

Galdar could see just how much pain this caused him. But she didn't move to help him. He watched her the whole time. His eyes didn't waver. Not once. Finally, he said, "Help me." He held the short length of bandage up from his hand and nodded towards it. "I can't tie it off myself."

Galdar nodded and came over to kneel beside him.

The Assassin's unmasking revealed a face of white death. Her eyes were still open. There was a froth of blood on her lips. She had done this, the hollowness in Galdar's stomach spread, guilt taking its toll.

The man held the bandage out to her.

"Split the end and tie it off with a knot. Quickly. We don't have the luxury of time. The Raiders will be on us very soon if they realise we survived. Sooner maybe."

Galdar did what she was told with the bandage as she spoke, "Survived? Survived what?"

The man tested the tightness of the bandage and seemed satisfied with her work. He looked up. Galdar followed his eyes up, up, and up to the Riven Bridge a mile above them, just visible in the clouds.

"How did we get down from there?"

"A good question, but one for another time. We must get away from here, now."

He rolled the dead Assassin onto her stomach and drew the black-steel blade out of her corpse. He kissed the blade and sheathed it with his others, before taking up his pack. He began to lead them out of the ravine without waiting to see if Galdar was following.

Galdar's head was clouded with shame and confusion.

What is it about this man?

He hadn't even offered his name, and yet she followed him blindly?

"Who are you?" she called forward as they reached the treeline.

There was a path that would lead them down into the fertile valley, but the man was deliberately moving away from it. It took her a second to realise why: it would be the first place the Raiders would look for them.

"I have had many names, but you can call me Shryke. It's the one I use now."

Galdar waited for him to ask hers, but there was no curiosity about the man.

"I am Galdar," she said. "Curate of the Church of Safehome."

"Short names are best."

"No, what I meant— "

Shryke, looked around, his grin broad and his eyes smiling.

The same feeling she'd felt when Carlow had laughed at her welled anger and hot embarrassment.

"You're a very serious girl, aren't you?"

"I am not a girl. I am a woman."

"My apologies," Shryke smiled again. A look not dissimilar from the one she'd seen in the eyes of the Raider played across Shryke's face. Galdar balled her fist, ready to lash out. What was happening to her? Violence wasn't the way of her Order. It wasn't her way. Or it hadn't been. First busting Carlow's nose, then attacking the Raiders before they killed the boy, and *killing* someone!

She felt completely out of control.

Shryke stopped and looked at her.

The amusement draining immediately from his face. "What troubles you girl?"

"Stop calling me girl! You're not much more than a *boy* yourself!" Her voice echoed through the trees and off the valley walls.

Shryke sighed and held up a finger to silence her, which only served to infuriate her all the more, but she fell silent. They listened. For a moment nothing beyond the usual sounds of the forest, but then…

A *crash.*

Then the neigh of a horse and a thunderous beat of hooves echoed all around.

"Well done," Shryke rasped. "Well done indeed…*woman.*"

The hoof beats clattered as they struck rocks. The jangle of weapons and spurs came next and then one voice shouting: "I will have my fifty *skelling* crowns. Mark me!" And Five Raiders, on horseback, burst through the trees, weapons drawn, and bore down on Galdar and Shryke like the minions of death itself.

CHAPTER 6

B arl lay on the timbered deck of the skiff looking up at the woman in black.

His hair was plastered down by seawater that dripped stingingly into his eyes. Out of the water, he could see that there was a definition to the sky that he wasn't used to in *God's Heart*.

The white light appeared to be a ball of rock, with a rocky, uneven, surface that hung far away, set on a velvet sky that had been scattered with tiny gemstones. Whorls of them drifted and collected into patterns, gulfs and spirals. It was the most beautiful thing he'd ever seen.

Until the woman shook back her cowl, revealing her face for the first time and he reassessed his understanding of beauty in that moment.

Barl had never seen someone so *perfect*.

Even his Mother, Shaj, who was lauded as a beauty among his people was almost ugly beside her.

The woman's features radiated nobility and serenity.

Her skin shone darkly, her hair braided in curls and whorls that were more than a match for diamonded sky's perfection. But, when it came, it was her smile that took Barl's breath away. It was like being brushed with a warming summer breeze. It spoke of good harvest, full bellies and happy life. It was the smile of a God.

"Who... are you?" Barl managed.

"I have a thousand names," the woman kindly. "But you may call me Summer."

It was if she had been reading his exact thoughts about her. If all the best things about the summer could be poured into one body, it be *hers*. Barl immediately felt calm and safe.

He sat up.

Summer knelt and dried him with her cloak, and within moments, he was warm and dry, as if the cloak had drawn the seawater from his garments then released it onto the air around them.

Summer sat beside Barl on the deck, putting her arm around his thin shoulders and drawing him close.

"Better?" She asked.

Barl nodded. He didn't know whether to look at the sky or up at her in the hopes that Summer might smile again so he could wallow in the wonder of it.

"Where are we?"

"Where you travelled to."

"I don't understand."

"You travelled."

"You keep saying that like it should mean something to me, but it doesn't. I don't understand any of this. Why is it happening to me? What is it that's happening to me? Why?" He had so many questions.

"How is not yet important, the time for that will come. All you need to know at this point in time is that you travelled, and I followed."

"Why?"

"It is my duty to follow you in these early days. If you are like the others, it is possible you will travel more times before you settle. I was exactly the same."

Her words made no sense to Barl, not as words, but there was a feeling behind them, a sense that eventually all would be well, that was overwhelming. He rested his head against her shoulder as if it were the most natural thing to do. As if he had been doing it all his short life.

His life.

His life in *God's Heart*, with his parents. His family his friends.

The memories crashed back like waves in a storm and he felt as lost and scared as he had ever done. It was too much.

"It will take time, Barl," she assured him, her gaze focussed on the dark sky. "But the joy is that we have all the time in the universe." Summer reached behind her back to pick something up. It took him a moment to realise it was a pewter tankard, almost identical to his father's.

It was as though she had drawn it from out of Barl's memories and offered it now as a gift that might somehow make him feel at home wherever he was now.

"I understand this is something prized by your people?"

Barl took one sniff of the liquid in the tankard, recognised the hoppy aroma and without needing so much as a mouthful this time gagged and vomited over the side of the skiff.

Barl wiped the back of his hand across his mouth. The stuff was drying with the salt on his lips. He looked earnestly at Summer and said: "I want to go home, please."

Summer sighed. "If only it were that simple, kid."

"You brought me here. Take me back."

"You aren't listening to me, Barl. I didn't bring you anywhere. *You* travelled here. It was all *you*."

He shook his head. "It wasn't. I didn't open a trapdoor in my world. I didn't leap out into *nothing* so my heart froze. I thought I was dead!"

"Ah, well yes. I did do that. But, believe me, kid, you were never in any danger, though I do understand it can be scary the first time it happens. But you will get used to it."

"I won't," Barl said, and stood up, compensating for the gentle swell of the waves rocking the skiff. "Because I'm going home." Barl refused to be drawn in by Summer's smile. There was something magical about it. It wasn't merely a smile... it was more of a tool. An enchantment she used to calm him, to sway his thoughts and make him forget his fears. Right now, Barl didn't want to be calm, he wanted to be home. He wanted a normal life that began and ended with his village, his friends, and most importantly of all, his family.

"I want to go home!" Barl snarled in her face.

Summer didn't flinch from his anger or try to pacify him. She got to her feet, towering over Barl, and raised her cowl to hide her ebony skinned face. "That is not going to happen, Barl. We have much to do, you and me. And none of it involves going back there."

Barl felt bereft without Summer's face to comfort him. In that moment it felt as though he had lost the most precious thing that he...

NO.

It was another trick, another enchantment or tool, some sort of mechanism to lull him. He was already wise to the effect it was having on him. He wouldn't succumb to it. Not now, not ever. Barl reached over the side of the skiff and splashed cooling seawater on his face, set his jaw, balled his fists, turned. He didn't know what he was going to do next. He didn't allow himself to think about it. He just ran, screaming his pure hatred at Summer.

And because he didn't know, Summer couldn't anticipate or expect the explosion of fist and feet that he battered her with. She fell back on the decking, Barl landed on her, windmilling his arms, his fists pummelling Summer's too-beautiful face trying to unmake that unnatural perfection.

Within one tenth of a second, Barl's fist was punching bare wood, the impact scraping the skin of his knuckles raw.

He looked around wildly.

Summer had moved impossibly from beneath him. She stood

over him now, shaking her head. "Stop this stupidity, boy," she barked.

She reached down and then threw the still punching Barl over the side of the skiff into the water.

The shock of the cold stilled him; he clamped his mouth shut and began to let himself drop through the water.

If she wasn't going to let him go home, then he wouldn't stay here. He would rather drown...

Before the cold could really grip his lungs Barl was rolling onto his back, on the deck, water crashing around him as if he and half of the sea had been gathered up from the depths and dumped unceremoniously in the skiff.

He lay there, coughing his guts up as the water ran away across the deck and drained back out into the sea through the scuppers.

Summer stood over him, exactly where she stood before. "Barl. I'm telling you to stop this."

Barl roared and launched himself yet again at Summer. It was futile. His arms and head sliced through empty air—and before he could catch his balance a blinding burst of light and heat hit him. It felt as though he had been hurled into the heart of a roaring inferno...

As he hit the ground, he rolled across sand; it stuck to his wet body in patches where the seawater persisted.

Sunlight burned the sight from Barl's eyes. He could barely squint, the sudden brightness painful as the night was banished in favour of an endless vibrant turquoise. He pushed himself up onto his hands and knees. The sun-baked sand burned immediately into his palms. He rocked back as though stung, staring at the red welts on his palms in disbelief. It wasn't more than three seconds before the heat of the dune where he'd fallen began to radiate intensely through the knees of his trousers.

With a yell of pain and frustration, Barl got to his feet, trying to make sense of everything. He had no idea where he was, how he'd got here or how the sea could suddenly dry up, replaced by burning sands, or how night could turn into day in the space of a heartbeat, or anything else that was happening to him.

Mercifully, the thick soles of his best boots protected his feet from the blistering sand.

Looking up, he saw that there were three suns in the sky. They ran in a line to the horizon. One was red and swollen. It didn't hurt to stare at it. Indeed, he thought he could see the livid, boiling disc seething with black spots and great arches of fire. The other two suns were hot bright lenses of white, impossible to focus on.

Barl scanned the horizons. In every direction, sand. Nothing but rolling dunes, frozen waves on an endless silent sea of orange and dust. He turned. It was the same in every direction, nothing but sand from horizon to horizon and in the greeny-blue sharpness of the sky nothing to look at but the suns. Not a cloud. Not a bird. Nothing.

Barl had never felt more alone in his life.

"Summer?" Barl shouted, his voice carrying for miles on the wind. Not really knowing how he thought she could hear him, or if he even wanted her to. She was the only point of familiarity in this hot and hellish place, assuming she came back to find him, but even if she did, he had to face the truth: she wasn't taking him home.

Barl felt like crying, but realised in this heat, he couldn't waste the tears.

If he didn't find water soon, he would die.

Barl was being squeezed between the crushing plates of the sand and the suns.

His body felt like it was seizing up in the heat.

Each step was an agony, each breath a stinging, cooking blast in his lungs.

Even though his eyes were open, he dreamed of water.

Even the salt-water of the night ocean where he'd stupidly tried to attack Summer would be preferable to this deathly heat.

His thin body trembled.

His back seared.

The sand his feet scuffed up as he walked stung at his hands at face.

He walked away from the three suns.

He tried to pull his shirt up over his head to protect it, but that only succeeded in exposing his back to the searing triple heat from the sky. As much as he dreamed of water, he dreaded the feel of his skin reddening, cooking and turning to crackling like the skin of a pig on a spit. The world was dunes all the way to the horizon.

A horizon that didn't gently curve up into a solid wall as it did in *God's Heart*.

It was proof, more than anything else, that he was walking in a different world.

You have travelled.

Her words came back to him.

Barl walked on.

He didn't know where he was going, or even why, only that it was imperative he kept on moving because to stand still meant dying here.

Barl fell to his knees.

Got up.

Stumbled down again.

Hour after listless hour trailing through fine sand, the end was approaching, and he knew it.

Perhaps if he just lay down here, closed his eyes, he might be able to remember home?

Perhaps if he curled into a ball, drawing his knees up to his chest and clasping them tightly in his arms he could imagine the flattened corn of the Festival venue? He could almost remember the stalls and the wrestling tents and the bright banners and snapping pennons.

Perhaps if he concentrated really hard, as his small, inconsequential life ebbed away into the sand, he could see his parents again?

Their faces smiling down at him, tending to him in this fever. Mopping his forehead with a cool cloth, dripping chill water into his mouth, putting a balm on his cracking lips, mother sitting on the edge of his bed where he was curled, stroking his hair and singing him lullabies. Perhaps...

Barl opened his eyes.

The corridor was dimly lit and made of metal.

The shock of the cool air in his lungs had Barl clutching at his chest as pain crawled up inside him. He fell onto his knees, gagging and retching up the last of the desert heat from his lungs.

He knelt there, head down, unmoving.

How was he supposed to deal with this?

Was this just a dream?

Or more likely a nightmare?

Was he going to wake up in his room back in the village drenched in sweat, trembling with fear? Wanting the night-light back?

"It's no dream, Barl," Summer told him.

Barl lifted his head to see that she was leaning against the metal wall of the corridor, picking at her nails with the edge of a small knife. She was no longer in her cowl and cloak. She was still dressed in black, and in the dim corridor, it was difficult to see where the material of her clothes ended, and her ebony skin began. She was dressed in a way more appropriate to the conditions, a blouse trimmed with fur at the collar and wrists.

Barl got up, hugging himself as the chill set in.

The air in the corridor tasted stale and used.

There were other aromas, unfamiliar, metallic, and in the distance the dim roar of a huge and mighty furnace, burning all the trees of creation to generate power.

"You can see inside my head," Barl said. It wasn't a question. He'd felt the not so delicate probing of Summer's mind pushing away at the fringes of his thoughts. He resisted the temptation to ask how.

Summer nodded. "Not always, but sometimes. When you are uncertain or scared you open up like a flower and I can reach right inside."

The very idea that someone could do that, look deep inside him, made Barl feel even more vulnerable.

"Once you've learned a few coding-spells of your own you'll be able to resist it, but as I'm the one who'll be teaching you the codespells, for now, well, I'm afraid that I'll peek inside you whenever I want, but at least I'm being honest about it."

He tried to push the thought from his mind. "Where are we?"

Summer looked around. "You've been a devil to keep up with. I only found you in the desert a moment before you went again. Luckily, I caught your ripple very quickly and rode the wave through the Quantum Aether to this place."

"I have no idea what you're talking about."

"Let me put it at its most basic: you travelled. I followed."

Barl knew that there was no point in using the anger he felt rising in him to attack Summer. It was pointless. She was too powerful. Too fast.

"But perhaps we can use our heads, take a look out of the window and see if it gives us an idea?" Summer pushed a blinking light on the corridor wall that came on has her hand reached it. With a hiss and clank the whole wall split in two, grinding open on rusted hinges.

Behind the wall was an impossibility: a huge silver ball, hanging in blackness.

It was difficult to get a sense of his true size from here, but Barl felt it in his guts that the ball was *enormous*.

"What is that?" he asked, knowing the answer before Summer answered.

"You call it *God's Heart*. That's your home."

CHAPTER 7

Shryke pushed Galdar hard, drawing his sword at the same time.

She clattered into a tree-trunk and slumped, dazed, to the ground, but not without realising Shryke had just saved her life.

Again.

Five horses, their mounted Raiders brandishing javelins and crossbows charged towards them. The tree, which a heartbeat before she'd been standing in front of, trembled beneath the impact of crossbow bolts.

Metal *sang*.

Two horses dropped almost immediately. Shryke thudded to his knees and struck out with his steel. The Raiders, unseated from the animals, hit the ground hard.

Shryke was over them in a second, gutting both with cruel strikes.

Even as another bolt hissed through the air, aimed squarely at Shryke's spine, he moved. It wasn't some wild roll or desperate lung for safety. He simply moved, just a side-step, which took him out of the bolt's trajectory. As the missile flew wide of the mark and disappeared into the undergrowth, Shryke took a dagger from one of the lifeless Raiders, and cast it underarm, with grim accuracy into the throat of another. The dying Raider rocked back-

wards in the saddle, and as his horse bolted, still hung in his stirrups, being dragged as the animal burst through the trees, every
twist and kick smashing the Raider's body sickeningly against
trunks.

Corpse, she amended.

"You should ride away," her saviour said, calmly. He wasn't
even out of breath despite his injuries and everything they had
been through.

"Should we now?" one of the last two surviving Raiders
mocked. "There are forty more of us in these mountains and only
one of you. You aren't walking away from this."

"Besides," his companion said, "I want my fifty coin."

"And if I offered you sixty to ride away and forget you saw
us?" Shryke asked.

"Where would be the sport in that?"

"I'm trying to give you a chance here," Shryke said. She
couldn't understand why he was wasting his breath trying to
reason with these killers. "Not that you deserve one. If you are in
such a hurry to die, let's get on with the killing, shall we?" The
lead Raider kicked his mount forward, levelling his lance on
Shryke's bulk.

Smiling coldly, Shryke threw down his sword, and waited as
the great horse's hooves clattered across the ground. He breathed
deeply, centring himself, then closed his eyes.

She couldn't believe what she was seeing.

He inclined his head slightly to the left, like he was listening to
the charge, and then, at the last possible moment, his hands
moved lightning-fast to grab the point of the Raider's lance,
though it could surely only be inches from impaling him and
thrust it back towards the Raider's chest, using the rider's
forward momentum to lift him clear of his saddle and into the
path of the second rider. The screams as the man was impaled on
his companion's lance were wretched. Shryke cut them short with
a single short slash of black metal. As the Raider fell away, the last
of them dropped his weapon and raised his hands, as though to

make peace. "You don't need to do this. I can just ride away," the Raider said, looking down at his friend's blood on his hands.

Shryke shrugged. "That would have been best for everyone," he said.

"I can still do it," the Raider nodded as though seeing the light.

"I don't think so," Shryke said. "I'm tired of walking. I want your horse."

"Take it," the Raider said. "It's yours. I don't mind walking."

"The problem is, I don't trust you to just walk away. I think you're the kind of craven soul that would get some stupid idea in their heads about avenging their friends, and then you'd do something even more stupid, and try and come for me."

"I wouldn't, I swear," the Raider said. As last words went, they weren't the most profound. He held the hilt of the dagger that buried itself in his throat, his mouth chewing blood as it gurgled out over his lips and spilled down his tunic.

Shryke didn't waste time watching him die, he caught hold of the swinging bridle of the dead man's mount, then helped him out of the saddle. He stepped over the Raider as he hit the floor and deftly snagged the bridle of his companion's horse, and brought the skittish animals to a standstill, whispering in their ears and stroking their mains as if what had happened was nothing more than the natural order of things.

Perhaps in Shryke's world it is natural, Galdar thought as she got to her feet. *But not mine.*

"Can you ride?" Shryke asked as she looked about, a little lost.

Galdar nodded.

"Good," he handed her the reins of one of the two animals and helped boost her up into the saddle as if she weighed nothing.

Getting on to the other horse, Shryke kicked on and led Galdar away through the trees at a gallop.

They rode for three hours before Shryke allowed them to rest.

He didn't look back over his shoulder once.

It was deep into Halfnight, a chilly breeze coming down off the Climbs.

The storm had long since passed, but the ground was still sodden underfoot and there was no chance it was drying before Firstsun.

Galdar had wanted to speak to Shryke, wanted to speak to *anyone* really, about the turmoil raging inside her. She was struggling to cope with the emotions killing that man, but more, the guilt that came with not being able to carry out her regular devotions to the God of Safehome was chewing her up.

But the words wouldn't come.

As a diligent curate, she'd made sure throughout the Congregation's quest for Safehome, whatever the privations or the situation, that she'd been able to Pray and Take Dirt. It was the most sacred of their ritual beliefs. But this headlong flight had made it impossible to do anything but run. She needed to try to explain, try to make amends and ultimately seek some sort of forgiveness for taking a life. She needed to be heard.

Shryke seemed to kill so *easily*. The act itself didn't touch him. There was no shame, no pain. She couldn't help but look at him and wonder if the man was hollow? That was what they called empty souls; Hollow Men. She couldn't understand how he could live with himself. But he had saved her, and for that Galdar resolved to put Shryke front and centre in her prayers—when she finally rested long enough to say them.

Shryke slowed his animal and jumped down from his horse. In the weak loopmoonlight, he indicated for her to do the same.

He took his pack down, including the javelin and crossbow he'd acquired from the dead Raiders, and the gourds they used for nourishment, he slapped both horses on the rump, sending them running into the night.

Galdar was confused.

Shryke hunkered down, back against a tree. Seeing her confusion, he said, "Too easy for them to track us on the horses. They manufacture heavy quantities of spore. And they're more likely to keep on hunting us if they think we stole their beasts. We're better on foot from here on. Once we've made it through the valley to the river, we can find a boat to take us downstream and on to Saint Juffour."

Galdar shook her head. "I have to return to my people... our Quest for Safehome..."

Shryke closed his eyes. "No. And before you go getting all self-righteous and holy, every time you speak without thinking you risk bringing those scum down upon us." She started to object, but he silenced her. "This isn't up for debate, *woman*. I need you to think before you speak, but better yet, say nothing, because we are a long way from being safe. Words travel. You understand? They betray us."

Galdar bit back on her curse she wanted to spit, and just nodded.

Shryke's black eyes bored into her.

Looking at him now, he couldn't have been more than a year or two older than she was, despite the way he spoke, but those eyes told a different story. They were the eyes of a man who had seen more than a lifetime's worth of pain.

"This Quest...what is it?"

She appreciated him moving the conversation to safer ground. She felt comfortable talking about her religion and devotions, "I am a curate in the Congregation of the Movable Church. Our scriptures tell us that somewhere on one of the sixteen links of Chainworld, God was born. That place is called Safehome. When we find it, we will make our new lives there. The Moveable Church will no longer have to move."

"How long have you been looking?" This was a question Galdar was used to, so many times she had heard it asked over the years from people they had met along the way—the questioners sometimes earnest, sometime sarcastic—she couldn't tell which flavour Shryke was, but was there a glimmer of mirth in his eye? "It's not the length of the quest; it's the quality of the destination," Galdar said, setting her chin defiantly against ridicule.

"How long?"

"One thousand eight hundred and forty-six years."

"Across how many links of Chainworld?"

"Five, not counting this link."

Shryke nodded, smiled to himself, but said nothing, letting the silence squeeze against Galdar's temper. She trembled but did not rise to the bait. She was determined to keep her anger in check and to act like the devout soul she professed to be. "Shall I gather some firewood?" she asked, instead.

Shryke looked at her in the same way you might pity a dying dog.

"No. It's night. The light and smoke would only draw unwanted attention."

She nodded. She should have known that. She wasn't a stupid woman. But this man... he unnerved her.

"This quest of yours that has been going on for nearly two thousand years, were you born on it?"

"Yes of course. I'm not a recruit. I'm First Family."

"Help me understand something, after so long, why have you not found the birthplace of the God of Safehome? Don't you fear that after all this it might not be there to be found?"

It was a common enough argument. She'd had it with the lots of people their quest met across the Links. "There's no time limit on faith, Shryke. We have the Oracle's Prophesy. It tells us that as the Chosen we will find his birthplace, somewhere in the Sixteen Links. In the last five hundred years we have surveyed three Links in the Chain. This Quest will take many generations to complete. We knew that when we first embarked upon it. Faith is not repaid with immediate gratification; it is repaid with the knowledge that keeping faith is the reward within itself."

"Which is all well and good, but that doesn't answer my question, does it? I asked what do *you* think?"

"That is what *I* think."

Shryke snorted again, "Do you know what you sound like? You sound like the victim of indoctrination," he said before she could answer him- "But you've known no other life, so of course you buy into it. Why wouldn't you? It's not like you can think for yourself or anything."

"I pity you," she said.

Shryke looked down, "As I you."

"Tell me which direction to go in at Firstsun."

"You're serious?"

"Yes. I need to return to the Congregation."

"Why?"

"It is my life."

"And the journey back there will almost certainly rob you of it."

"That's a risk I am prepared to take...so tell me, which direction? You'll be better off without me. We both know that I'm only going to slow you down."

"I passed the Congregation's encampment on the way up from the Fallow Pass. If I read the land right, they were in the process of breaking camp. They weren't looking for you. I wonder, why would that be?"

Galdar's face reddened and she looked to the wet grass around her knees.

"So, I could cut you loose, but if I did, and you somehow found your way back to them, would they even want you back?"

It was a cruel question.

"I don't know. I left in anger. But I will return with contrition. I will throw myself on their mercy."

Shryke nodded.

"Why would you *want* to re-join people who made you so angry that you fled the safety of their camp, got yourself lost and almost murdered?"

"Because I need to confess." Galdar didn't want to say the words.

Shryke said nothing.

"The woman I killed…"

He nodded. She knew that he was judging her.

"The assassin that you killed to save me. If it's forgiveness you need, then I forgive you. A hundred times over. And if it is thanks, then I thank you, from the bottom of my heart."

"It's not *your* forgiveness I want, or your thanks."

"Aren't they worthy?"

Galdar put her face in her hands. Rubbed her eyes and bit on her lips. Shryke wouldn't let the matter drop. "Tell me."

Galdar didn't want to say the words. She knew already they were unfair and wrong, but she had no others right now. "You kill like other people breathe. I saw you. I know what you are. Forgiveness from you would be…worthless."

Shryke considered this for a moment. "Perhaps we can discuss this the next time I have to save your life?"

The conflict inside her raged on, opening out into a knife-edge sadness that sliced deep into her emotions. Here was a man who had done more to keep her alive than any other person in the Sixteen Links and he was anathema to her. He had no faith, had no purpose that she could determine. And yet, he was strong and brave and skilled. And without him she would have been passed from Raider to Raider for their sick pleasure, then killed when her usefulness ended.

She picked a small sliver of dirt from between the grass blades between her knees, dried it between her fingers and ate the grains. Connecting again to the natural world, leading her thoughts from this unnatural one. Taking Dirt was the baseline rite of her faith and the religion of Safehome. The taste and the action of becoming part of the land from which Safehome was made. Becoming an extension of Safehome. Becoming safe.

She felt a calmness for the first time in hours.

And out of it Shryke exploded into action. He leapt over her with a hiss and crashed to the ground five yards away, rolling around; the wet plants and weeds soaked the back of his cloak.

There was a snap and a groan.

As Shryke came up Galdar saw he held a young wood-pig in his hands. Its head lolled on its broken neck, eyes glassy with death.

"Perhaps we'll risk a small fire. Pig has got to be better than eating dirt," he said, and she knew he was mocking her, but she didn't care. The hunger pangs twisted her stomach.

In the end Shryke waited until dawn before he lit the meagre fire beneath a thick canopy of brush and branches in an attempt to dissipate the smoke as best he could. The trick diluted it enough that, with luck, it might not betray them. He gutted the wood-pig expertly and cooked thick cuts of meat that smelt like heaven in Galdar's nostrils.

After the fighting and their frantic flight, Galdar hadn't had time to feel hungry, let alone register that she hadn't eaten for nearly four quarters now, but with the meat on the flames the meat sang beautiful songs in her mouth and filled the gaping hole in her belly with its warm succulence.

Shryke ate like a dog. He was ravenous. He tore at the meat, scoffing down huge succulent fatty chunks. When the meat was finished, he broke the bones and took the marrow, sucking it out of the bone, then ate the pig's innards with relish. When he finished sucking out the last bone, he burped contentedly and patted his stomach. The only word he said before getting up and kicking dirt over the fire was, "Good."

Shryke climbed one of the taller pines, looking out into the valley and the mountain climbs. He stayed up there for several minutes, watching the land, before he jumped back down, satisfied that the fire hadn't given them away.

Galdar took a deep breath and tried to bolster her courage. It would be the last meal she would eat for a while, of that she was sure. "So, you didn't answer my question last night."

Shryke was tying up his weapons, "What question was that?"

"Which way back to…what did you call it…? The Fallow Pass? If I can at least find my way back to where the Congregation made camp, I should be able to pick up their trail."

"You won't make it," he said, matter-of-factly. "The Raiders are all over this land. They are hunting. I can't remember the last time I've seen them this far from Port Rain or the Heartlands. If I cut you loose, you die."

"I've told you, Shryke, I don't care. Which way?"

"I won't have your blood on my hands, woman."

Shryke put the pack across his shoulders, adjusting the straps for comfort. He sheathed the weapons and put them across the top of the pack. He pointed at the sheath with his thumb. "Tighten that for me, would you?"

She owed him that much, at least. Putting aside her growing frustration, she quickly tightened the weapon's sheath. "Please," she said again. "Just tell me where I need to—"

He cut her off. "Have faith."

He was so damned infuriating. She felt a scream of rage rising, her hands making fists.

But…

No.

Galdar pushed the anger back down.

She refused to sink to his level. She wouldn't give him the satisfaction, not in the same way she had with Carlow. She was better than this. "Fair enough." she said turning. "I'll find my own way."

A hand fell firmly on her shoulder.

Shryke turned Galdar, and again fixed her with those eyes that ached of centuries, not years. "That's better," he said. "If we're going to find the Congregation at the Fallow Pass, avoid Raiders, and whatever dreads or travails might harry us, I need to know that you're going to be able to keep a check on your anger. There are times to be angry, woman, of course there are, and times where the only choice is to vent your frustrations. But if you're determined to do this, and *not* get us killed in the process, you need to learn how to master the anger inside. And it looks like you are actually beginning to grasp that."

"You're coming with me?"

"Of course, I am. I didn't save your life three times only to let you die because of your own pig-headedness."

"All this? It was a test? You were goading me to see if I could control myself?"

"Yes."

"And now I'm supposed to be grateful that you're not actually the complete bastard you've been pretending to be."

"That's the general idea," Shryke said, earning himself a slap from Galdar. "I guess I deserved that," he said, rubbing at the red hand rising on his cheek.

CHAPTER 8

B arl looked down upon *God's Heart*.
Its silvery surface was lit by its own deeply buried lumi-
nescence.

Barl had been staring at *God's Heart* for what seemed like
hours.

He knew the metal corridor in which he stood was part of a
larger structure moving through the diamond littered blackness
towards the vast object, but they didn't appear to be getting
appreciably nearer. The sheer size of *God's Heart* drained the
energy from the view. It sucked the power out of their forward
momentum. They could travel towards it forever without the
view changing, such was its vastness.

It was just *too* big.

"*God's Heart* is a constructed world," said Summer matter-of-
factly. "It surrounds its host stars, presenting a massive inner
surface where a billion or more tribes live and thrive within an
enclosed eco-system. You could live a million lifetimes and never
explore a thousandth of it. My employer's people have been
studying it for a hundred thousand years and have barely begun
to understand what it takes to open a door. Beyond that it is a
mystery."

"The door you took me through?"

"Yes."

"Was it built by God?"

"Certainly something *like* a God," she said. "As powerful and Godlike to your people as you are to simple bacteria."

"Bacteria?"

A smile. "We have a long way to go, you and I Barl. For now, just watch and enjoy the view."

The sheer expanse of *God's Heart* continued to grow in the window as they approached. And, incredibly, before too long it stopped being a huge ball in space; he realised that it was flattening to fill the whole view. With a sharp feeling of awe in Barl's gut, the thinning edges of blackness around *God's Heart* disappeared and all that was left was the surface of the object. Smooth and endless. Stretching up and down, side to side. Just *God's Heart*. Nothing else.

"I thought you said I couldn't go home?"

"You can't, I'm afraid. Consider this a…hmm…*flying* visit." Summer said, looking slightly amused at her own choice of words.

"But we're here. Now. Just let me go back inside."

"You're right, we are here now. Your jump was well done."

"Put me back inside."

"No. Just watch. You'll miss it if you don't concentrate. Trust me."

Barl wanted to argue. Wanted to plead. Wanted to do anything he could to persuade this woman to just let him go home. Being this close to his *God's Heart*, knowing he could almost reach out and touch it was more punishment than he could bear…

"Look…" Summer grinned and pointed to the surface of *God's Heart*. Moving across it Barl saw a small black blur racing over the material from which the sphere was constructed. It gradually came into focus. The edges of the shadow began to define. It was arrow shaped to begin with, but began to elongate, keeping the pointed tip as the body of the shadow stretched out thinner and thinner in its wake to form a long block of shade. As they came closer, the edges of the shadow began to open out until they were no longer blurred. Barl saw crenulations and variations in them; one section looked curiously like the battlements on a castle wall, which reminded him of the history books his mother collected for their lessons and thinking of her brought a pang of sadness slicing through Barl's chest. He pushed it back inside.

The shadow *whooshed* meticulously straight and blisteringly fast across the landscape. They were close enough to see tiny variations in the surface of *God's Heart*. It wasn't as perfect as it first appeared from distance. When Summer had said that it had been 'constructed' Barl hadn't grasped what she'd meant, but closer, it looked as though vast, precision-made elements had been fitted together on a scale that was unimaginable to Barl.

The whole thing was so bewilderingly immense he couldn't fit the size of it into his head.

Even when he'd been at home on cool spring evenings, when the sky was as clear as it could possibly have been, Barl had never once imagined that on the other side of the sky was a perfect reverse face of land looking back at him. Or that maybe on the other side of that sky, there might be a boy, in his own spring, staring up at his own sun not imagining that, too.

Barl reached out to steady himself on the lip of the window, a deep sense of instability undermining his balance. He forced himself to concentrate on the rushing shadow, powering ever faster over the outer surface of *God's Heart*.

"The shadow...what *is* it?"

Summer put her hand on Barl's shoulder. "Us," she said simply.

Barl blinked. It didn't make any sense; it didn't look like them...

"Of course, it doesn't look like us silly," Summer grinned, reading his thoughts again. "We're *inside* it. You're looking at the shadow of the *Liston Nine*. A Whole-Environment-Class Colony Cruiser of the Vellotrax Confederacy. They fly in on *God's Heart*, skim the surface at half a million klicks, throw up a fusion light behind it to cast the shadow and put on a show. The tourists *love* it."

"I..."

"Yeah, I get it. It had a similar effect on me the first time I saw it. It's really quite something. If the Captain is in a good mood, sometimes she'll throw up seven or eight fusion lights with multi-flares and spectrum-bursters. Makes the parties on the Ob-decks go with an absolute bang..."

"There isn't a single word coming out of your mouth that means anything to me," Barl admitted. He needed both hands on the railing to steady himself.

He felt as if his brains were draining out of one of his ears.

The shadow of the *Liston Nine* began to fade as the light casting its image dimmed. The shadow blurred as *God's Heart* began rapidly to change from a flat surface back into a vast curve.

They were moving away.

Leaving...

Barl's insides twisted. Everything he knew was collapsing in on itself. It was as though he had lived his life on the surface of some huge ice-covered lake, deep beyond imagining, and now Summer, and the heat her name suggested, was melting that ice, and Barl was falling through the cracks in the surface of his experience.

"Come on," she said. "Let's head up to the Guild Protectorate and I'll teach you how to make real magic from thin air."

Summer took Barl gently by the hand and led him away without resistance.

He was drowning.

On the journey through the corridors of *Liston Nine*, Barl felt like the shadow powering across the surface of *God's Heart*.

His body and mind were all blur with very little definition.

The metal corridor ended in a glass tube into which Summer

pushed Barl gently with two fingers at his back. His feet lifted free of the floor, and he floated slowly forward.

Just another miracle in a universe of new miracles.

Barl moved in the air as if he were back in the water, swimming. With a firmer nudge, Summer propelled the boy along until he'd built up enough speed in the frictionless environment to travel without her help. The tube ran out above free air. They were passing over huge cities illuminated in the artificial night. Lights and buildings miles below; horseless carriages moving along wide roads, some of them were even flying around between buildings. The cities were inside a huge walled room miles and miles across. Cities clung to those walls, and when Barl looked up within the tube, he saw even more of them, cities piled on cities hanging from what he took to be the ceiling.

He wanted to puke.

Once through the tube, Summer pulled Barl down onto pavements on which he didn't need to walk. The pavements did the walking for him. Moving on silent metal plates.

Everywhere was opulence and beauty.

Everything seemed to be made from gold or other precious metals and inlaid with gems that blinked with their own inner lights.

It was hellish.

The moving pavement brought them down a wide spiral into the streets of one of the cities. At ground level, the city towered over Barl, making him feel tiny. He found himself holding Summer's hand as if she, even as Trickstery and evasive as she could be, was the one point of familiarity he required to stay calm and sane.

The streets of this city moved with a thousand different faces and peoples. There were beings who looked just like Barl, with the same colouring and numbers of limbs, but there were many more who were nothing less than *expanded* humans. Tall, lithe, with eyes where their mouths should be. One waved a greeting at Summer. She was known here.

Other species came and went as they travelled towards the heart of the city. Short Tripods that bounced and moved like excited dogs, their craniums just one large unblinking eye, the size of Barl's head.

They stopped at a stall where Summer bought Barl a bowl of a sweet, dessert-like confection. It tasted like solid yellowberry milk; a winter treat in Barl's Village. But this treat wasn't made from milk and crushed yellowberries. It had been squeezed from a gland in the neck of a jolly, round bodied creature with a ruddy face and more thin tiny arms than a bushel of corn. Barl had been suspicious at first, but Summer tasted some, and then spooned a tiny amount into his mouth. He didn't know what he'd been expecting, but certainly not this explosion of sweet beautiful flavours in his mouth.

"It's *wonderful*," Barl said.

"It all is, "said Summer, casting her arm wide over the brilliance of the city.

As they walked, Summer explained more to Barl about the nature of where he had come from and where he was going, "*God's Heart* was made too long ago to remember who made it. There are many old and forgotten races in the universe, but whoever built your home are among the oldest and most forgotten of the lot. Most of *God's Heart* defies any kind of investigation so we can't really tell how old it is, but looking at the other stars in the cluster…"

"Stars?"

"You've never seen a star. Of course. Understood. Moving on. *God's Heart* is the big ball inside which you lived. We don't know how old it is, but we suspect *very*. The people in this Slice have decreed that only on very special occasions, like when we came for you, can anyone contact the people on the inside. As you appreciate, it's a bit of a culture shock coming from inside the *Heart* to the wider universe."

"Then why did you take me?"

"Because you can travel. And ones who can travel are...useful."

They stopped by the side of a wide road along which many well-lit horseless carriages travelled. Summer waved at a blue shiny bubble on wheels that appeared to be empty. A red light on top of the vehicle came on and it rolled smoothly to a stop beside them.

A door opened in its bulbous side. "In you go," Summer encouraged.

"Guild Protectorate Passport Control and Immigration please," she said seemingly to no one. The door swung closed, sealed with a hiss and they accelerated into the traffic. Barl dug his fingers into the rubbery material of his seat. What he *wanted* to do was close his eyes and scream but managed to keep the terror at moving so fast against a stream of other fast moving and zigzagging carriages, in check. Barely.

"We let the people on the inside of the *Heart* keep themselves to themselves, though we do some covert surveillance, looking for Travellers, and when we spot one, we bring them in. You're the Guild's two hundredth and sixth recruit from *God's Heart*."

"I don't understand what any of this means."

"I know, but I'm enjoying your confusion."

"I'm glad you find it amusing."

Summer called the peculiar unmanned cart a Taxi. It moved through the city, oblivious to the other vehicles around it, heading for its destination with a mechanical determination that Barl didn't understand. How could it work without horses and someone to steer? And yet Summer seemed relaxed, so gradually Barl relaxed his grip on the seat, still uneasy but trusting that the Taxi knew what it was doing, where it was going and how to get there without killing him.

"This city," Summer explained, "And the seven more like it are inside a ship."

"We are on water?"

She shook her head, her smile gentle now. "Now, sweet child, remember the shadow? We are flying through the heavens."

He tried to wrestle the thought into shape, putting words on it that made some sort of sense to him. "So, we are in a heavenship?"

"Close. We are in a spaceship. We call the heavens space."

"We are flying through space?"

"We are," Summer paused as Barl's face creased, but he chose not to throw out more questions. Summer looked for the words to help him understand, but in the end settled for, "Space is just that, *space*. It's the blackness on the outside of *God's Heart*. It's where we plucked you from when you fell through the door, and it's what we're travelling through now on our way to Geronterix. Once we are there, we'll hitch a ride on a much smaller ship for the planet hop to Pantonyle and the full Guild Nest. They'll want to examine you, of course. And assuming you don't fail the examination, that's where you'll undergo your training."

The words made even less sense than anything else Summer had told him. They were travelling inside a ship that sailed on the heavens, away from a god made world to some other place where he'd be tested?

The Taxi stopped and the door hissed open.

Barl climbed out onto the pavement. They were on the far side of the city, outside a huge stone building that was constructed like a castle, with turrets and battlements that were lit with beams shining up from the lush grounds surrounding the walls. Banners fluttered from poles on spires. Stone lions guarded the entrance over which a huge, but rusty portcullis, was suspended by thick chains.

Summer ushered Barl into the building.

Away from the street, the stone walls turned the warm air cool. Their footsteps echoed through the high-ceilinged entrance.

"Those on the outside have a certain view of the way the Guild operates, hence the image. The fortress. It brings in the customers. I think they like the aesthetic. Makes them feel like they're buying into something ancient."

Summer paused and waved to a window high up one stone wall.

A human face appeared behind the glass and a hand was raised in return.

One entire section of the wall cracked open and turned back on a silent hinge. Summer let go of Barl's hand, and he wiped the sweat from the surface of his palm across his tunic.

Light blazed beyond the crack in the wall.

Indistinct figures moved around in a large open courtyard that was somehow lit by sunlight despite being inside. The figures, wearing the same black cowl Summer wore, fought across the courtyard, their swords a blisteringly fast whirl of steel. The clashes chimed out in the music of mortality. The dance of blades was hypnotic. Barl couldn't look away from the bodies, with their incredibly defined musculature and precision of movement as the fights raged back and forth. Others, he saw, were stripped to the waist and engaged in hand-to-hand combat.

In groups around fountains, smaller, childlike figures sat in ordered semi-circles hanging on every word as they were instructed by adults.

A glass barrier rose as the door swung back fully.

In the gap that created, armoured guards in magnificent ceremonial armour barred the way. The lacquer on the black plates was blindingly shiny in the artificial sunlight.

Summer led Barl towards the guards, taking some papers from inside her robe.

She pushed them into Barl's trembling hand.

"Welcome to the Protectorate Vellotrax Embassy," Summer said as she pushed him forward, towards the guards. "Welcome to the Guild of Assassins."

CHAPTER 9

S hryke was amused by the girl.
He'd seen her kind a thousand times over on the Chain.

She was earnest and honest, but more naïve than she'd ever want to admit, or more accurately would want to be accused of being.

He hadn't had lustful thoughts in... how long? There was nothing stirring, emotionally or physically. That wiped the amused look off his face. There was still a huge gap in his memories—between arriving in the Thalladon Climbs and rescuing the girl from the Raiders. Some kind of trickery had been played upon him, and it was unnerving.

Shryke looked away from the girl as she followed him up the rubble-strewn path. Against his better judgment he would take her back to the Fallow Pass where he's last seen the Congregation and was prepared to set a brutal pace to be done with it so he could move on. The most direct route was by far the riskiest. It was logical to assume that any pursuing Raiders would have parleyed with other groups, so word of the price on their heads would have begun to spread, painting a target on their backs.

Which meant staying off the well-travelled paths.

The Raiders generally moved in packs of five or six, which he was more than able to handle if push came to shove, but a force of fifty or more, like the one they'd run afoul of was an unwelcome development.

The fresh wound on the back of his hand ached, the tendons stiffening beneath the Assassin's Turban bandage.

He dared not use any Magic to heal it so soon after the last ripple he'd sent out into the Quantum Aether. Sending more signals to the Guild betraying his whereabouts was stupid. He would just have to live with the threat of corporeal dangers; they were considerably less dangerous than the threat posed by the Guild. With their arcane powers they could dispatch a full force through the chain, making him a dead man several times over.

"You haven't told me anything about yourself," Galdar said, as they made their way up a rough scree of skittering stones and split granite.

"You haven't asked," said Shryke.

"I'm asking now."

"Perhaps I have nothing to tell you."

"I don't believe that for a second. A man with so many enemies has more than one story to tell."

"Is that from your holy book?"

"If violence is the only thing you understand, then perhaps the only way for me to understand you is through violence. And no, it's not from my book. That's pure me."

Shryke laughed. "Maybe I could grow to like you, Galdar. You are surprising. Who knows, maybe you were worth saving after all."

It was Galdar's turn to laugh. "I'm flattered, I think. So, come on then warrior, tell me about you."

"Like you said, I'm a warrior."

Galdar waited.

And waited. "That's it?"

"What else is there? I fight for what I believe in, and some-times I fight for things I don't believe in. I get paid to ease my conscience."

"You expect to get paid by the Congregation?"

"That is how business works."

"We have very little gold. And Carlow will tell you to keep me."

"I see you make friends wherever you go," Shryke said with a grin.

"I hit him," she admitted.

"Then I assume he deserved it?"

"No, it was a mistake."

"Then you learned from it, so it was worth it."

They walked on companionably.

"Where were you going when you found me?" she asked after a few more minutes of scrambling across the treacherous slopes. More loose stone skittered away down the slopes behind them.

Shryke bypassed the dark hollow in his memories and dredged up a past he could talk about with some reliability as it felt as fresh as yesterday in his mind. He wasn't ready to admit to himself that his memories had been manipulated and wasn't about to share that with the girl.

"Forthana. A Prince there in the ninth district has employed a new Mage. I was to go there to protect him."

"The Prince or the Mage?"

"Both. What can I say, men of power have many enemies; several court Mages who have been killed over the last few years, seemingly unconnected events, granted, but a Mage is such a rare and useful person it is hard not to mark the coincidence. Wars have started in the wake of these murders. There are Links on the far side of the Chain where total war is happening. Someone is stirring things up. Someone seems to have a vested interest in bringing chaos."

"And you protect these people? For money?"

"Sometimes. Yes."

Galdar hesitated, drew a breath.

"Are you a good person, Shryke?"

"I am not a bad one," he said, which he knew wasn't an answer to the question she'd posed. Shryke knew what the next question was going to be but waited to see if she had the courage to ask it.

She did. "Do you kill for money?"

How best to answer this? "If I'm asked to protect someone, it stands to reason that people can die in the process," he said.

"That's not what I meant and you know it."

"I know. What you want to know is if I am an assassin, no? In which case my answer is yes. Sometimes I kill for money. It's a job like any other."

"It's not."

"I admire your sense of morality, but you are wrong."

Galdar caught hold of his arm and turned Shryke to face her properly. He looked her in the eye. "You're a good person. I can *feel* it. You saved my life."

"Tell that to the others I killed to keep you alive. Who is to say which one side of that equation is good and which is evil? I don't have your faith or your book to answer my questions." There was an edge to his voice, but it wasn't unkind. Just lost.

"Perhaps if you read it, you might find what you are looking for?"

"Don't waste your time trying to save my soul."

"Why not?"

"I don't have one."

The conversation was over.

Shryke picked up the pace, trying hard to shake off his frustration.

She had a knack for getting under his skin.

He didn't like it.

He pushed the thoughts of past horrors from his mind even as they rose up in vivid colour, turning his memories to a wasteland. He buried the guilt. It was a familiar routine; wake screaming, hit something, drink. Forget.

It had worked for the last few thousands of years admirably.

What he needed was a drink. That would make it go away.

"Your people. Do they drink?"

"We have wine. For ceremonies. Other than that, no."

"Pity. Wine will have to do."

The path through the scree began to level out. Shryke used the opportunity to get his bearings. The uplands hereabouts were mainly scrub and gorse that sprouted between bare black rocks. He scanned the high ridge. In the far distance he saw the Riven Bridge swinging uninvitingly over the ravine. A dark slash of black, a familiar robe, and the clash of blades skittered across his vision, sending Shryke recoiling. He stumbled on the uneven ground and would have fallen but for the fact that Galdar caught his arm. She steadied him and helped him sit.

Shryke closed his eyes and the dead Assassin sat up, the sword coming through the front of her robe wet with her heart's blood.

Damn the girl and her questions.

He pushed Galdar away, "Leave me alone. I just need..." Shryke's voice trailed off. He didn't know what he needed, but he knew he didn't need this.

The yawning chasm between his memories was affecting him more than he dared admit. He quite literally wasn't himself.

Galdar sat on a rock beside him, not touching Shryke, but too close.

"I'm a good listener. If there's something you need to say."

"I'm not a good talker."

"You surprise me," she said, not unkindly. "I can see it in your eyes, you aren't content. You wear this brave face, and when you're fighting and killing, I truly believe you are as close to content as your soul has ever known, but in the quiet moments like this you are tormented."

Shryke half-turned, seeing it in his mind's eye: the strike, just a single blow. One sweet and harsh blow and her face bursting into blood, neck snapping, her body falling limp to the gorse...

No.

Shryke never even raised his hand, but the possibility was there fever-bright in his mind as he licked his lips and shook his head, trying to banish it. He pushed himself to his feet, looking to the Secondsun to get his bearings. Without a word he began to walk. He didn't care if the girl followed or not.

Galdar watched him go.

For the first time since he'd saved her, she wasn't sure if she wanted to follow him, even though he was going where she needed to go.

The rage in his eyes had been fierce and frightening.

It was barely held in check, the anger burning through his self-control.

It was the first sign of weakness she'd seen in him since he'd saved her. In a way it made him seem more human. More vulnerable. But she didn't like it. Human wasn't necessarily *better*. Galdar realised then the truth of what the years and experiences behind those eyes represented: horrors beyond imagining that haunted him.

She'd never be able to save Shryke, not in the way that he had saved her, but perhaps she could help exorcise some of his ghosts?

She owed him at least that much, didn't she?

So, picking up her water-skin and walking staff, she followed in Shryke's footsteps, assuming he was leading her to the Fallow Pass.

They saw no sign of Raiders as Secondsun made its way down between the Overchain and the looped horizon.

A chill wind whispered of a harsh coming winter, but tonight at least there was no more rain.

There was no time to stop for rest.

Shryke set a determined pace. He was intent on delivering her to the Congregation and moving on.

Secondsun fell, but the plain was lit well by the two Halfnight Loopmoons that rose in its wake. She felt more exposed in the darkness. Vulnerable. Off towards the lowland pines Galdar heard the cries of two wolves howling to each other. Were they telling each other about the two tasty bodies walking across the plain? Were they calling the pack to close in for the kill?

Muscles burning, throat parched, Galdar jogged on, forcing herself to move faster until she closed the gap to Shryke.

She found herself growing accustomed to his mood swings, and even when he was in this stay-the-hell-away-from-me humour she knew it safer if she kept him in touching distance than let him sulk off and leave her trailing in her wake.

Another wolf howl cut across the plain.

This one, she realised, sounded considerably nearer than the last.

Galdar cast a look back over her shoulder, but kept walking, straight into Shryke.

"The wolves?" She said, rather than apologise.

"They're not interested in us. Look"

They had reached the edge of the plain. Before them, a slope led down, lit garishly in the moonlight. She saw a deep path carved in between two high walled faces of rock. "The Fallow Pass," said Shryke, meaning they'd reached their destination. "And beyond..."

Galdar strained to see where the Congregation had made camp. She realised what was so fascinating to the wolves: The Congregation had dug a waste pit to put all their rubbish in from their four-day stop. Three hundred people needing to be fed and watered created a lot of waste over those hours. The Congregation always tried to leave a campsite in the condition they had found it. It was something they took pride it. That pit should have contained left over food waste and night soil. Nothing more. Bones would have been set aside in a separate pile for the wildlife to scavenge without disturbing the ground digging into the pits.

But the wolves pawed and clawed at the land, churning up the freshly turned ground.

"What are they doing?" What she meant was surely there were bones aplenty nearby, easier sustenance, so why dig? What she didn't *want* to know was the answer to her question, because there was only one reason wolves turn their noses up at easy bones.

"Nothing good," Shryke said.

Shryke didn't wait for her, he set off down the slope making a godawful noise and waving his arms, drawing the attention of the animals. She thought for one moment their possessive nature would have them guard whatever it was they'd found against his intrusion, but it was as if they recognised a greater predator in Shryke and ceded their find. The animals scattered, running for the trees as Shryke drew his sword. She reached the edge of the pit.

"Well we have the answer neither of us wanted, girl," Shryke said grimly.

She didn't bother correcting him this time.

She saw three fresh bodies half-buried in the pit. Each had been stabbed through the heart. She saw the marks of torture on their flesh. They hadn't died easy.

But far beyond the terror of their deaths was the horror that came with recognition. She knew these people. That sick recognition hit her with the brutal force of an iron flail across the heart.

Galdar fell to her knees, the Prayer of Absolution mumbling from her lips even as she sobbed and rubbed at her eyes, blinking back the tears. Between each verse, she picked and dried a crumb of earth to eat as she murmured more words, needing to believe in them, to believe that they would make a difference for the dead.

Shryke looked around, wary. "I'm sorry, Galdar. We can't stay here. Even if the wolves don't rediscover their courage and come back, we don't know what killed your people."

Galdar finished her prayer, felt the tears running down her cheeks and the trembling of her bottom lip.

"They aren't just people, they have names. Novice Klab, Curate Shul and Pastor Dyne. Slaughtered and discarded like trash. Who would do this?"

Shryke climbed down into the pit, examining the bodies more closely. He moved their slack jaws and felt their broken bones, then looked back up at her. "This was all done before death. Time was taken over it." He was telling her they were tortured. "Their mouths and throats are untouched by violence, see? They were expected to talk. I've seen wounds like this before."

"Of course, you have," she said, more harshly than she intended. He didn't take it as a rebuke. "But what could they possibly have said? We have no secrets of worth."

"There's a life lesson here, Galdar. It doesn't matter how little you have to tell if the person forcing you to talk believes you know more." It was hard to argue with his logic, as ugly as it was. "And these tortures were inflicted by people with no small skill in this stuff."

"Raiders?"

"No."

"Then who?" And then, the question that would answer the first. "Where have you seen such tortures?"

Shryke, standing there amongst the dead, knee-deep in corpses, told her, "The Assassin you killed was not acting alone."

"His people want revenge? Are you saying I caused this? By saving your life I killed my people?" The horror of the thought rose in Galdar, overwhelming her; the very idea sliced her open deeper than any blade could have. Those tears became wracking sobs. She cried for her friends, for cheeky, happy Klab, with her blinding smile and infections laugh, getting them both in trouble when they were small girls for giggling at the back of the Movable Church on Prayer Day. Devout and serious Shul, a finger-wagger and tell-tale, but who had been great comfort to Galdar when her mother had passed over from River-Fever. Shul had sat with Galdar for days, not saying anything, just listening, helping her make the required devotionals to her dead parent. Lastly, noble, wise, Pastor Dyne. A towering figure, but as gentle as a butterfly kiss on your cheek. A man-mountain who never used his size to intimidate or threaten, a man who listened to all points of view before deciding that truly was for the best of all involved.

When Galdar had begun having difficulties with Carlow, Dyne had been the one who most spoke about the good qualities Carlow possessed, and assured her how one day he would be a great leader, and how she, Galdar, complimented Carlow perfectly—together they were a whole and wonderful entity. If only they could just find the time to *like* each other.

Galdar loathed the idea that Dyne had gone to his death sure that Galdar was a murderer who had shamed herself.

But mostly she cried for herself.

She knew it was selfish, knew it was pointless, but she cried until it felt she had used up all the tears in the universe.

Shryke didn't move to comfort her. He wasn't that kind of man.

He was the kind of man you wanted at your side when you sought justice for the lost.

CHAPTER 10

The journey to Geronterix passed in a blur of colour that succeeded in very little beyond numbing Barl's mind.

The Guild Protectorate sang with magic and wonder. Most days he was left to himself to wander within. He didn't have the necessary clearances to leave the turreted castle. Summer told him to: "Get out there, watch, and learn what you can. It'll serve you well for the test."

But he wasn't sure what he was supposed to be learning? About the nature of space, stars, and the worlds of the universe? He watched the Trainees and their Tutors make magic and war and felt like he could never possibly belong.

The building itself was full of wide well-lit spaces where the Guild's trainees were put through their paces by their Tutors. There were as many different races as there were trainees and teachers. The first time Barl saw a Trainee reaching into the air, make a complicated sign, whisper a codespell and pull from the very atmosphere a double handed sword with an edge as keen and lethal as any smith could fashion, Barl's jaw fell open, slack. His eyes widened enough to hide his eyelids deep-set in his skull and his legs buckled, sending him crashing onto his backside. The trainee who had just summoned the sword from nothing laughed and reached down to him with her hand. "Don't worry," she said with a smile that could stop hearts, his especially. She was blond haired, with the face of an innocent, so wide, so natural. "You're the first fool to fall at my feet," she said, grinning. Before he could sputter some kind of protest that he wasn't some farm boy hick, her grin spread even wider and she shook her head. "The first time you've seen someone cast a Spell of Creation?"

He nodded.

"It doesn't get any less incredible," she promised him. "But you do get used to the miracles."

"I'm not sure I want to," he told her.

Barl scrambled to his feet without taking her proffered hand and left the training area. He watched his feet and *only* his feet. What was happening to him here? What *were* these creatures? Because they surely weren't like him.

After a few days of seeing this sort of thing around almost every corner, he began to realise that simply hiding out in the frugal room the Protectorate provided wasn't really an option. If he was going to survive this experience, and pass whatever test they intended for him, he was going to have to prepare because these others were so far beyond him in every aspect and he couldn't imagine ever being a match for them without *experiencing* everything this place represented.

The curious sense of vertigo didn't last. Soon enough he could walk the cool stony corridors and brightly illuminated cloisters of the building without wanting to throw up his last meal, even if the instinct to simply hide under his bed refused to go away.

He forced himself to explore.

One of the most fascinating places in the entire Protectorate were the Aether Stages. The raised platforms were covered in runic symbols Barl had no hope of deciphering. As best he could understand, they were the platforms from where fully trained Assassins were dispatched on their missions to the worlds which the *Liston Nine* was in reach of. The Assassins sent on solo missions were dressed in black from toe to turban, the only concession to colour the red jewel they wore in the centre of the headgear. They cast the Incantation of Creation to fashion a weapon before striking a battle stance and seeming to blink out of existence, vanishing into the Quantum Aether. The operation was completed with quiet efficiency. There were many squires in attendance. Some Assassins, he noticed, blinked back almost immediately, their missions complete. He couldn't imagine how they could be so ruthlessly efficient, given he barely had time to scratch his arse and they were back, the target dead. Some came back with terrible wounds and were carried away by the squires. Others, like the tall blonde-haired Assassin holding that lethal black-bladed sword didn't come back at all.

The squires consulted instruments and crystals. He saw their faces, crestfallen, as they moved on, and realised what those expressions meant: not every Assassin was successful.

Summer came to check in on him from time to time.

He wouldn't know when she would appear at his shoulder, and more often than not, failed to mark her approach. She either moved silently, or just stepped clear out of the air at will, like an Assassin from an Aether Stage. It was more likely than not a combination of the two, judging by the other miracles he saw regularly in the Protectorate.

This place was unlike anywhere in *God's Heart*.

On the sixteenth morning, while Barl foraged in an ornamental garden that appeared to be outside on a bright summer day beneath blue skies and white clouds, but in truth was accessed through a door off one of the main thoroughfares of the castle and was, he knew, still within the walls of the Protectorate, Summer tapped him on the shoulder. "How's tricks?"

Barl spun around.

Summer stood between him and the gnarly bark of a huge tree Barl knew could not be real. Summer smiled that infuriating smile of hers, her dark skin every bit as enchanting as the false morning sun.

"There are too many of them," Barl said gloomily. "This whole place is nothing but a trick. If a trick is another word for a lie."

Summer laughed gently and put a slender arm around his shoulders. They walked through the ankle high grass, following a well-trodden walk down towards the stream. The bright waters washed over a perfectly jagged spur of rock.

As they approached, Barl realised that the water was so clear he could see the smooth stones, the same colour, make-up and arrangement, of the stones that made up the walls of the Protectorate, on the bottom. It was further proof that the entire construction, even though Barl felt like he could squint and shade his eyes and peer off into a far distance, was a *lie*. He didn't know how they did it, these people, but they seemed to be able to manufacture anything with their strange magics. The entire place reeked of the stuff.

"You seem to be settling in." she said.

"Appearances can be deceptive," he said. "I'm getting used to it, that isn't the same as belonging here."

"Good point well made."

"I miss my home."

"Of course, you do."

"I've been watching the Aether Stages."

As though she read his not particularly deep mind, she said, "You don't want to be running before you can walk, kid. Concentrate on getting to Pantonyle first. Worry about the Stages later."

Barl ploughed on. "Some of the Assassins don't come back, do they?"

Summer looked down at Barl. "Listen, you really…"

"They're dead, aren't they?"

"It's complicated."

"It's not *that* complicated. I don't want to die far away from home."

"Then you'd better make sure you don't," she smiled gently, taking the barbed edge off her words.

"It would be easier if you just used the Stages to take me home, wouldn't it?"

"No. But how about we do something useful with your time, like talk about the Test."

Barl's eyes dropped.

"I don't mind admitting that I was never good with tests. They unnerved me and I ended up making mistakes," Summer said.

"I haven't thought about the Test."

"Really? That surprises me."

"Why? I've been too busy watching kids like me magic weapons out of thin air."

"Ah, yes. It can be a little... difficult at first."

"If you say so."

Summer stood, "Get up." Her whole demeanour and attitude shifted in those two words. Suddenly there was steel in her voice. Barl immediately felt the ice beneath the sunshine. He did as he was told.

"Hold out your hands. Palm up. Like this." Summer placed her elbows against her sides, lifted her hands and turned the palms up, extending her long fingers.

Barl mirrored her.

Summer closed her eyes.

Her lips moved for a moment, and words from a language he had never heard before, whispered between them.

He felt something: a shiver in the air around him. It prickled against his nerves.

Summer reached into the wound she'd woven in the air with her words, her arm disappearing to the elbow.

Barl had seen this kind of trickery over the past few days, but only from a distance. This was the closest he had been to any sort of codeweaving. The air sizzled and sparked around Summer's flesh. Light distorted and flared. With a grin of satisfaction, Summer pulled a small but overflowing punnet of Yellowberries from the air and put it down in Barl's palms.

"Try one," she said.

Barl hesitated.

"Now," the steel again.

Barl reached into the punnet and snapped off a berry.

It felt cool and ripe in his fingers.

With some trepidation, he placed the fruit on his tongue and bit into it.

The tastes and flavours of home burst into his mouth, flooding his memory so completely and utterly that with that single bite he was taken back home, in town, the sun on his back, and he heard the *clip-clop* of hooves on the dried mud of the high street. For just a second, on the breeze, he was sure he heard his mother calling him in for supper...

But then he opened his eyes, and the punnet dropped from his hand.

His legs gave way beneath him, but Summer caught him before he could fall.

"Did you feel it?" She asked.

Barl nodded, looking at the upended punnet and the yellow fruit as they rolled down the banks of the stream into the water.

"You can go home like that whenever you want, Barl, and we will teach you how."

Barl looked beyond Summer to the stream.

The fruits bobbed in the shallow ripples that weren't quite waves, and in them saw the metaphor, he was the fruit sailing away in currents over which he had no control, to a destination that he couldn't guess at, and wouldn't be able to escape.

A chill ran through Barl.

Although Barl heard the word Geronterix many times over the month it took to travel there, he hadn't really considered *what* it was.

A vast screen in the Protectorate announced the ship was now, "In orbit." And that: "Disembarkation for the journey to the Guild Nest on Pantonyle should begin immediately."

Summer appeared at the door of his room with a holdall and a new coat.

Barl took the bag. "Thank you."

"Ready?"

"If I knew what I was supposed to be ready *for* it would be easier to answer that question."

Summer switched off the light and the room became a memory.

She walked with Barl through the Protectorate one last time.

It seemed like nearly everyone was leaving with them for the journey down to the Nest. Beings were packing away equipment in large metal-cornered cases that then rose up, seemingly of their own accord, and floated in neat lines behind them. Non-magical weapons were sheathed and everyone, except Barl and Summer, appeared to be in uniform, marking them out as belonging. Yet again he felt like he had no place being here. The uniforms were black and gold, with red sashes that he assumed denoted rank within the group. "Don't worry," Summer whispered conspiratorially into Barl's ear as they joined a long line of Trainees and Tutors heading towards the central square of the Protectorate, "You'll get your own uniform when we get to Pantonyle."

"I wasn't worried," Barl lied.

"Man, you're hard work sometimes, kid, you know that?"

They stood in the square for a few minutes until the stream of bodies slowed to a trickle and the Main Screen's Disembarkation notice changed to a countdown from one hundred.

"The Guild have a rather overblown sense of the dramatic," she said, looking at the clock above them.

"What's happening?"

"In the most prosaic sense we're getting off this ship and getting onto another."

"But...?"

"But rather than do it like normal people, walking, taking a travel tube, or even teleport if there was the technology in the Slice. But not the Guild."

As the countdown moved inexorably towards zero, Barl felt his knees start to tremble and the muscles of his legs loosen. He was determined not to show weakness or fear. He planted his feet firmly and followed the heads of everyone else as they craned their necks to look up towards the ceiling.

Except, there was no ceiling now.

With a rush of wonder, the entire thing blinked out of existence. A gulf of stars reached off into universal expanses past a blue-green planet that held vast oceans, enormous continents above which white clouds sailed and danced.

Between the planet and the opened ceiling of the Protectorate, a complicated arrangement of cubes, spheres and rectangles, held together by a web of silver and golden filigree was turning in the vacuum. It moved closer at a sedate and steady speed.

"The Guild," continued Summer, "like to keep up the mystique, but what they also like is to make an *exit*."

As the countdown reached zero an alarm sounded and everyone in the square lifted off the floor and flew slowly out into space.

If Barl had been near the ground, instead of flying up away from the wide expanse of stonework, his backside *would* have thumped into it.

CHAPTER 11

S hryke wasn't used to comforting crying women.

Galdar moved away from the bodies and, as the tears rushed down her cheeks, she grabbed him, burying her face in his chest.

He didn't move for a moment, then dropped his steel into the soft earth, and folded his arms protectively around her. This kindness only served to make the girl cling onto him all the more fiercely. He felt her tears through his clothing. Her sobs echoed off the rocks of the pass.

Not sure how best to progress from here, Shryke fell back on ingrained routines: he searched the immediate area for signs of danger, then scoured the ground for any indication where the girl's people had gone after burying their dead.

In the bright moonlight, he picked out tracks and signs that told the story of a rushed exodus, not a panic, but one driven by fear all the same. But, some of the Congregation were alive, several moving as though injured, judging by their scuffed tracks, dragging feet, and in some, old blood dried.

There had been a battle, though not much of one. They had tried to defend themselves against the Assassins' onslaught, but they couldn't hope to do that for long, meaning the Assassins either had the information they had come for or had grown tired killing the fools of the Movable Church. That was as much a blessing as his people would bestow upon this faith. Compared to the alternative, leaving their corpses by the side of the road, it was not necessarily a kindness.

Galdar rubbed the tears and snot from her face. Her eyes wide with anger and her mouth barred with spit. "These...Assassins... they're not looking for *me*, are they? They're looking for you!"

"Yes," he admitted. "They're looking for me."

"What kind of friend are you?"

"I don't know," Shryke replied truthfully. "Not the kind you thought I was."

Galdar's composure was returning. She began to pace. "If I hadn't killed that woman when you were on your knees... this wouldn't have happened? My friends would still be alive."

Shryke nodded.

"Does it matter whose fault it is?"

"Yes!"

"Then blame me if it helps," he said.

The silence grew between them again.

Shryke was more comfortable with this; the anger that comes after a terrible grief. He'd felt it himself on so many occasions. He could see Galdar was still bereft and struggling to find a balance in her mind that would allow her to function. It wasn't helped by the proximity of danger, which twisted her instinct to grieve against her need to reach out to him for protection. The Assassins would eventually track them back to these shallow graves, and then onwards wherever they went. How could they not when they had the gift to be anywhere and anywhen within that quaint notion, time?

Galdar did her best to stifle the sobs, and Shryke was prepared to take the brunt of her anger if it got them moving.

"Which way did my people go?" Galdar looked for clues he'd already found, but without his skillset she was lost. Shryke pointed. "Downloop. We can follow. Judging by the blood..."

Galdar closed her eyes, bit her lip.

Shryke found himself admiring her for the first time: he could see the effort she it took not to break down again. He thought better of acknowledging it so carried on. "...and how it has dried; at a guess they left here no more than twelve hours ago. If we travel fast, we'll catch them by the second-sunrise."

Galdar nodded. She didn't look back. She set off in the direction Shryke had indicated without a word.

Shryke smiled grimly.

Perhaps this girl was more of a woman after all? And a strong one at that. A warrior.

He heaved the pack onto his back, picked up his steel and followed.

They walked through the night, making good progress down through the mountainous terrain.

The chill helped to keep their thirst at bay and gave them fresh impetus when a soft breeze struck up just before dawn. They crossed a mountain stream from which Shryke took a moment to refill his gourds. Galdar refused the opportunity to sit and rest. While Shryke stood knee deep in the gently working water, she paced the riverbank, eager to be moving again. He saw the pent-up energy, her eyes fixed on the route ahead, not willing to waste a moment between now and finding the survivors of her Moveable Church.

Shryke was keen to get going too.

He'd lost several days to the journey, and however much his feelings towards her had changed, the reality of his own situation hadn't changed. He still had his own mission to complete, even if he couldn't remember *what* that was, or why the Guild would be sending hunters after him.

When Galdar was back with her people, he would take the time to prepare for the battles he knew were waiting, and weave the codespells he needed to unlock his memories.

But that was a far-off thought.

Right now, they had more pressing concerns: if a small force of Assassins were already on the Chain then that compounded the immediate dangers ten-fold. Raiders on one side, Assassins on the other, and Galdar and Shryke in between. It wasn't a pleasing prospect.

"Come on!" Galdar stopped pacing. She pitched her voice low, but harsh, demanding, across the water at Shryke.

Shryke waded towards her and climbed out of the stream, hanging the gourds back on the packs.

Firstsun was starting to send shivers of light through the valley mist ahead and the hazy, distant mirage of the Overloop was slowly picked out in the dawn sky. If Shryke squinted, he could see high above to the Crossloop of the next link in the chain. That was the link where Shryke had arrived on the Chainworld. A loop very different to this one. Cities of golden spires, sapphire seas, and vast trading economies. Commerce carried out in baskets slung below airships propelled in the skies, moving against the thrust of brass screws turned by steam engines. How Shryke wished he had an airship now. They would make the escape from the Thalladon Climbs in a tenth of the time it would take them on foot.

He resolved to steal a horse at the earliest opportunity.

Morning bloomed bright and fresh in the valley.

Galdar stalked on ahead, with Shryke only occasionally having to call for her to change direction, following the more subtle signs of the Moveable Church's passage.

At midmorning, they found where the party had camped for the night.

Hearths were still warm and smoky. A pit had been dug for refuse, this time without any bodies left to rot.

This renewed Galdar's spirits. She broke into a loping trot, pushing herself to close the distance between them and her people. Shryke could understand the desire. His home and his people... so long ago. In such a distant time. He couldn't remember their faces now. It had been such a very long time since he could call them to mind with any clarity. And the village where he had lived? That was lost to the smear across his thoughts that was the past. A brightening line of indistinct colour on his memory. When he thought of it now, it didn't conjure any specific images, but it *felt* like home. And that was in many ways all he needed; anything else would only dull his purpose and deflect him from his end-goal.

Though every time he did dredge through his memories, he came across that huge gap where more recent life should have been.

How had he come to the Climbs?

Why?

On what mission?

The chill of it went up and down his spine. He daren't use any magic to investigate his mind further, but the temptation was there. And it was strong. Shryke was uncomfortable in his own head. He felt like an unwelcome visitor inside his own skull. This was not a something he could allow to continue indefinitely.

Shryke liked simple solutions.

If only there was someone's head he could remove from a set of shoulders to fix it, that was the kind of answer he was more than capable of finding.

The tracks of the Moveable Church veered into scrubby woodland.

Shryke assumed the survivors had felt the open valley was too exposed, especially given their numbers, and so had decided to take a route through the trees in the hope of throwing off any pursuers.

Shryke smiled inwardly, these religious observants were not skilled in the ways of war or hunting.

Going into woodland would make the task of following them easier.

"Slow down," Shryke called to Galdar as she sprinted through the trees. There were signs of passage even she couldn't miss—the broken twigs, the flattened ankle grass and the half prints in the wet earth. She didn't need Shryke. In her mind safety was within arm's length, but not his arms. She didn't listen to him; she was in a headlong rush, plunging deeper into the undergrowth.

Shryke strained to differentiate the different sounds in the forest, trying to hear beyond the noise of her crashing footsteps. He heard something… a low…singing?

Were these people imbeciles?

It struck him then, they were worse than that, they were fanatics. They'd gone into the forest to hold some sort of ceremony or rite, not to hide at all.

Shryke shook his head.

He hefted the pack high onto his shoulders and began to run after Galdar.

Knowing that no amount of calling would get her to slow down, he had no choice but to move as fast as she was, and that meant crashing through the trees in pursuit.

He surged on, pushing back branches as they slapped at his face and body, hurdling deadfall, and blundering forward, trying to keep her in sight as she ran towards the voices.

He heard something else, but before he could grasp the implications of the sound, or what was behind it, a gnarled branch swung whistling through the still air, and hammered into the back of Shryke's skull, sending him tumbling in an explosion of pain that opened the way to the cold, starry blackness of unconscious.

CHAPTER 12

B arl looked at his hands.
Palm up. Elbows in.

Sweat broke on his brow.

His lips trembled.

A tear appeared in the corner of one eye; he felt it trace a line down his hot, red cheek.

He forced himself to stare *into* the flats of his hands, working his gaze into the cracks between his fingers, zeroing in on the lines across his palms as he tried to see beyond the skin into the inner realms of his being. Without understanding what he was trying to do, he was doing it anyway, dismantling the very atoms that made up his body and opening a gap through the particles of his existence.

The sweat poured from him.

He felt it pool in his armpits. Felt it trickle down the inside of his shirt, Felt the thin material cling to his skin.

His ears hummed and his mouth dried.

Nothing.

With a rasp of frustration Barl dropped his hands, spun around, his body twisting in the half-gravity of the ship, and drifted towards his bed.

The *Inter-Star System Freight and Passenger Assemblage*—'Minu-

lar' was, Summer had explained, a ship the Guild had chartered to take the Trainees from Geronterix to Pantonyle. Apart from the lack of full gravity, Summer had described it as "a fairly normal ship—if a lot smaller than the *Liston Nine*." There were no cities inside for one thing, and the Guild had just three floors in the accommodation sphere rather than a whole Castle Protectorate. But the level of technology and the dizzying array of the alien inhabitants more than matched those of the Colony Ship.

The Bantoscree themselves, the species that owned and crewed the *Minular*, were nine-foot-high sacs of pulsating flesh that floated gently around the corridors and living areas of the ship, polite and helpful, and on occasion dryly funny. However long they had been in contact with humanoid species, the Bantoscree had never stopped finding the ideas of limbs both limiting and hilarious.

When Barl edged past a Bantoscree in a corridor, taking care not to bump into it, the creature would invariably laugh and wave a coiled tendril in the direction of his Barl's gangly arms or flapping feet, trying to get purchase in the low gravity environment. His gawkiness amused them constantly. He was getting used to it. For the first few days onboard, Barl had felt like a newborn foal trying not to fall over. One Bantoscree, Gharlin, had been assigned to his quarters as guardian or observer (it was never that clear which, meaning it was probably both) and had taken a shine to the boy. He was almost telepathically present in the corridor when Barl left for the morning. Every morning. And would float alongside him to the Guild Training Deck. Barl couldn't help but wonder if the creature had been waiting out there all night for him to emerge?

Perhaps Gharlin had.

Who knew how these creatures spent their time when the Trainees weren't round them?

Maybe waiting in corridors made them happy?

It wasn't his place to question them.

It didn't help that the things stank, like rancid cheese, which only made him all the more determined to avoid physical contact.

"You appear to be acclimatizing," Gharlin said on the seventh morning of the journey, floating alongside Barl, who took enormous, loping strides towards the Training Deck.

"It's not so bad after a while. Once you get used to it."

"Let us hope you remember how to walk once we arrive at our destination. The Bantoscree cannot visit Pantonyle without a Pressure Gravity Cage, so I would not know. Tell me. Your legs? Why do they only bend in one place? That seems to be a flaw in your evolutionary design."

Barl looked down at his knees. He'd never thought about why they bent like they did. "I don't know. What's evolution?"

The Bantoscree sighed a puff of putrid gas and shivered the purple of sarcasm, "What are they teaching the young Trainees these days?"

"I know how to milk a goat," he said in all seriousness.

"What is a goat?"

Barl smiled, "What *are* they teaching young Bantoscree these days?"

Gharlin shivered a yellowy red and its tendrils curled and uncurled. Barl assumed that's what passed in its species for laughter.

Barl was a long way from laughing right now, however.

The frustration of another failure had him bury his head in the pillow and cover the top of his head with his hands. In the warm dark Barl imagined *God's Heart*; the sound of corn rustling in the breeze, the lowing of the cows coming in for milking; the bleat of goats in their pens. His father's voice saying words he couldn't hear, and in a faraway dreamy distance, his mother waving to him across the warm evening. She was pleased to see him coming home, walking up the track towards town…but…

Barl thumped his hand down hard on the mattress, the recoil lifting his body clear of it. He hung there for a moment, not exactly weightless, twisting in the warm air, before he fell back towards the bed with a groan of frustration.

Summer had spent much of yesterday showing Barl more magic; transporting herself invisibly from one corner of the Training Deck to the other, creating weapons from nothing but the air they breathed and using the reduced gravity to *fly*.

Prolonged time spent weaving the codespells forced Summer to draw on a lot of her internal energies. After a few hours of showing Barl what could be possible in his future if he didn't fail the coming test, she was spent.

They rested against the bulkhead and watched the other trainees going through their rituals and routines. As fast as some created weapons, others used newfound skills to dissipate the blades and barrels into smoky nothings with the whisper of an incantation on their lips, and an almost imperceptible gesture.

Summer breathed heavily, a sheen of sweat sparkling on her dark skin. "Nothing's free, kid," she said, smiling. There was a lesson in this she wanted him to learn. "Every spell you cast *costs*. And the greater the codespells you weave the higher the price you pay in energy and emotion."

"In…emotion?"

Summer nodded. "Oh yes. It takes a toll, believe me. You'll be visiting the Plain soon enough. You'll understand then, in ways I can't explain beyond saying you will be forced to fight for your spells, and battle for your energy."

"I don't understand what you mean."

"I know you don't," Summer drew up her knees and rested her chin on them. Her whole aspect sank; not changing to steel this time. It was as though she had deflated. Breath hissed from between her teeth.

"Does it hurt?"

Summer shrugged. "Everything hurts." With that, Summer got up and pulled Barl to his feet. "Come on. Hands!"

This instruction had become a familiar one on the *Minular*. It meant that Barl was to place his elbows in, turn his palms up and try to make something, *anything,* appear in his hands.

Summer held her hands at the ready and nodded. "Go."

Barl concentrated on his palms, but as fiercely as his focus was internal, he still felt Summer's eyes boring into him.

A small ornamental knife blinked into existence on Summer's palm.

And still nothing on his.

Barl concentrated harder. Pushing his thoughts into his hands.

Summer dismissed the knife into silver, acrid smoke. "You can do it. I know you can. It's in your bones."

A golden goblet filled with chilled wine appeared between Summer's palms. She drank down the wine in a single swallow and threw the goblet over her shoulder, unmaking it with a nod of her head before it could hit the floor.

Barl pushed harder, but the images would not come.

There was a grey emptiness within his mind. It engulfed and smothered his thoughts.

Summer willed him on. "When you've done it once, it will become easier, I promise."

"I thought you said I had to pass the Guild test first—before I did this."

There was a twinkle in her eye as she told him, "If you don't tell them neither will I. *Come on,* Barl be the devil I know you are."

Barl fought his thoughts hard.

He dived into the grey.

Kicked at it.

Punched at it, but it absorbed everything.

It was nearly a minute before he realised his tongue was trapped between his teeth and that his incisors were slicing into it. The iron taste of blood seeped into his mouth and whatever progress he might have made in that moment was lost.

He let his hands drop.

When he looked up through blinking, sweat-stinging eyes, Summer had gone.

Barl was alone on the Training Deck.

A door clanged closed behind him, making him jump.

He looked around, realising that all the other trainees had gone, too.

Even Gharlin wasn't lurking in the corridor waiting to escort him back to his room.

He'd seen neither hide nor hair of another soul in the hour since.

Barl got up from the bed, sighing deeply.

He placed his feet firmly on the deck, dug his elbows into his side and turned his palms towards the ceiling. If he had this power, as Summer was adamant he had, then he was going to uncover it. Not because he wanted to become a Guild Assassin, but because if it were as powerful as Summer's magic, then surely he could use it to go home to *God's Heart*.

God's Heart.

Those two words thumped in his chest like love.

The endless view into the hazy distance, the ceaseless fields, the tracks, the hills and the people. The gentle upward curve of the far horizon. The suns and Shadewalls, the warm nights, the festivals and the…

Barl felt a weight in his palm, as if there was something resting in it although he couldn't see anything, but it was there, and it was urgently trying to make its presence known. It weighed in his hand. It had proper weight. It felt rough against his skin. There was genuine texture. And as Barl looked, a shimmering, out of focus line of blurry air wavered above his skin and a blue fissure tried to open in the air; it shivered and warped. With the hand not weighed down by an invisible object Barl, daring not to blink, moved his fingers warily towards the shimmering. He held his breath and kept his thoughts focussed on *God's Heart* as he reached into the void between atoms.

A cascade of yellowberries settled in his palm.

Before the rent in reality sealed again, an empty wicker punnet fell out of the air and dropped directly to the floor plates. He dropped the berries in the shock of it. But that didn't matter.

He'd done it!

True, it wasn't a weapon. It was a fruit salad.

But it was a start.

Barl allowed himself the first smile in what seemed like forever. At last, proper progress, something tangible. Real. Finally, he felt a little surer of himself and the powers Summer was so sure he had. He was going to get *home*—of that he was convinced —however long it took.

Barl's mouth was suddenly full of saliva.

His belly grumbled, aching with pangs of hunger.

The yellowberries looked like the most delicious food he had seen in his life. He bent to retrieve one…

But before he could get a finger on the shiny yellow fruit, the *Minular* shook so fiercely he was thrown against the wall. Three muffled explosions tore through the structure, resonating from the distance, the vibrations shivering all the way through the metal underfoot and the walls and ceiling all around him. The sound amplified, tortuously loud, as the ship shook violently. Barl was battered around like a tumbling dice in a gaming cup. He reached out trying to steady himself as everything around him lurched away beneath him, smashing bodily into another bulkhead and hanging there stunned as the full gravity turned on.

CHAPTER 13

S hryke's head pounded and his ears buzzed with a mad tinnitus of silence. He was in darkness. It was absolute. There were no shades, no shadows no chinks of light.

He tried to move a hand, reaching out in front of him to feel the immediate area around him, but couldn't. He was bound hand and foot. Not chains... rope? It felt coarse against his skin.

If he couldn't move, or see, he needed to rely on his other senses to tell him what had happened to him.

First, there was the smell.

By all that was holy, what was it?

It *reeked*.

The stench clawed in his nostrils, it cloyed at his taste buds.

He shook his head trying to shake off the foetid odour, coughing and hacking and gagging as he struggled to banish the stench.

"He's awake."

A man's voice. Young. Snotty. Arrogant.

Shryke didn't need to open his eyes to dislike him.

"Shall I hit him again?"

You can try it, he thought, braced for another unseen blow. His head thudded, senses dulled. The base of his skull burned, sore from where he'd been struck. For a flicker of a moment, not even a full heartbeat, Shryke thought about travelling to The Plain to battle for more energy to weave escape magic, but the risk of lighting up his position so soon and drawing the Guild's warhounds was too much, especially as he was chained. He needed to think rationally; if his captors wanted him dead, he would already be dead, not waking up bound, nursing the aches and pains of their ambush. Which meant they weren't Guild. His headless body would already be on the way back to the Nest on Pantonyle or to the Protectorate on the *Liston Nine* if they were.

"No. Please don't."

Galdar.

"Please. He's not a threat. He's saved my life. He helped me. He didn't have to do that."

"Be quiet," the snotty one rasped. "When we want *your* opinion, we'll ask for it."

"Do you want me to punch you again, Carlow?"

He began putting the pieces together, remembering her stories and the personalities of her Moveable Church. Carlow was a name he'd heard before.

A ripple of laughter came from a number of voices, male and female.

"Carlow."

A new voice. Female. Older. Authoritative.

"Yes, Reverend Yane?"

"Take the bag off his head."

"But…"

"Do it or I'll *instruct* Galdar to punch you. And you know she will enjoy that."

Rough hands removed the dark leather bag from Shryke's head,

He blinked in the bright light. The bag's interior was stained with traces of rotten food. Fish scales glinted around the lips of the opening, smeared over the drawstring that had been tight around his throat, which explained the sickening stench; they'd covered his head in a bag used for carrying dead fish.

Delightful.

Once he'd shaken his head clear of the humiliation, the warrior took a proper look at his surroundings. They had tied him to the thick wooden pole holding up the central area of a large tent. There were maybe fifty or so people in various tunics, hose or religious garb, habits, surpluses and the like, staring at him, and a makeshift altar between Shryke and the entrance.

Galdar was close, and standing near her was a thin faced, black haired, spotty boy, who was nineteen summers old at best, sixteen at worst. The runt stared at Shryke with intense suspicion. He held a large tree branch, which had been stripped of bark and extraneous twigs, to fashion a crude club. Being taken out by a snotty nosed kid with a stick wasn't his finest moment.

Shryke cursed himself for being so fixated in catching up with Galdar that he'd left himself vulnerable to a damned stick. There would be a reckoning with the boy, he promised himself, but not yet.

First, he had to get free.

Standing a few feet removed from the crowd, closer to him, was a tall, well-appointed woman in a red habit. Her face had that care-worn tiredness of leadership, but her eyes still sparkled with fierce intelligence. He noticed a chalice in her hands, which appeared to be overflowing with fine dirt. Shryke watched as she closed her eyes, picked some crumbs of earth from the chalice and put them into her mouth. Her lips moved in prayer. She waited a moment and then looked at him.

"Tell me why we shouldn't burn you now?"

Shryke considered the woman, Reverend Yane. He needed to rein in his instinct to sarcasm in the face of religious fervour. These people were zealots of one stripe or other, and they'd just seen some of their congregation slaughtered. "Is your God a vengeful God? Are you a vengeful people?"

"Three of our number have been killed and many injured in an attack. Novice Galdar tells us this action was in retaliation for her saving your life by killing one of their own. Should we not kill you for them? I believe it would keep us safe."

"It wouldn't," he said, telling the truth. Handing his corpse over would achieve nothing.

Carlow turned. "I'll go and prepare the pyre."

"No," Yane raised her hand to stop him. She levelled a bony finger at the boy. "Your bloodlust is disappointing, Carlow. Now be quiet. I need to think."

They weren't going to burn him, Shryke knew. This woman, Yane, was clever. He knew what she was doing; she was trying to bond with him, to make him scared and then offer salvation, a pardon to make him beholden to her mercy. It was a reasonable tactic, and it would have work with many others.

"I don't want to die, Reverend Yane," Shryke began, "and if you let me go, I will travel far from here. The Guild will not need to bother you again."

"Except to exact more death and destruction on us for letting you go?"

"It's not their way."

"How can you be so sure, Warrior Shryke?"

"Because I'm one of them."

There was a collective gasp of shock. Carlow boiled with frustration; hefting his branch from hand to hand, ready to beat Shryke's face to a bloody pulp should the order be given.

"Is that why they want to kill you?"

"Yes. You don't leave the Guild. And…I left. They will spend eternity hunting for me."

"Perhaps you would be better off dead."

"That is almost certainly true."

The tent fell silent. Reverend Yane took another benediction of earth. "And yet, you do not want to die?"

"I do not. I have much to do before I can allow myself that luxury."

Reverend Yane sighed, handed her chalice to another novice

and clasped her hands, fingers interlocked, in front of her. "Carlow..." she began.

Carlow needed no second bidding he raised the branch and stepped towards Shryke, murder carved into his face.

"...release him."

Carlow froze.

His eyes stuttered from side to side as he processed the command. Shryke could almost see him struggling, unwilling to believe he had heard correctly. But he had no choice but to lower the branch and step up to Shryke, doing as he was told. The boy produced a small knife from his belt which he used to saw through Shryke's bonds.

"I'll be watching you barbarian," he whispered in the Quantum Assassin's ear.

"I'm flattered, honestly, but you're really not my type," Shryke whispered back. "I like a bit more meat on the bones."

Shryke was taken from the Moveable Church, to the Reverend Yane's personal tent. As he was led through the camp, he saw that it had been struck in a forest clearing. He assumed not deep within the forest. Fires burned, and vegetables roasted on spits above them. The camp filled the space, and some of the Congregation were busy building rough shelters and covering them in fern leaves to insulate them from the worst of the elements. Shryke had guessed right; they had left the open valley for shelter rather than protection, but more than safety the decision was underpinned by devotional needs. The Congregation would obviously be staying here for a while. After the Guild's attack they still had wounded to tend to and companions to mourn. They needed the rest, but lack of forethought made Shryke uneasy. They were targets. His very presence increased their risk—not just from the Guild, either. The Raiders would not forget what he had done to their number and would seek to humble him. If they realised

Shryke was among the Congregation their kindness would bring doom upon them.

The tent was fur lined against the cold, and small enough to be cosy while offering room for a Church Council. Galdar was there, but not, he noticed, Carlow. Yane sat across from Shryke with a small, smoky fire in between them. She was flanked by Church elders. Galdar appeared out of place, her cheeks puffy and eyes red from where she'd been crying; finally mourning her dead friends. The relief of reaching the Congregation had at last allowed her the space to remember and regret. She gave him a wan smile as he sat down. Perhaps she had found some small space in her heart for forgiveness? It would be good for her if she could. He could live without it, of course, but then forgiveness was never about the one being forgiven. Shryke smiled back and their eyes met. It was plain their shared journey that had taken its toll on them both.

Shryke was surprised at how much that moment of eye contact comforted him.

He realised there was a bond growing between him and the girl that might even lead to a pure friendship.

He liked that idea.

"I am sorry that you were hurt and bound, Shryke. It's not our way. But I will speak plainly with you; the attack by your people has left us scared. I apologise for Carlow's rash attack, but you must understand he believed you were chasing Galdar and intended her harm." He nodded. "He acted without thinking, and because you were an unknown entity, despite Galdar vouching for you, we believed it best to secure you so that we might talk without fear before releasing you."

Shryke shrugged. "It's fine, honestly. I've got a hard head."

The flap of Yane's tent opened and several novices brought in plates of steaming vegetable stew. Shryke ate greedily. The food was good but simple fare, made all the better by being the first thing he'd eaten in days. The others give a prayer of thanks before eating.

Yane finally spoke again. "You do present us with something of a dilemma."

"I do?"

"Yes. I wonder, how do we protect ourselves against the Guild? As I said in Church—they will come for us whether you're here or not. So that they might chase you down."

Shryke could offer no comfort. "This is true. If it helps, I am genuinely sorry. And I have wrestled with the fact that had I'd left Galdar to the mercy of the Raiders…it might have been one life lost but many more saved."

"We thank you that you didn't…" she cut herself off in mid-sentence.

"But here we are."

They ate in silence for a while. Then Yane looked up. "Galdar tells us that you are a mercenary."

"Not the word I would use."

"But you are paid by others to protect them? To kill on their behalf and to outwit the enemies who would do them harm? Yes?"

"It's what I'm good at. I'm a terrible carpenter and blacksmith, but I am very adept at violence and reading the darker aspect of humanity."

Yane chewed on her stew, the firelight glittering in her eyes. Eventually she swallowed, put down her plate and wiped at her mouth with a napkin. "Warrior Shryke." Yane said firmly and with conviction. "The Congregation of the God of Safehome would like to employ you to protect us from the Guild of Assassins."

CHAPTER 14

B arl smacked to the deck plate, in an instant feeling one hundred times his normal weight. The impact was brutal. His lungs were crushed within their cage of bones and his limbs suddenly brittle, like rusted iron. Alarms fired off around the room. They echoed down the corridors outside. Raw. Desperate.

His face burst the handful of ripe yellowberries. The wooden punnet broke painfully against his belly.

Barl tried to raise his head against the crushing force of gravity pinning him to the deck. His neck muscles screamed in protest, but his head wouldn't come away from the cold deck no matter how hard he tried.

The *Minular* lurched sickeningly.

Barl was thrown, his special awareness undone as suddenly he was upside down on the deck, pressed up against the floor with the ceiling somehow *below* him. For a moment, as gravity reversed, and Barl hung above the room trying to make sense of the crazy perspectives and the free fall rush hollowing out his guts. He didn't know if he was going to vomit or piss himself. The strain on his body was incredible.

Then he crashed down on to the ceiling, smashing the side of his head against a brass light fitting.

A trickle of blood from the fresh wound brought him back to his immediate reality.

Two more huge detonations ripped through the ship, off in the distance, rumbling and shaking the very core of it, the aftershocks surging all around him. These felt *nearer*, he knew, and considerably more powerful.

A new alarm blared, and with it the voice of the Bantoscree captain shouting over the shipboard com-channel: *"Hull breeched on levels four to six! Abandon ship! Abandon ship!"*

Abandon ship?

Leave?

How? I can't move! His mind screamed. Barl tried to calm his racing thoughts and the panic surging through him. What was he supposed to do?

There had to be some sort of escape capsules, surely? A way out or why would the captain be shouting for them to abandon ship?

He had no idea where they were or how to operate them. A few weeks ago, he hadn't even known what *space* or *stars* were, even as a concept, and now he was expected to survive a star-ship blowing up?

He was doomed.

Come on.

Come on.

Nothing was moving.

No part of his body possessed the strength to fight the increased and crushing gravity. Every breath had become a jagged struggle in his chest. The ceiling beneath him was a collection of raised whorls and sharp bumps.

Come on.

It was like laying against lacerating gravel.

Come on.

As the forces around him increased, pushing him ever harder until it felt like he was being pushed through the ceiling, Barl's clothes snagged and the skin of his forearms began to puncture.

The alarms cut out, but there wasn't silence in their place.

Something *fizzed* in the structure of the ceiling. He could smell acrid burning coming from somewhere beneath him.

Another explosion tore through the ship.

The deep rumble made the ceiling buck beneath him.

Barl's arm slid across the raised stippled pattern, skin splitting against one razor sharp corner. Agony flooded through his arm. He rolled away, clutching the wound with his other hand.

And in that move realised that the incredible force of gravity had relaxed.

He could move!

Barl got to his feet, still disorientated by the upside-down room, and spun around trying to remember where the door would be in this inverted landscape. He walked unsteadily towards it, not sure what he was going to find in the corridor outside but knowing whatever was out there had to be better than the inevitable death that waited for him if he remained here.

Barl palmed the door mechanism hard and the door swished up onto a scene of icy horror.

The smell hit him first.

The rank odour of bile and fresh vomit, mixed with...he couldn't even begin to guess... It was awful. He saw that two Bantoscree had been crushed... *smeared*... across the corridor wall opposite his room. Their innards dripped like slime down the walls, their bodies split open, the gaseous sacs of their mid sections popped and deflated, tendrils hung down in limp tangles, their compound eyes crushed like thin ice on a winter pond.

Both were dead.

There was nothing he could do to help them.

Barl didn't know which way to go.

The only times he'd ever left his chamber had been to go to the Training Deck. That meant he knew little of the geography of the ship. The Training Deck was towards the centre. Logic dictated any escape capsules would probably be towards the outer decks of the *Minular*.

Signs on the wall pointed in various directions in an alien script.

Barl walked along the corridor ceiling, heading away from the Training Deck, hoping that it would take him towards the periphery of the ship and a way out of this charnel house. He found more Bantoscree corpses littering the corridors. He side-stepped to avoid light fittings and engineering conduits.

Engineering conduits…

Two words that he did not recognise, but that he seemed to know.

Other images flooded his mind as he half-ran, a door surrounded by yellow lights, a panel next to it in alien script that resolved into words he *could* read. Suddenly the words on the sign were made from letters of the alphabet his mother had taught him in *God's Heart*.

ESCAPE CAPSULE. PRESS TO ENTER.

It made no sense.

A sick feeling rushed through his stomach. Barl had to stop. His knees buckled and he pitched forward steadying himself by throwing out a hand and grabbing at a pipe running along the wall.

'We're being attacked. Keep going kid. Don't stop.'

Summer. Her voice loud in his ear. He spun around, slamming his knee on a maintenance conduit hatch beneath his backside.

The corridor was empty. There was no sign of Summer.

The nausea passed only to be replaced by a thumping headache that stole his breath away.

'You have less than a minute before the Minular shreds to atoms. I don't have the power to get us both out of here, too much dicking about on the Training Deck. We're going to have to do this the hard way. So, run you little prick! RUN!"

Barl didn't care how she had found a way inside his head, he trusted Summer. He scrambled to his feet and ran for his life, head down, arms and legs pumping furiously.

Explosions rumbled in the decks below, the ceiling beneath his feet shook again, tremendous forces at play, and *cracked*. Jets of scalding steam spat up, drenching him in boiling vapour. He screamed but ran on. The corridor flipped again and Barl crashed to the floor plates, winded again, but not willing to let even this slow him down.

He leapt to his feet and pelted along the corridor, running faster than he had ever run in his life.

He dodged between huge billows of steam that gushed down at random intervals along the widening cracks in the ceiling.

He approached a junction.

"*Left!*" Summer's voice screamed in his ear.

Barl used a pipe on the wall to swing himself around the corner and launch himself down a smaller tube-like corridor, lit only with red emergency lighting.

Emergency lighting?

"*Stop asking stupid questions! I'm sharing brain-space with you, you idiot. You're piggybacking my thoughts! JUST RUN!*"

Shaking his head to clear the fog of panic, Barl charged down the tube.

Blue arrows ran alongside him on the walls.

The nearest explosion yet boomed right above him. The tube split along its full length, torn in two. For a heartbeat—before fast sealing vacuum foam invaded the gap and stopped the violent decompression of the ship's atmosphere—Barl saw *directly* out into space.

The temperature in the tube surged brutally down well to below zero, and down more, until he felt frost crystalizing on his lips.

The tube swung violently to the right.

The claustrophobic red lighting pulsed faster and faster.

And at the far end of the tube, Barl saw the door of the escape capsule—exactly as he had seen it in a memory he didn't remember happening.

He ran headlong towards it, his heart hammering against his ribs like a woodpecker trying too…

"Woodpecker…?"

'Don't even think…'

The tube twisted, but not of its own accord; it was breaking apart. Another direct hit on the outside threatened to tear it clear away from the body of the ship. Seven more blasts ran in destructive concussions the length of the corridor.

A gout of flame crashed in from outside.

Particles of hull crashed through the metal walls like gunshots, peppering every surface in molten metal.

The vacuum boomed in from outside.

A fog of freezing air billowed the length of the tube.

Barl stopped in the icy, fast draining atmosphere.

He watched in horror as the escape capsule as the end of the corridor collapsed as if it were a beetle crushed beneath a giant's thumb.

The end of the tube broke away into space, leaving the open corridor waving widely across a star-scape filled with one-man fighters buzzing around the *Minular*, firing volley after volley of explosive missiles at it.

The explosive decompression reached Barl with its wintry fingers. Grabbing him and dragging him towards the hard vacuum. There was no chance to resist, there was no opportunity to grab onto anything, and even if he could, the speed he had already built up would have ripped his arms from their sockets and sheered through the skin leaving him dead.

His last thought before he was hurled from the wreck of the *Minular* into the cold drifts of space was that he'd never taste yellowberries again and that made him unimaginably sad.

CHAPTER 15

S hryke watched from the back of the Movable Church while the Congregation held their evening service.

It was like a dozen other pointless services he'd witnessed over the years.

The Church Leader moralised over one point or another, the worshippers nodding along, and then clapping and singing their happy songs.

There had been further benedictions and rituals—but they didn't look any different from those Shryke was used to. One type of worship was very much like another as far as the assassin was concerned.

At the end of the service, everyone had their taste of dirt to show their level of importance in the unfeeling universe, and then trooped out looking happy, smiling and animated with chatter and laughter.

Shryke wondered what they had to be so happy about?

There was the constant danger of attack by the single best-trained killers in the galaxy, a single one of whose number could kill every person here with their bare hands before they'd had a chance to finish a worthless prayer. The very fact that they were all still alive after the encounter, told Shryke that the Guild Assassins had been called away which meant they could well feel they had unfinished business with the Congregation.

One of the uglier truths about his people was that there were some of their number who *enjoyed* their jobs and that love of violence may yet prove to be the Congregation's demise.

Yane's request itched its way to the front of his thinking as he watched the Congregation clear the tent.

Initially, he'd given her a blunt refusal, dismissing her request with a snort and a half laugh, but Galdar had thrown him a pleading look. He had agreed to take a day or two to consider the offer properly. The fierce hug of thanks Galdar had given him outside Yane's tent, without tears, shaking or wild accusations, had been… pleasant. She was a surprising woman. Or was it his reaction to her that was surprising?

Shryke had been given a shelter on the edge of camp.

This part of the forest was near indefensible. He would have felt better if they at least found a hill or a rocky outcrop, something they could use to protect their backs. But if he started getting involved in strategies for their best defence, he'd be telling Yane that he agreed to her commission, and he wasn't doing that. So, he kept his mouth shut about the inadequacy of their defences and his steels within reach. He sat through the prayers with a short sword across his knees.

Galdar had been one of the novices attending at the ceremony.

She carried out her tasks with reverence, everything about her calm and unfussy. It was obvious to him that she was a deep believer. She took her minor role in the rituals seriously.

Shryke thought he'd caught her eye at one point, as she had walked past waving smoking incense sticks in the air, but she had looked straight through him, immersed in her spiritual duties.

Carlow helped at the ceremony but was nowhere near as focused on his worship as the girl. Shryke felt Carlow eyes, hot and unblinking, boring into him like bolts from a crossbow, lips thin with distrust and distaste.

There was genuine hatred in there.

He'd waited until Carlow left the tent before he crossed the dirt floor to where Galdar was folding beautifully embroidered cloths.

She opened a large metal-banded trunk and carefully placed the cloths inside. As she laid each one inside, she touched two fingers to her lips, and then placed the fingers onto the cloth. She repeated the little ritual several times as Shryke watched. He waited until she closed the trunk and locked it with an ornate key she produced from with the folds of her robes, before he spoke.

"You do this every day?"

"Three times. Yes. Sometimes four if there is a special service of remembrance. Tomorrow there will be an extra service for the three who were murdered by your Guild. We will celebrate their lives and works." Galdar got up from her knees, smoothing down her robes where they had creased. "What do you believe in Shryke?"

"Everything and nothing."

"But what does that mean? It sounds like an excuse."

"It is. Do I believe in Gods...?"

"God." Galdar corrected.

"*Gods*...no. I don't. Do I have all the answers? No. I don't even have all the questions."

Galdar picked up the trunk and walked towards the door. "Perhaps you will find them here, with us, if you stay."

He followed her towards the tent flap. "I doubt that."

"Why so sure? Isn't your mind open to the possibility of a greater power than you?"

"That's not why I'm unsure."

They came out of the Church into the chill evening. Torches burned, illuminating the camp, smoke rose from fires, steam rose from pots.

"Then why?"

"I won't eat dirt for anyone. Least of all an invisible God."

Galdar sighed and they parted company there.

Shryke watched her go. He hadn't meant to antagonise her,

but he couldn't help himself. He'd already given himself up to a greater power in the Guild Nest all those years ago. And look how that had turned out.

Shryke wasn't going to make the same mistake again.

Galdar didn't *want* to walk away, but she wasn't going to beg the Warrior to stay.

His flippant answer about eating dirt had both angered and saddened her.

She had felt herself warming to the tall raven-haired warrior for some time; since before they'd discovered the bodies. He was a compelling soul. She found herself drawn to him in a way she did not understand and could not deny. The bond between them seemed to grow stronger all the while, and Galdar would never admit it, but she found herself hoping more and more that Shryke would take up Yana's offer to stay with the Congregation.

Galdar was in her eighteenth summer now and knew there would be pressure soon to consider couple-bonding. She had always assumed she would be forced to join with Carlow; a thought which while it didn't exactly fill her with dread did little for her hope of happiness. The Quest for Safehome had been going for nearly two thousand years now across several links of the Chain and relied the seekers intermarrying and breeding to continue. Shryke, for all his faults and non-secular nature, was turning her thoughts to matters of the flesh, and that was a new feeling for her.

She allowed herself the tiniest of smiles and looked about surreptitiously to see if anyone in the Congregation had seen the emotion play across her face. She was terrible at hiding her true feelings. Her body and her expressions gave her away time after time.

"We don't want him here."

Galdar stopped, looking up, startled.

Carlow emerged from shadows between the tents.

He still clutched the branch which had felled Shryke.

Weapons of any kind were forbidden for curates.

Carlow would weasel out the excuse it was firewood or had been protection when Shryke had woken in the Church, but it was obvious the branch was meant to serve as a threat.

"That's not for you to decide," Galdar held her ground, but gripped the trunk tighter, ready to use it as a shield if Carlow decided to turn the threat into action. She tensed her arms, placed her feet a shoulder width apart, a stance that would give her the stability to fight—or run.

"Yane is a fool."

"*Reverend* Yane leads us, Carlow. You would do well to remember she is the head of the Church."

"Why? She exposes the Quest to danger? This…warrior…is a viper ready to strike at our heart. He is *one of them*. One of the killers. Surely you understand the danger she is putting us in?"

"Again Carlow, you have your opinion, but it's not one I share. I have travelled with him. I have seen him fight. Not just fight but fight for *me*. I know that he *will* protect us."

Carlow took a step forward. "He might protect *you*; it's the rest of us I fear for. Once he's saved his broodmare, what chance for us mere mortals?"

Galdar's anger welled up like a blazing hot fountain of lava from the depths of her guts, but, somehow, she kept her mouth closed.

Carlow saw the effort she was making. If he expected her to lash out and hit him again, it didn't show. "I've seen the way you look at him. I've heard you beg for his release and for us to trust him." Carlow reached out with the branch, touching it on Galdar's inner thigh. She wasn't about to give him the satisfaction of flinching. She wasn't scared. She was blisteringly angry.

The branch moved higher.

Galdar remained still.

"No point in him being tied up all this time is there? Especially if you want to welcome him to your tent with open legs."

Galdar knew the words were meant to provoke her into lashing out. She had already been censured by Yane and the Elders for striking Carlow once, and for running away. If she let her angr loose again, it could see her banished from the Congregation. So instead, she remembered the change in Shryke's attitude towards her when she'd first mastered her anger, and sought to do it again, biting back on the rage of emotions churning her up inside, forcing them down until, finally she was calm enough to etch the ghost of a smile on her lips. "I hadn't thought of that, Carlow," she looked down at the branch. "But now you say it, I'm sure he has a better *weapon* than yours."

The branch dropped.

She sidestepped the fool and walked on, seething still, but in control.

She knew Carlow would continue to goad her at every opportunity, but if nothing else, the last few days travelling with Shryke had taught her more about her own strengths than years around the demeaning battery of Carlow and his kind had taught her about her weaknesses.

Shryke settled down beneath his fern covered shelter.

His belly was full, the bedding fashioned from saplings was comfortable enough, and the wine he had shared gave him pleasing inner warmth. All the conditions were in place for him to travel into a dreamless sleep, and yet he could not find the route.

Shryke's ears were alive to all the sounds of the forest: the low murmur of voices from the members of the Congregation who were still awake and the distant sounds of the river in the valley below, waters dancing over rocks. Perhaps at Quarternight tomorrow he'd be able to rest, once he'd been with the Congregation a little longer and become more accustomed to their strange ways.

A little longer…

That surprised Shryke. Was he really coming around to the idea of staying with the Movable Church as some sort of mercenary bodyguard? Would they expect him to observe religious niceties—or worse, to convert?

He rubbed his tired eyes.

I'm just exhausted, he thought. *That's what's making my mind wander.*

He tried to think of other things.

Out in the camp, a robed female figure moved among the sleepers, touching those on the forehead who were already sleeping, bending her head in prayer and placing stones on fires to put them out for the night. She was dressed in a red habit; perhaps it was Yane moving among her people, transmitting strength to them in the certain knowledge that she had their best interests at heart?

The dimly lit figure moved on. Bent. Touched. Prayed. Put out a fire. Moving towards Shryke and his tiny pyre of burning twigs. The flames in it guttered. It wouldn't take more than a handful of dirt to extinguish it.

Yane moved on. Bent. Touched. Prayed. Extinguished a fire.

Was she coming to him to persuade him to stay?

Would she look to bribe him with a retainer? For all the Church's protestations of poverty, there was always money to be found.

Bent. Touched. Prayed. Put out a fire.

Shryke rubbed his eyes again—looked at the figure in the habit moving through the camp. It wasn't Yane. Now that she was nearer, he was sure of that. The woman's frame was wrong, less stiff, less formal.

Was it Galdar?

No. Too short. She walked with a limp.

The shadows around her face were too deep for Shryke to make a clear identification, but she was coming ever closer.

A flash in the dark hole of his memories.

Something…

The paw of a wolf.

Bent. Touched. Prayed. Put out a fire.

Shryke could follow her path through the camp. A line of extinguished fires directly through the centre, heading inexorably towards him. Shryke tried to rise, but his exhaustion was total, he yawned, his eyes smarted with campfire smoke and his limbs felt as though they were made from lead.

The snarl of a wolf, leaping out of the blackness in his head.

The robed nun continued her approach.

There were no fires now between her and Shryke.

As she drew closer, a cool dread seeped into his bones, growing up from the ground up.

It came out of the earth.

A damp and scathing chill rose into his body, sitting tight in his throat, blocking out any scream that may have been born there. With rising, impotent, panic, the robed figure came close to Shryke's paltry fire.

The fire lit the skull raw face inhabiting the folds of the hood, pieces of dried flesh clinging to the bone in strips. Dry puckered eyes moved slowly in crusty sockets.

As the full force of the *dread* overtook Shryke's paralysed body, a bony, fleshless hand reached towards his forehead, ready to burrow into his skull and end his life where he lay.

It was The Mother Superior.

CHAPTER 16

H ard Vacuum.

As the air rushed out of the tube so did all sound.

Barl was deaf to the destruction of the *Minular* as it disintegrated around him.

Cold unlike anything he'd ever experienced thudded into his young body and he felt his eyes begin to frost as his vision crystallised.

The irony of someone who did not know that the space outside *God's Heart* had existed just a few short months ago, now being ejected into it—for the *second* time—wasn't lost on him. Either he was the unluckiest boy in the universe, or God herself had a terrible sense of humour.

The muscles in Barl's neck hardened. He lost the ability to turn his head.

His vision was at the mercy of his slowly spinning body and even that would be lost to a patina of ice in a few seconds.

Then everything blinked out.

Went dark.

WHAM!

Air rushed in.

It slammed into his ears with sudden fury.

The ice on his eyes boiled away.

He hurtled into a soft crash-couch inside a small, spherical room, the air battered out of his lungs by the impact even as more surged in. He rolled in agony off the crash-couch, thudding to the floor.

Summer's unconscious face greeted the mist of ice retreating from Barl's pupils. Her mouth was slack, and thin trickles of blood ran from the corner of her mouth, her nostrils, her ears, and to Barl's distress the corners of her eyes.

Summer was crying blood.

"Summer?" he tried to say, but his voice was nothing more than a crack of sound. Dry and broken. It hurt his larynx to make even that little noise. His skin itched all over. His spine protested as he tried to sit up.

Reaching for Summer, he touched her braided hair, stroked it.

She stirred but didn't wake.

Her lips moved on a couple of soundless words and then were still.

But she wasn't dead.

Barl knew enough to grasp that bleeding from the eyes wasn't a good thing.

But he couldn't see any other signs of injury.

Her clothes were intact. No tears. No blood seeped out from any wounds.

Barl's neck had relaxed enough to take in his surroundings.

He was inside a ball-shaped room covered in soft, safe looking surfaces. Gravity felt normal for the *Minular*. As he looked up, there was a glass porthole through which a star-field moved.

He looked around for something he could use to warm Summer.

Was this the escape capsule?

Barl had no idea how he'd arrived here but looking at Summer and the blood seeping from her eyes and ears he could make a guess. She'd taken herself to the very limits of her strength to bring him in here, and it had taken a terrible toll on her.

Unable to see anything he could easily put to use, Barl took off his thin jacket, folded it a few times, and placed it under Summer's head as a pillow. The blood on her face was drying in the warmth of the capsule. It didn't appear to be free flowing. That had to be a good sign.

Barl stood and looked around.

There were thin instrument panels designed to be used by Bantoscree tendrils, and small instruction signs—or at least that was what he assumed they were. He could no longer read the alien script. He didn't dare touch any of the controls in case something he touched inadvertently fired off a door or vented the air into space or something.

Barl jumped up in the low gravity, stretching to reach the porthole and peered out into the void.

What was left of the *Minular* hung dead and dark in the vacuum, lit only by distant starlight.

The small fighters had gone, their vicious work done.

Barl tried to see if there were any other escape capsules floating nearby, but if there were, he couldn't see them. The star field outside the porthole wasn't only slowly revolving, but the distance between the capsule and the wrecked *Minular* was also increasing—quickly enough to suggest that soon he would no longer be able to see the ship with his naked eye.

Barl craned his neck to give himself the widest spread of sky to scan.

Milky gulfs of stars crossed vast bands of night in one direction.

In another, a misty patch resembling gargantuan gas cloud, lit internally by a lush pink glow, pulsated as he looked on.

Barl couldn't tell, as he had no frame of reference to measure, if the gas was within touching distance or a billion miles away.

His gaze swung back to the wreck.

The *Minular* had been opened up like a goat on a butcher's table: gutted and stripped. There were no obvious signs of life. Not a light or a fire. Sections of it spun into each other, crashing together and breaking apart to fly off in new directions, while others were held to the main wreck by silver filigrees of tortured metal.

Barl thought of the Bantoscree Gharlin, crushed by the sudden increase in gravity and then torn from the ship, thrown into the merciless vacuum.

He hoped against hope that at least some of their kind had escaped but knew that was unlikely.

If Gharlin was dead, Barl thought, he owed it to his friend to visit *he, she, its* family and tell them what a wonderful soul Gharlin had been. But he doubted he would ever manage to make that visit. He hoped he lived long enough to prove himself wrong.

Barl let himself sit back down on one of the soft crash-couches.

He felt enormously tired, as if all the life in him had drained away. He felt the heaviness of exhaustion in his limbs, and the call of sleep. The feeling pervaded his bones, and yet just seconds before he'd felt wide awake and alert but now…

A thin dribble of drool made its way from the corner of his mouth down his chin. He didn't care, didn't have the energy to wipe it away…

Barl caught a flash of movement in the corner of his eye and for a few seconds his heart leapt, thinking that Summer was awake and recovering, but that didn't make sense, Summer was still unmoving on the deck of the capsule beside him, her head resting on his folded-up jacket.

Barl wanted to turn his head but didn't.

It would take too much energy.

It would…

The movement again.

Like a swish of a dark red robe.

As though someone stood beside him.

But that *couldn't* be…?

He was alone in the capsule with Summer.

Barl's eyes closed. He fought to open them again.

Why fight?

Surely, I deserve to sleep? It's been a terrible day. Sleep heals and…

With supreme effort Barl turned his head to where the swish of red robe had last been.

Don't look.

He kept turning his head.

Don't look.

There was more robe. A figure. Someone was there.

Barl could only see the folds of dark red. He couldn't see limbs or a face.

He needed to look…

Don't look up.

…up. But sleep. Sleep was so warm. So beautiful. Everything would be all right if only he slept.

If only…

The face was a grinning mask of skull, smothered in decayed flesh. Insects moved in the mouth, in and out of the gaps in the teeth. Eyes, revolved in the scabbed crusts of the sockets, staring through Barl.

Something dry and dead pushed itself into Barl's mind.

A thin, bony arm bereft of flesh disappeared out of his vision. Those fingers reached through his hair. He felt the crackling knuckles scrape against the inside of his skull, felt the invasion within his brain, tapping against the inside of his face.

Barl wanted to scream.

Don't scream.

Terror. Pain. What was…

Don't scream.

The voice was a dead whisper inside his throat; it filled his mouth with a fist of white bone fingers. It pushed down his tongue, closing his lips with a sharp pinch from the inside.

Barl's eyes swept crazily side-to-side, tears bubbling from the depths of the sockets. His breathing rasped and tugged at his chest. His heart cowered from the bone fingers reaching towards it. Down. Down. Through his gullet, expanding his neck to the point of splitting.

The red robed abomination leaned in …

Don't scream.
I want to…
Just die.

Summer crashed into the robed skeleton and tore it away from Barl.

The boy fell limp to the deck. She had no way of knowing if Barl was aware of what was happening, only that he couldn't help.

The creature was thrown back against the porthole, but not before it reached into Summer's guts and twisted and yanked at the strings of intestine. She screamed through the sheer blinding agony of it, but kept on fighting. She punched the skull. The jaw cracked and hung limp. She kicked it in the belly, and then conjuring a battle-mace, thick and heavy from the air with a whisper of the codespell, smashed it into the creature's body, slamming the damned thing back against the porthole.

The creature passed through the glass and travelled outside the capsule as if the wall wasn't there.

She didn't understand.

How?

She closed the distance to the hull wall.

The creature's eyes blazed before her in the half-heartbeat before they blinked out of existence and the red robed creature of ethereal bone was gone.

Summer dropped the battle-mace and then dropped herself, falling back onto a crash-couch. Fresh blood streamed from her nose and eyes. The pain was beyond bearing. It tore through the muscles of her midriff.

As Barl looked on helplessly, blood began seeping through the material beneath Summer's fingers, blooming there like a deadly flower.

"No. Not that one. The next one along." Summer's voice hissed through pain and gasped breath. She was sitting up; her knees wedged against her guts, in what Barl feared was an attempt to stop them spilling out of her body.

Summer directed Barl to get a Medipac from one of the storage containers in the capsule. She didn't have the energy to piggyback his mind and share the meaning of these unfamiliar words. Barl had a thousand questions about what had attacked them, both in the capsule and back on the ship, but finally free of the influence of the creature and able to move again, he knew he had to act fast to save Summer.

"Yes. That one. The latch. It's on the side." He fumbled with the latch, struggling to open it. "Come on. *Dying* here."

He finally sprung the lock.

Inside he found a complicated looking piece of machinery that was easily the size of his hand, fingers outstretched, "Is this it?"

"Yes. Now throw it down!"

Barl unclipped the Medipac from its cradle inside the locker and dropped it into Summer's open hand.

Wincing in pain, her fingers trembling, she worked at several switches on the device's shell, and crying out, pulled up her tunic to expose the gaping wound that sliced deep through the layers of her belly. The blood and the muscle and loops of grey gut was terrifying. She set the machine down on her belly and sank back against the wall, letting the Medipac do its work.

Barl had to look away.

The machine whirred to life with a deep buzz that hummed through the entire chamber, and a wild whizz that sounded like blades chopping madly against each other. He couldn't look at Summer.

He was sure she was going to die on him.

After several minutes, the mad chorus of noises stopped.

He heard Summer slump to the deck, unconscious or dead.

He finally looked at her and saw that the Medipac had slid away from the wound, still clinging to her skin above it. A pattern of lights blinked slowly on and off, is if the thing were somehow listening to what was happening inside her. The wound on Summer's belly was closed and stitched with crazy lightning-jagged lines of suture thread. Blood still oozed between the stitches, but she was alive.

Barl felt utterly helpless. And more than anything, scared.

With Summer unconscious what would stop the creature returning?

Barl sat beside Summer.

He picked up her hand and squeezed it to his chest, unsure if he were comforting Summer or himself...

CHAPTER 17

D*on't scream.*
    Shryke couldn't move.

The Mother Superior's festering face and white bone arm snaked with cruel precision from her red robe into the top of his head. It was his whole existence. It blotted out the sleeping Congregation and the camp. There was only Mother Superior.

Don't *scream.*

Just *die.*

Shryke's helplessness, his inability to fight back against the bony intruder defiling his skull, grew into a harsh panic deep down in his guts. Somehow, she was stopping him even attempting to flee to The Plain to beg for new reserves of energy, new codespells. New hope.

If he tried working at the very edges of his ability, he could barely summon the will to lift the tip of his index finger from the bedding, but that wasn't enough to muster even the smallest of resistance magic to conjure an escape.

Shryke looked away from the suppurating visage above him.

He tasted the rancid breath that even rushed out over the blackened teeth set in the Mother Superior's insect infested mouth.

He could barely make out the tip of his short sword sheathed beside the bed.

It was only inches away, but it might as well have been miles, such was the extent of the crushing paralysis.

His vision tunnelled down and down into the black of death.

The bone hand punctured the roof of Shryke's mouth, on its slow, inexorable path towards his heart.

Shryke knew that if the fell hand of this crypt creature reached the beating organ it would rip it out of its bone cage as easily as an eye from a month-dead pig.

The Sky-Shrine of Thalladon…

Shryke dismissed the morsel of returning memory.

This was not the time or place…

The fist snaked into his throat.

Shryke felt the muscles of his neck howl in agony.

He wanted to cough but he was choking. He wanted to gag but was denied even that petty rebellion. The Mother Superior's mouth, lipless and fleshless, turned from a rictus grimace into a cruel smile of triumph as her vile hand burrowed deeper into him.

Just die…

And that's when the battle-mace smashed into Mother Superior's spine, snapping the damned bones in half beneath the crimson robes.

The arm, dislocated from the creature's shoulder, slithered out of Shryke's skull and lay writhing in the dirt outside his shelter.

The creature howled.

Gathered up its fallen bones, the Mother Superior disappeared with a crackle of lightning and the delicate crash of distant thunder. As the air sizzled and sparked, Shryke saw a striking ebony-skinned woman with braided hair and a gaping stomach wound, holding a battle-mace cradled in her arms like a baby.

His saviour dropped the mace at her feet.

As the air rested, the woman disappeared too. Whether blinking into the Quantum Aether or just walking away, Shryke was too lost to tell. She left a dim shadow on the ground—it existed as a doom-laden wraith of darkness that needed no light to cast it. The wraith lingered, a second, two, three, longer, before it dissipated into nothing.

Shryke fell back. Mouth dry. Head pounding. Heart trying to escape his chest.

It had been forever since he had seen her.

So long that he had lost his memories of her to the seasons.

There were no signs of attack on the freshly killed bodies in the camp.

It was though death had visited them in the night and gently taken the souls without a struggle.

There had been much wailing and chest beating alongside the discoveries, but no one spoke of an enemy in the night.

Not one of the Congregation had witnessed the slaughter, sleeping through the entire Quarternight without waking. The dead had just…died…with no obvious reason or cause. There were no apparent injuries. Some whispered fearfully of poison, but everyone had eaten the same food and drunk the same wine, which made it unlikely.

Once the shock and the grief had given way to confusion, the mystery surrounding the deaths whispered around the camp. It didn't take long before the finger of suspicion pointed at Shryke, but as the first eyes fell on him, they saw a sleeper slowly waking, as oblivious to what fell evil had stolen into the Church to claim those souls as the rest of them.

Reverend Yane regarded the corpses of friends she had loved like her own and felt nothing beyond pain. The dead were like children to her. She had seen them brought into the Church and raised on the Quest. And now saw them as corpses, faces covered by shrouds, carried on biers by dozens of mourners. Her eyes sparkled with tears as she contemplated what she was going to say, knowing that no words could give succour to her people.

How was she supposed to assure them of their safety when something like this could happen while they slept? How could a man like Shryke protect them from such evil?

It was a thought echoed by Carlow, "So much for our *protector*," the Curate gloated.

Yane threw him a bleak look.

Galdar felt the hollow of loss and regret—she wanted to argue with Carlow, tell him it wasn't Shryke's fault, but the all-enveloping pall of sadness which covered her, stilled the words. There would be enough time for them later.

Galdar looked to the back of the Church as the rest of the Congregation filed in for the service, hoping to see Shryke sitting where he had for the evening service a Quarternight ago. He was not there.

The service was low key and reverential.

Yane spoke of good people called before their time. She talked of God's will. She reminded them of the fine works completed in the years the dead had been with the Quest. She remembered how all of them, in their own ways had lessened the burdens of others. She shared stories of how they had comforted the scared and lonely. She mourned their deaths but swore that they would not deter those left behind from their sacred mission to locate Safehome. Yane promised that was exactly what those taken in the night would want.

Galdar heard a snort of derision from Carlow. As much as she loathed the pathetic little man, it was hard to deny that Yane's words felt thin and empty in the shadow of last night. Platitudinous would save them. She would never admit that to Yane, though.

Scanning the Congregation, Galdar looked at the faces of people who had had enough of death and the misery of grief.

She felt the same.

The Congregation parted silently, Carlow walking out with a face of foul thunder.

The bodies were prepared for burial.

Galdar wandered amongst the Congregation. Everyone was silent. A few fires were lit, a few gathered around them, but most sat alone in contemplation or in small circles resting their heads on each other's shoulders.

A forbidding gloom of grief hung over the clearing.

Galdar just wanted to be free of it.

Shryke lay in his shelter, facing away from the Congregation.

Galdar couldn't tell if his was awake or asleep.

His small fire had gone out, but she saw the sheen of sweat on his back, as though he burned with fever.

Was that what had happened? Some brutal illness that had swept through the Congregation? A contagion that even now spreading amongst the survivors?

Galdar bent and touched Shryke.

In a startling moment of explosive movement, the assassin was up off his bedding, had Galdar by the throat, swept her feet out from beneath her and slammed her into the ground, the razor-sharp edge of his black blade at her throat.

"Stop!" Galdar choked out, desperately hoping that no one in the Congregation had seen them.

Shryke blinked. She saw it in his eyes. He hadn't been here. In that moment he snapped back into the *now*.

He relaxed the point of the sword and sank back onto his haunches, before he cast the sword aside and rubbed his eyes.

Was that sweat he wiped away or tears?

Galdar couldn't tell.

When his hands came away from his face, she saw his blood-shot eyes. The skin around them was raw.

Shryke was uncomfortable with her gaze on him. He got up and turned away. "What do you want?"

"I came to see how you were. Do you have a fever?"

"No."

Shryke still couldn't or wouldn't make eye contact with Galdar.

She got up and rested a hand on his back again. She felt him stiffen against her touch, but it was his only reaction.

"Why can't you look at me?"

"I can hear you. Isn't that enough?"

Galdar was confused. Shryke seemed so…vulnerable. It was unsettling. This wasn't the man she had come to know on their journey. She moved around him, standing on his bedding and looking up at his face. Still, Shryke avoided her eyes. She touched his cheek.

His hand came up and grabbed her palm, not to share in the comfort but to deliberately take her fingers away from his skin.

"I don't want to be touched," he said quietly.

"What happened? Why have you changed? What did you see last night?"

"Nothing. I haven't. I was asleep. I saw nothing."

"You are accustomed to death, Shryke. I'm not a fool. I know that. Death is your life. I don't believe for one second that five people dying, people you don't know and have no connection to, is going to twist you like this. So, tell me, Shryke. Tell me what has changed?"

Shryke took a step back, still avoiding Galdar's concerned gaze. "Bad dreams." He said, which was no kind of answer at all.

Galdar took the plunge; if he wasn't going to talk to her because they were friends, or possibly more, then perhaps if she goaded him, she might get the answers she wanted? "Children complain about bad dreams. Not warriors."

She got a reaction, but not the one she had expected.

Shryke pushed past her, retreating into his makeshift shelter. He buried his head in his hands and wept.

Later, after Galdar had relit his fire, warmed him some soup in a crude bowl, and the sobbing was reduced to memory, Shryke took the proffered food and sat cross-legged with her in the entrance to the shelter. He was embarrassed by his earlier show of emotion.

"I do not cry easily," the assassin said.

Galdar sipped her soup. She nodded rather than interrupt.

"Truth be told, I can't remember the last time I cried. Perhaps it was when I was boy… in the first days after I was separated from my parents and taken to the Guild Nest for training." He shook his head. "I don't remember. The years have stolen those early days from me. If I did cry, then it was through grief and loneliness. I was in a strange world, forever changed. I could never go back to being who I was. I would never be that innocent boy again. But today I was not crying from sadness, nor loneliness." He leaned forward, his voice sounding so much weaker than it had in all the days she had known him. "I wept with *fear*, Galdar. Fear. Stone cold fear. And that is something I have not felt since it was battered out of me during my training. Fear is a luxury. Fear makes a warrior hesitate. Fear allows doubt. Fear kills men like me. *I do not fear…* and yet… I was afraid."

Shryke took a sip from the soup cooling in his bowl.

She was no longer hungry.

He used the moment to collect himself, slowing his racing mind.

Galdar took a sip of her own soup.

"Last night, I dreamed that death visited me here. I dreamed that its hateful face and cold hatred invaded not just this clearing, and your Congregation. It was inside my flesh. I dreamed death reached inside my body, cold fingers clawing deep within the tissue and muscle in search of my heart—and I knew it was going to tear it out of my chest and there was nothing I could do to stop it. I couldn't move. I couldn't speak. I felt that chill hand inside me." The fear was there in his eyes as he shared the memory. This was no mere nightmare he recounted. "If the woman hadn't woken me in that moment I would have died. Not only in my dream state, but here, in this woodland. She saved me."

"What woman?"

"She was tall. Striking. Some might say beautiful. Her skin was ebony black, so perfect it shone like silver in the moonlight. She wore her hair in fierce warrior braids. She shook me from my dream and saved my life."

Galdar's confusion must have been evident on her face because Shryke lowered the bowl from his lips without taking a second sup. "What?"

She shook her head. "There's no one like you described in the Congregation."

"Impossible," she was here, "look."

Shryke put the bowl down and scrambled back to reach under his bedding for some half-buried treasure. "She left this." Shryke placed the battle-mace in Galdar's hands. "She *was* here," he insisted.

CHAPTER 18

B arl wasn't sure exactly how long Summer slept before the Medipac fell away from her body, but is was long enough for him to sleep, wake, sleep, wake and sleep again. It felt longer than it was because he'd been unable to find any sort of toilet in the escape-capsule and been forced to improvise. He didn't feel good about his solution, but it was better than the alternative.

He had tried to calm himself enough to open a wound in the air and weave a sense memory of yellowberries so that he might get some sort of sustenance, but no matter how fiercely he willed it, there was no sudden feeling of weight in the air, and nothing appeared on his upturned palms.

Fear had robbed him of any power.

Fear of the red-robed skeleton.

The Mother Superior, a voice whispered in the recesses of his mind. He had no idea where it came from, or how it named the demon death, but he did not doubt the veracity of those three little words.

When Summer finally awoke, Barl was hungry and weak from thirst.

The first words out of her mouth, weak and phlegmy, were, "What is that damned *smell*?"

Barl pointed with some embarrassment at the locker he'd been using at a cess-pit.

"I couldn't find a toilet."

Summer stood slowly and rubbed at her face vigorously to restore circulation and wake herself up. "Bantoscree don't need them."

"Surely they…?"

"They excrete gas. And right now, I'm wishing you did the same."

Summer went to the locker, opened it, made a sign in the air, uttered a few brusque words through gritted teeth, and Barl's waste disappeared. She kicked the locker closed, stretching her back, "How, long was I out?"

"I don't know," he admitted. "A long time."

Summer nodded. She looked up through the porthole, making a few quick calculations in her head. "Hungry?"

Barl nodded.

With a word and a turn of the wrist, several meaty sandwiches and waxy fruit appeared before Barl. With her other hand, Summer wove two pitchers—one of wine, one of fruit juice, and two ornate goblets. They would not die here, he realised, tucking in greedily to what felt like a feast.

He heard a *whoosh* in the air behind him.

When he looked, there was a crude toilet with a curtain rail above it.

Barl looked at Summer. Summer looked at Barl and shrugged. "Don't flush while in space dock," she grinned, and he couldn't help but laugh.

The food was good; Summer ate sparingly, rubbing the stitches in her stomach as she did so, obviously still in pain despite the fact her wounds appeared almost healed. She picked up the Medipac, spun a few dials on it and began to run her finger along several lines of read out. She sucked in her breath. "I was lucky, kid." She didn't need to elaborate. If he hadn't got to the Medipac when he did, she'd have been stinking the place up worse than his waste, and he'd be slowly starving to death.

Grimly she put the Medipac down. "Go on, ask."

Barl stopped in mid-chew.

He hadn't really wanted to think about what happened, but now it all came rushing back. The horrific skull, the skinned arm reaching down through his body...

"What was that *thing*?"

"I don't know. I can guess, though. It was bad magic."

"Bad...?"

"Yes. And powerful at that. That creature wasn't really here, not in the physical sense, but it had enough corporality to get inside you and rip out half my guts."

Barl shivered. He put down the sandwich. Suddenly he was no longer hungry.

"But there's a more interesting question," Summer said.

"There is?"

"Yes. Who sent it, and why go to so much trouble to kill *you*?"

"Me?"

"Yes. You. They weren't looking for me. The attack on the ship was one thing, in the grand scheme of things it could have been any of many causes, but you survived..."

"Thanks to you."

"Thanks to me. Yes. And don't you forget it," Summer ruffled Barl's hair and gave him a wide white smile. "So, they sent something else to finish their dirty work. Not a whole human, but *enough* of one. That can only mean it was projected from an incredible distance, or it would have had all the skin it required."

Barl was confused.

"To send a *whole* Assassin over extreme distances requires an enormous amount of power. If you don't send the whole Assassin, but just enough of it—half in the reality, half out of it—then you have considerably more chance of it getting to where you need it. Remember what I told you on the training deck about how much it costs to create the energy for magic?"

Barl nodded. "Yes. You transported me here when the *Minular* exploded didn't you? That's why you were unconscious and bleeding when I got here, right?"

"Exactly that. It almost wiped me out."

"Your eyes bled."

"Which is not a good thing. My strength was so depleted I had nothing left to protect you with against that thing. I got lucky."

"I reckon we've used up our luck for a while."

"A couple of lifetimes' worth, at least," Summer agreed.

Barl had another question, one that he probably wouldn't want to hear the answer to, but he needed to ask it. "Are we going to die here?"

"Not if I can help it." Summer said. "We're still light-years from Pantonyle in deep interstellar space, if my calculations are even close to right. The problem is escape capsules have no motive power of their own, except for thrusters to get them down safely onto a planet. So, as we're not near any planets, the thrusters aren't going to help us. There are communication arrays in the capsule, but nothing that will cover the range we need—the emergency beacon will have tripped, but that does have a hyper-space component, so I'm not convinced the beacon will reach far enough to tag a ship—even if it's heard by one willing to get involved."

"That doesn't sound promising."

"Sorry about that," Summer picked up a goblet of wine and took a healthy swallow. Smacking her lips, she said, "Good job we haven't used up two lifetimes' worth of luck already, eh?"

Days passed slowly in the escape capsule.

Days where Summer healed and grew stronger. Days where Barl became more convinced that the space in which they were trapped was poorly named. They could no longer see the *Minular*. Summer explained that this was a safety measure. "When starships are destroyed there's a lot of dirty energy expelled from reactors and weapons arrays. The escape capsules are as shielded as they can be for their size but need to put distance between the wreckage and themselves if the dirty energy isn't going to undermine their integrity, so they are jettisoned in the direction of the nearest planet."

"Does that mean we're heading towards a planet?"

"It does. But you'll be very dead by the time we reach it. A thousand years give or take, at our current speed."

They occupied themselves with Barl's continued training.

"Time for you to be a modern man, Barl. Hunt and gather," Summer laughed, turning his palms up and pushing his elbows in. Barl tried his hardest, willing any sort of sustenance to take shape in his hands, but on the few occasions it did work the only food he could scavenge were yellowberries, and rather than satisfy him, his constant failures and half-successes only served to frustrate and exhaust him.

After yet another frustrating attempt in which Barl could only manage to conjure sweat and bitter bile at his failure, he sat down heavily on a crash-couch and asked Summer to tell him not how to weave magic, but what it actually *was*.

"In all honesty, we don't know. Some people are born with the ability, sometimes they find out for themselves, which seldom ends well. They end up killing themselves by accident or starting wars. The lucky ones might make a fortune in a casino and think they're just very lucky. Less often, the Guild pick up flavours and indicators of someone with the first primitive stirrings of talent. Like you. For some reason *God's Heart* has a propensity for creating magicians and mages. We don't know why that is. But we keep Guild ships in the vicinity and when that...flavour...that taste emanates...we go in and..."

"Kidnap..."

"Rescue."

"I can't say that I feel particularly rescued."

"It's a better word than extricated. Seriously, kid, imagine if this power had come to you unbidden? I've seen kids just like you who've gone out of their minds because they diced their parents up in a fit of anger because they gave them extra chores to do in the kitchen. This stuff is dangerous. A thought. A word. The will behind it. It's even more dangerous because we don't know where it comes from, or why it's there or what it's for. We've had priests and scientists working on it for thousands of years. The magic seems to be a fundamental force of the universe. We haven't found a limit to these magics yet, just to the energy required. If you have enough energy, we suspect, we can do anything."

"Anything?"

"Then why don't we put our energies together? *Now.* See if we can get out of this mess?"

Summer was taken aback. "Together?"

"Yes. We've both been resting for a week. You're healed and when you first took me, I jumped to three different worlds, remember?"

"They were close by."

"But I jumped, yes?"

Summer considered.

"Out of control and with little direction, but yes. You jumped worlds."

Barl held out his hand. "Then let's see where we can jump ... *together.*"

CHAPTER 19

Galdar led the disbelieving Shryke among the defeated and heart-wounded Congregation.

Unless he set eyes on all of them, she knew he would never accept the truth: the woman who he described, the one who had saved him and left behind the battle-mace, was not one of their number.

Galdar tried to hold Shryke's hand, but he was having none of it. "I'm not a child." So, she settled for sliding her arm through his as they walked, selfishly enjoying the closeness that afforded.

Shryke, for all his warrior's power and physicality, shivered beside her. And though the woodland was chilly, it was not from the cold. Galdar felt it pass from his frame into hers as they moved. She squeezed his arm with hers. He would settle, grimly walking on, looking from face to face in search of the ebony skinned warrior with her braids. She couldn't imagine what manner of threat could transform the man who was a colossus of a fighter into a shadow of himself? The change both appalled and fascinated Galdar.

She was grateful they didn't encounter Carlow in this bitter trawl through the sorrowful ranks of the Congregation, fearing that Shryke would snap at his insults and remembering all too vividly how he had leapt at her when she'd tried to wake him. It wouldn't end well for the smart-mouthed Curate.

Shryke insisted on walking through the encampment twice before he finally agreed to sit down and take some water.

He was agitated and obviously suspicious of those around them.

He kept rubbing at a patch of skin on the side of his neck, so much so he had made it raw.

"You might want to bathe that and put some cooling balm on it before you scratch all the way through to the bone."

"No," he said, dismissively.

He kept moving his eyes from face to face around the camp.

Wary. Anxious. Scared.

Galdar knew Reverend Yane would call for them soon. Yane was anxious to find out what Shryke's answer would be in the matter of becoming the Congregation's protector, though Galdar knew it was a hopeless endeavour. Shryke was in no fit state to protect his own skin let alone three hundred worshipers. She said nothing.

Shryke picked up the battle-mace.

Its surface was intensely detailed. Raised lines and curved pictograms slithered over its angles and faces. The metal was alive with movement; it shimmered in the morning light, as if it were a silvery layer of metal beneath the sheen of clear mountain water. The handle was completely enclosed in leather strapping, which was black and well oiled. The whole thing looked freshly made. As Shryke turned it repeatedly in his hands, ever faster, Galdar felt her gaze becoming lost in its delicate whorls and incomprehensible sigils written into it.

She had to reach out and stop Shryke's twisting the weapon before she became utterly mesmerised by it.

Shryke looked up at her. She couldn't tell if his red-rimmed eyes were on the verge of anger or madness. One or the other. Shryke opened his mouth to say something, but in the end chose silence.

He threw the battle-mace down onto the bedding of the shelter and went back to worrying at the raw patch on his neck, fingernails revealing small specks of blood.

Galdar felt utterly helpless.

If Shryke had been a member of the Congregation, perhaps he would have found solace or succour in prayer and contemplation. They could have carried out calming rituals with each other, perhaps gone into the church to worship together, or make confessions to one of the priests. But faithless, what could he do to unburden his conscience? How could he return to himself? He'd given her no indication over the past days that he believed in anything except himself and his duties as a warrior. If he worshipped anything it was the abstract concept of honour. Or perhaps money, as that was something he was willing to kill for?

As Shryke scanned the faces nearby, Galdar took a few crumbs of earth from the ground beneath her feet and offered a prayer to Safehome on Shryke's behalf.

She left Shryke then, the assassin clawing at his neck.

He said nothing but looking at him she saw desperation and fear in his eyes.

It broke Galdar's heart to see it.

When she returned a few hours later, she wondered if Shryke had moved at all.

He sat cross-legged in the entrance to his shelter, next to a fire that had long since burned down to ash. Thick black scabs were forming over the wound in his neck, but at least he had stopped digging at it. Galdar placed a basket of small winter fruits down at Shryke's feet along with a jar of wine.

Shryke was unmoved.

His eyes darted.

His tongue moved like a snake across his lips.

She could see the fine trembling of his muscles.

Through the service, Galdar had agonised about asking Yane to give Shryke more time to consider his answer to her proposition. Perhaps by Quarternight or Secondsun he would be recovered enough to consider taking up arms for them. But she didn't want the reverend to lose confidence in the warrior. So, with a confused and worried heart, she chose silence. For a while she toyed with the idea of asking Lastag the Doctor to come to see Shryke; perhaps there were soothing balms or potions that might settle his angst? But Lastag was a cousin of Carlow, and worse, a gossip. Going to her would damage Shryke in ways that went beyond mere shivers.

She bit into her knuckle, desperate to think of some way to get through to the hollowed-out warrior.

She didn't understand what had happened to him.

Perhaps there were forces at work? Evils she didn't dare guess at?

The Assassins?

Assassins use poisons, don't they?

Perhaps…

Galdar heard footsteps approaching through the twilight. Determined footsteps. Shryke was unmoved as she saw her worst fears realised.

Carlow with his branch and his twisted grimace of distaste.

"I've told Yane all about him, you know."

Galdar wasn't about to let Carlow get under her skin with his goading. Shryke needed her to deal with the things he couldn't right now. She had to be his strength.

"Told her what, *exactly*?"

"About you and him."

She felt relief flood through her veins and relaxed. Carlow was still obsessed with the dark twist of his putrid imagination—good. Let him obsess about who she took into her bed. The more he stewed over that, the less likely he was to see the change in Shryke's demeanour.

"I saw you."

"Saw me what, Carlow? What has your jealous little brain dreamed up for us, eh?"

Carlow spat with derision. "Jealous? Don't make me laugh."

Galdar took a risk and stroked Shryke's bicep. He stiffened, but didn't move, "I'm sure a man like this could make us both very happy Carlow. What a specimen."

Galdar dropped her hand before Shryke could shoulder it away. He reached up again to pick away at the edges of the scab. She felt him tense beside her, wary. And not because of Carlow's presence. He cocked his head as though listening to something on the wind.

Galdar looked back to Carlow but tried to keep half an eye on what Shryke was doing.

"Your filth won't be able to pollute the Congregation much longer."

"Oh really?"

"Absolutely."

"And how did you work that out? Yane isn't going to banish either of us for falling in love…"

Shryke did react at that, but not in the way Galdar intended. The trembling in his muscles intensified. She saw sweat breakout on his brow. He continued to listen intently, moving suddenly up onto his haunches…alert…ready.

But for what?

"Love! Ha! Don't make *me* laugh. His kind don't love anyone. He hasn't even looked at you since I got here. Maybe you're a good roll in the ferns, but nothing more to a man like him. You're *nothing!'*

Carlow fell back as Shryke leapt up, grabbing the battle-mace as he did so. "I am betrayed!" He rasped, so much pain in those three words she thought his heart would break.

Four Assassins on horseback burst into the clearing, swords drawn and wearing faces like masks of death.

They circled and hollered.

"Over here! He's here!" Carlow called to them and backed

away with a smile as wide as his heart was tiny, levelling a finger at Shryke.

And suddenly it was obvious why Carlow had been absent from the encampment all day.

The worm!

But before she could leap at Shryke's betrayer and unleash all of her pent up and clawed fury, Shryke pushed her down onto the bedding and stood astride her, swinging the battle-mace.

The Assassins, following Carlow's call, kicked their spurs into their mounts' flanks and galloped towards him.

They were upon Shryke in seconds.

The battle-mace sailed and whistled in the air, but whatever dread had over-taken him since last night had diminished him.

The mace sailed through empty air.

Shryke took the full force of a shield to the side of the face, battering him to the ground.

All around the campsite, the members of the Congregation began to run blindly for the deeper trees—anywhere that might hide them from the death come riding among them again.

"They're back!" Jacka screamed, "They've come back to finish us! Mercy my Lord! Mercy!"

Shryke managed to get up on one knee, but only to meet an Assassin's boot as it thundered full into his face rupturing gristle and bone as it drove him sprawling back into the mud.

An ebony hand came out of nowhere, grabbed the battle-mace, and swung it with all the fury of the Gods.

One moment she wasn't there, the next she was.

The woman with the ebony skin and braided hair, stepped into reality from the world beyond.

And she was a demon.

Or an angel.

She was incredible. She fought with such ferocity, unleashing the fury of the seasons upon the four Assassins, ending them.

Her eyes blazed and her mouth roared.

Galdar couldn't move. She was rooted to the dirt, sure she was about to become one with the earth she worshipped.

But the ebony warrior pulled Shryke from the ground, lifting him easily to throw him over the back of a horse, and lashed him there with the reins before she whacked the beast on the backside, and sent it galloping off into the twilight.

Before she disappeared, the warrior woman lifted Galdar into the saddle of another, said "Get to the Sun-Machine. The Dreaming Army is there. Make sure they *stay* asleep. Shryke will know what I mean. And girl..." Galdar didn't know what was happening but the woman's earnest and kind eyes told her all she needed to know about whether she should follow her instructions.

"Y...yes?"

"Attend to his neck. If you don't, he *will* die."

With that, the woman warrior placed the mace in the saddlebag of the horse and disappeared.

Without another thought, Galdar kicked the horse into motion and crashed on in to the trees.

CHAPTER 20

S ummer's outline shimmered.

Her existence wiped out from top to bottom until the air was clear and all Barl could feel on his hand, where a millisecond ago her hand had been gripping his, was the impression of a ghost.

But then...

With a rush and a gust of chill, mountain air, redolent of pine needles and wood smoke, Summer was back as if she'd never been away.

There was a sharp crackle of energy between their palms and Summer was blasted backwards on a massive thunderclap.

She slammed into the crash-couch as the echo of sound reverberated through the tiny capsule, amplified by the walls encasing them.

Barl sucked at his throbbing fingers and went to Summer.

"What happened?"

Summer shook her head, trying to shake off the confusion, and sat up. She scratched her scalp and looked at the readings on the chronometer she wore on her wrist. The dials spun crazily, the readouts spiralling in intense flashing green and red, in languages Barl had no hope of deciphering. "I have no idea." Summer said,

followed by a low whistle of incredulity. "But it was mental....
Where did you send me?"

"Send you?"

"Where did you visualise before you blasted me who knows
where?"

"I don't know what you mean. I didn't send you anywhere."

Summer looked at him hard. "You didn't?"

Barl shook his head. "No. I didn't do *anything*. I didn't think
about anywhere or visualise anything. One second I was holding
your hand, waiting for you to tell me how to jump out of here, the
next you were gone."

"For how long?"

"Less than a second."

"Okay. That's something, at least."

"Where did you go?"

"I don't remember. It stank of horseshit though. Have I told
you how much I hate horses?"

For the next few minutes Summer paced around the capsule,
scratching her head and tapping her chronometer. Eventually she
stopped. "None of this makes any sense. I have no idea where I
went. I have no memory of how long I was there, and no idea
how I was brought back here. If you didn't do it, who did. And
why did they do it? Don't worry, I'm not expecting you to answer
that."

"Good, because I've got no idea either."

Summer sat down, crossed her legs and held out her hand.
"Right. Let's try that again."

Wind blew across a blasted and exposed moor.

A sick, red sun hung livid in a cloudless grey sky like an open
wound.

The air tasted foul.

Barl wanted to spit the taste away.

His feet were in wet, coarse, straw coloured grass.

Mud and water squelched below him as he walked. The water soaked into the bottom of his trousers, filling his boots, and making his toes cold and uncomfortable. Against the horizon, where the sun hung as if hacked into the very sky, he saw the silhouettes of armies fighting. Bannered pikes swung and danced, swords hacked, and volleys of arrows flew into the air like startled field-birds, over and over and over, filling that vile grey sky with a deadly steel-tipped rain.

The wind carried the clash and clang of steel.

Huge dragons, flying on impossible wings circled the battle breathing gouts of smoky flame. The beasts were incredible. The membranes of their wings bloody red, stretched thin as they banked and turned, riding the thermals. Wicked incisors longer than he was tall, scales thicker than any manmade armour. How these things rode the air, even with the displacement caused by the beating of their mighty wings, never mind how their flight skimming across the heads of the warriors could be so majestic, was a miracle Barl didn't think he'd ever understand.

He didn't know what he was doing here.

He wasn't a warrior.

And yet, when he looked down at his hands, he was aghast to see a short sword, balanced for a boy, resting in his palm as if it was meant to be there.

"Summer?" he called out.

He looked around desperately hoping to see that she was near.

The last thing he remembered was sitting in the escape capsule, Summer telling him to close his eyes. Anything after that was lost until the moment his eyes opened here on this plain, half a mile from a raging battle with a sword in his hand and his boots filling with water.

"Summer!" He tried louder.

A hand fell on his shoulder. "Come on kid, are you trying to get us killed already?"

Summer stood next to him in the wet marshy grass. Her upper

body was covered in a black breastplate, and armguards. She held a metal shield inscribed with an ornate dragon, and on her head, she wore a protective helm which seemed to match the grim face of the flying beasts above them.

Summer fingered the material of Barl's thin sweater. "We'll need to teach you about the benefits of armour," she said with a wry smile. "If we live that long."

"Where are we? Where have we travelled to?"

"We haven't travelled at all. Our bodies are still in the capsule. This is The Plain. This is the inner world. The Plain of Heroes. The world of panic and pain. This is where we draw the energy to weave codespells and ultimately where we source the magic we need to travel."

Barl couldn't take it in. He looked around as the wind bit into him. The inner world? The Plain?

"If we are lucky, we'll find my Familiar quickly and she will grant us a quick death."

"That doesn't sound very lucky."

"The alternative is being burned alive by dragon fire."

"In which case I hope we get lucky," Barl said.

Summer set off across the grassy tussocks, her armour reflecting the wide grey sky coldly in the dying light.

Barl had no choice but follow.

The battle raged below them on the plain.

An endless sea of grey armour splashed with blood and ichor of all shades.

The grass ran red.

Streams foamed crimson.

As far as the eye could see, the armies tore at each other, blades biting deep, bones and flesh opened up. Barl counted a dozen different species of fighter in the near vicinity alone. Snarling dog-faced warriors, others with faces like balled leather fists, teeth and skin of every size and every hue. The weapons were bloody and rusted with age and stained by dead flesh. In the air, the dragons circled, breathing flame that scorched down across the ground turning that flesh and bone to cinder and ash as the majestic creatures flew on huge black wings. Volley after volley of arrows flew up from the field of battle, aimed at the dragons. They bounced off thick scales and skittered away harmlessly, answered by brutal gouts of flame that seared and scorched earth and archer just the same.

The Plain was tundra cold, but the air around the battle steamed it was so hot. And thick with the stench of carnage.

A litter of limbs and heads and entrails made a carpet of horror over which the warriors fought.

Hacking. Stabbing. Killing.

Barl was sick to the stomach just watching.

Even the destruction of the *Minular*, with its ruptured Bantoscree and brutal detonations was nothing compared with the savagery of this battle.

Barl looked again from the unfamiliarity of the sword up to the only point of understanding he could find in the whole nightmarish landscape—Summer—and even she in her black armour seemed *changed*. She was utterly different—as if the armour made her something *more* than Summer. Something *more* than who she really was.

Or perhaps this was who she really was, and the Summer he knew was somehow reduced?

"Why are we here?"

"To die. Don't you listen?"

Summer took a small telescope from her belt, opened it and surveyed the field of battle. After a moment, she said, "Yes. There she is."

She snapped the telescope shut and returned it to her belt, "Come on, kid. Time to do this thing."

'Remember piggy-backing?'

Although Summer walked away from him down the sloped

side of the small hill, and was swinging her sword to loosen her shoulders, her voice appeared in Barl's mind as it had done in the corridors of the *Minular*.

"Yes."

'Think it. Don't say it.'

Yes.

'Good. Fight.'

Barl ran to catch up with Summer and they launched themselves in the throng as if hand-to-hand combat was their only purpose in life.

And fight they did.

Barl felt his hands coming together in a two-fisted grip on the sword. It was as though he had always been a warrior. He was made for this. With one fluid movement, he parried a wild clubbing blow from a Dog-face, then rolled his shoulder and adjusted his stance to hack at the back of both its knees, slicing them open with the razor-sharp edge of black steel. The creature stumbled and fell, howling balefully up at the grey skies above.

Barl hadn't thought about any of that.

It was all instinctual.

A huge titan moved to block his way. The creature was seven-foot tall and towered over him. It was impossible to tell if its horns were part of a helmet or grew out of the side of its head.

Barl struck. He let muscle memory guide him, dancing through a thousand cuts, each one blisteringly fast, like lightning never striking the same place twice, until he opened the titan's belly and spilled its guts out onto the field of blood.

It went down with a howling crash.

Ahead of him, Summer cleaved a path through the endless tide of attackers, opening flesh with cruel precision, cleaving heads from shoulders and dispatching justice with staggering skill. The woman was a true warrior.

Barl heard her words inside his head again.

She pulled him under her shield to protect him from the worst of the fire raging down from dragons overhead. The heat shrivelled the flesh of the burning warriors it left in its wake, turning bone to ash.

'The Plain exists as a reservoir of energy. If you want to take something physically or magically away from here, you must expend the requisite amount first. Pay to play. The only way to get out is to be killed, and if you get killed too soon...'

You don't take enough energy out with you?

'Nice going kid, maybe you're not as stupid as you look.'

They fought side by side. Summer the aggressor, leading, piggybacking to give Barl the fighting skills to dispatch the enemies where they stood. But even with her inside him, Barl was tiring. He wore a dozen cuts across his body, but none life threatening. With Summer's help he was holding his own against ancient warriors.

Through the throng of combatants, Barl saw the endpoint of their journey: on a small hill stood a lone woman in blue robes. Her hair was golden, and around her neck, there were a complex chain of necklaces and symbols. She seemed incredibly vulnerable where she stood in the midst of the battle.

Both her hands were empty.

She didn't need a weapon.

As Barl watched, a phalanx of bloodied warriors rose from the throng and charged at her. Within two seconds, they were smouldering corpses slithering back down the slope of the hill into the bloody mire.

Barl hadn't seen her move her hands.

All the woman had done, as far as he could tell, was look at them and they'd erupted in flames, their spines tearing bloodily, intact, from the backs of their leather armour to writhe like snakes in the mud, the men themselves still blissfully unaware that they were dead.

By the time Summer and Barl reached the hill the spines had stopped moving and the woman with the golden hair was once again looking at the ground around her.

Barl began to climb, swallowing down his revulsion as he

realised it wasn't a hill at all. It was a mound made entirely from the dead vertebrae of warrior's spines. They rolled and clicked under his feet, squirming in grey meat and white gristle.

As he climbed, Barl tried to stop sour bile rising in his throat.

He failed.

Summer knelt before the woman, and tugged Barl's sleeve down to do the same.

"Summer," said the woman, "So, you have returned?"

"Afraid so. It's all getting a bit intense out there."

"When is it not?"

"Good point. Well made."

The woman smiled, but still didn't look at Barl or Summer.

"What do you require?"

"A hyperspace spell, something with enough juice to transmit our escape capsule to Pantonyle."

The woman considered.

"You wish to combine your energies with the boy?"

"Yes. Frankly it was his idea. He's saved my life—saving me a trip here—so he's already on a roll."

The battled wore on around them as the Familiar considered her decision. The foetid sun refused to move nearer to the horizon. They could have been waiting a week or a second before the woman spoke again.

"Very well."

'Hang on kid. This is gonna hurt.'

But.

The woman looked at him.

Barl felt his spine burst out from his back as his body was washed in flame.

Barl's eyes snapped open in the escape capsule.

His back blazed with agony remembered and his skin burned red raw, but he was not on fire, and his spine was still very much there beneath his skin. The agony was merely the residual memory of what had happened on The Plain.

Summer's eyes blinked open.

She squeezed his hand.

The Guild soldiers opened the escape capsule with cutting code-spells and brute force.

As the doors came off and the warm air surrounding the Nest rushed in, Barl had time to register a purple, livid sky, and a high, twisted building made from a filigree of gold. He saw a tall thin beast, walking on three legs and heard words emerging sluggishly from its strange mouth.

Barl was pulled from the wreck of the capsule along with Summer.

Summer bled again from the nose and eyes.

As the breeze hit his cheeks and he felt the blood drying stiffly on the skin, Barl realised that he was, too.

"Welcome to the Guild Nest on Pantonyle," said the three-legged beast, "You are Barl?"

All he could manage was a nod at first, but he realised words were needed. He tried to explain himself. "Yes. I've journeyed from *God's Heart* for the Test."

The beast's stern face broke into a dazzling smile.

"The journey *was* the test," said the beast, turning and walking into the Nest. It added: "My sincerest congratulations, young Barl. You passed."

CHAPTER 21

The horse pelted through the darkening wood, weaving a path between he gnarled boles of tree trunks without care for the low hanging branches that could have thrown Galdar from its back. She rode low, clutching the animal's neck as it swerved through boughs, trying everything she knew to calm the terrified animal.

She got her hands onto the reins and used the bridle to steer her mount as best she could through safer gaps between the trees, on the cusp of anger at Carlow's betrayal and the desperation against losing sight of Shryke's horse.

The words of the ebony skinned warrior woman rang in her ears. What was the Sun-Machine? What Dreaming Armies? What was so terrible about the raw patch of skin on Shryke's neck that he was going to die if she didn't attend to it—and how was she supposed to attend to it? She wasn't a doctor or a nurse. She had no skills with herbs or medicines.

The gloom descended as they raced through the trees.

Full night fell like a bad headache.

Up through the undergrowth she occasionally caught a glimpse of the Overloop; milky grey and dotted with clouds. Years ago, when the Quest had started its journey around that link, Galdar had been a toddler, but even now she remembered the wide plains, the deserts and oases of that quadrant of the Link. She'd been born there to parents who themselves were born a link and a half away. There were bright days, cold nights and the endless sand. Always the sand. Her parents spun her stories of other links. The Dragons and the Airships, the sailing barges and the golden canals, but all of that seemed so very far away. Now she had been tasked to stay with Shryke—to help him and keep him alive, and to do so without experience to guide her. *Her!* Weak and tiny Galdar! With her big mouth and her short temper. The Links of Chainworld, even those of the misty Overloop were more substantial and stronger than the links stretching now between her, the Congregation, and her past.

She thought, for a moment, about stopping the horse, turning in her tracks and going back to where she had last belonged—the Congregation.

What help could she be out here to a terrified warrior on the run from people who could step right out of the air to kill him?

She began to tense the reins, summoning the courage to give up, which took more strength than she had. Knowing that she was about to lose Shryke forever, she couldn't pull back on the reins. Up ahead, Shryke's beast cleared the treeline and galloped towards the crashing waters of the fast-flowing river that bisected the valley, his unconscious form bouncing and shaking on the animal's back.

The river was too deep for the horse to walk across, but that didn't stop the animal from entering the water. It began to swim. Lashed across the saddle, Shryke's head was submerged again and again beneath the water only to rise up as the horse's gait lifted it clear. The river was wide, and the horse was not a quick swimmer—if Galdar didn't reach him soon Shryke's neck wound wouldn't be the death of him. He'd drown first.

Galdar kicked her horse on, bursting from the treeline into the chill moonlit air of the valley. Using her knees, she guided the animal towards the river.

Galdar brought the steed to a halt on the bank and jumped down wading into the water.

The river was fast flowing and freezing. It churned a channel down from the heights of the Thalladon Climbs. The sheer shock of the temperature drop forced a gasp from her lungs and made her swallow a mouthful of foaming water instead of a breath. Coughing and spitting, she clawed at the river ever more insistently.

The frightened horse up ahead seemed to dance sideways in the current, half of Shryke's face visible.

She rode the current until the burning in her lings subsided, letting the undertow do the work for her until she caught up with Shryke and with fast hands, lifted Shryke's head clear of the water.

The wound on his neck glistened blackly in the moonlight.

It leaked thin bubbles of pus.

Pushing the thought of it from her mind, Galdar kicked along with the horse until they reached the opposite bank. The horse climbed out easily, dragging Shryke up with it. Galdar grabbed at its leathers before the animal could run off again and attempted to sooth it with quiet whispers in its fluttering ears. The animal's breath came hard, nostrils flaring. It was still skittish. Her non-words, and soft, soothing hands stroking at its coat eventually did calm the animal down and enough that Galdar was able to tie the leather reins to a bush. Her own mount grazed on the other bank, seemingly content with its lot in life so long as there was grass enough to feed on.

She checked Shryke's airways, and once she was sure he was breathing, Galdar dived directly back into the river, and swam to the back to retrieve her horse.

Once back with Shryke, she unlashed the assassin and eased him down gently from the saddle.

Galdar rolled him in a dirty, stinking, woollen blanket she'd retrieved from a roll on the saddle. It had survived the crossing under an oilskin, which had kept it dry enough for what she needed from it.

The animals were Raider's horses. The Assassins wouldn't have come through on the animals, she reasoned, which mean they had appropriated them as spoils. How many more Raiders lay dead behind them? How many were left to hunt Shryke to avenge the death and Assassin's doom he had brought upon them, if any?

They needed a fire, and they needed it soon.

She rummaged in the sodden saddlebags for an oilskin-covered tinderbox, still dry and ready to be struck.

Once she had a fire lit and warming them both, she wrapped herself in a corner of the blanket and used the light from the fire to examine Shryke. There was a fearful bruise on the side of his head from where he'd been kicked unconscious. The area around his eye was already swelling blackly and seemed ripe enough to burst.

Galdar examined Shryke's neck. The scab was black and cracking through to weeping red flesh beneath. She probed it tenderly. Dark fluid seeped onto her fingertip—burning a little on her skin. She told herself it was the cold.

She wiped rank liquid on the blanket and went back to the scab.

Trying to keep the unbroken crusts beneath her fingers, she pushed down again. She was no anatomist, but she thought she could feel out a harder lump of something beneath the surface. It seemed to squirm against her touch. She had no idea what to do about it. Whether it was to be removed or lanced or fed upon by leeches?

Galdar felt helpless again.

It dismayed her even more to see that the ooze she had wiped from the wound onto the blanket had eaten through the fabric, leaving holes as if it had been eaten by moths.

What was inside Shryke's neck?

Secondsun came with a pounding of hoof beats and wild yells that woke Galdar from a nightmare-filled sleep of pursuit, illness and death.

Shryke was still asleep. He didn't stir beside her. Was this new inertia part of whatever thing festered within his neck? So much sleep was unnatural, surely?

Should she wake him?

Galdar stood.

The hoof beats thundered closer. For a moment she'd dared to hope they belonged to their own mounts, that somehow, they had slipped their tethers, but that hope died the second she saw the black team of Raiders gathering on the opposite bank. She shook Shryke's shoulder, hard. He murmured, his lips twitching, but merely rolled over. He didn't wake.

"Wake up, Shryke! Please! Wake up!"

Nothing.

"Galdar! Don't run!" The voice carried easily across the still morning waters. It was a voice she recognised. And loathed.

Carlow.

She squinted in the still too-bright light, shielding her eyes from the cold sun to see the man she'd once thought she might marry astride one of the horses. He wasn't a good rider. He had no mastery of the animal. The reins, she saw, were being held in the hand of another Raider while Carlow was bound by the hands to the saddle's pommel. Looking down, she realised his legs were lashed to the stirrups.

Carlow's face was a mess of blood and bruises where he'd been beaten. His surplus was stained red and there were two tears in the shoulder as though he'd been stabbed there.

"You can't get away," he yelled, desperation in his voice. The last word ended in a brutal hacking cough.

The lead Raider led his horse to the water's edge and called across the river, his voice steely with certainty. "And, believe me, girl if you try, I'll cut your young friend's throat and happily watch him bleed out."

She was tempted to say Carlow was no friend of hers.

Every Raider was dead.

Blood, thick with clots and torn flesh ran through the coarse grass down into the water. From there it ran away in an oily slick of violence and pain.

The stench of death hung in the air like an accusation. Dead eyes looked up to the sky, still surprised in death. Slack mouths, broken and crushed, echoed the screams of their owner's last agonies. Hands, dead and frozen, grasped blackly for reprieve.

Galdar was on her knees in the blood.

Suddenly coming to, she dropped the battle-mace as if it had bitten her hand and scrambled away from it through the sticky grass.

She slid over the body of a slaughtered Raider and his dead horse.

Her hands and forearms were caked in gore; she felt stipples of it drying on her face in the gentle morning breeze.

Galdar only came to rest when she bumped into Shryke's unyielding body.

"What…what *are* you?"

Galdar looked up, wildly, ready to run.

Carlow, still wet from being dragged across the river, still bound by wrists and ankles, stared at Galdar with awe and fear.

"What…*are* you?" he repeated.

Galdar hugged herself. Thirty or more corpses surrounded her and Shryke like the petals of sick flower. Blooming death.

"You just… that mace…and you killed them all. Everyone. No mercy. You were murder made flesh."

Galdar struggled to grasp what Carlow was saying.

The last thing she remembered was Carlow on the opposite

bank being cut down from his horse and being dragged into the water.

Then…

Flashes.

Screams.

Darkness.

Bones.

Blood.

Silence.

"They killed everyone we knew."

Galdar blinked. "What?"

"The Raiders. They arrived just after you left on the horse. They killed everyone, Reverend Yane, Lastag. Jacka. Everyone. They only kept me alive to use against you… They were going to kill me when you picked up that…mace…and…"

Galdar fell sideways. A wrenching moan of anguish dredging up from her guts and blasting from her sick, raw throat. The wail echoed off the surrounding hills, running through the trees, scattering the birds into the air, and the animals through the woodland, running for their burrows.

She murdered the silence like she had murdered the Raiders.

"Galdar?"

Shryke stirred.

His eyes opened.

"Galdar…what's happened? Where are we?"

But she had no words.

She cried into Shryke's chest, the sobs shaking both their bodies and all Shryke could do was put his arms around her.

CHAPTER 22

"The Guild Nest has been on Pantonyle, the seventeenth moon of the Gas Giant Hanshavo Prime for seven millennia. The origins are not clear since the Archives of the Lost were destroyed."

Barl was sitting in a transparent bubble that hung from a curl of Nest super-structure listening to Guild Professor Vilow speak to the ranks of Trainees ranged on transparent benches all the way up to the back surface of the bubble. It had been Vilow who had met Barl and Summer when the escape capsule had materialised on an Aether Stage outside the Nest. It was Vilow who'd told Barl he'd passed a test that he didn't know he'd been taking. No one, however, not even Professor Vilow had explained to Barl what exactly had attacked them in the capsule. That thing hadn't been mentioned once.

Professor Vilow was a green-skinned tripod with three claws and a face as craggy as an ancient tree. His reedy voice whispered like the wind rustling through ancient leaves in some half-remember forest. Barl liked the sound of the voice but wasn't entirely happy with what he heard.

"History is not our concern today. Today you begin your Guild training in earnest. You will be measured soon for your exoskeletal battle-armour, and then begin your rotations through the various armouries to train at the hands of the battlemasters. They will teach you the vital skills needed to wield a thousand weapons. This truly is the first day of the rest of your deaths."

Vilow paused, hoping for a laugh. It wasn't as funny as he'd hoped, though it earned a polite ripple of unsure laughter. Sighing he ploughed on.

"Being a Guild Assassin is the most honourable vocation within the known universe. It is your mission to bring down, without mercy, the beasts who would subjugate and enslave us all. Your autonomy is sacrosanct. Your mission holy. Where beasts rise, the Guild have pledged to take them down with whatever means necessary. Go forth! Learn to kill!"

The class stood up in their pressure-cages as one, cheering and clapping.

Barl didn't share their enthusiasm. He intended to learn the skills he needed to escape, his only objective to return to *God's Heart*. But he had to fit in. He stood and cheered Professor Vilow with the best of them. The Professor bowed to the trainees and tripped out of the bubble with tripodal precision.

What Barl had initially thought to be a livid purple sky when he had been pulled from the escape capsule had not been *sky* at all.

Well not the sky of Pantonyle at least.

It was in actuality a massive planet. The surface of Hanshavo Prime was thinly banded with every possible shade of purple. It roiled with storms and constant flashing sparkles of lighting. Pantonyle orbited Hanshavo Prime every six days but kept one face towards its huge parent at all times. So, the massive gaseous monster was a constant fixture in the sky, day and night. Many of the planet's one hundred moons described arcs between Pantonyle. Some even came close enough to the Nest's host atmosphere to make out details on their rocky surfaces.

It was an astoundingly strange, yet beautiful vista, under which to live.

Barl couldn't help being thrilled by the sight—it couldn't have been more different from the sky above his home *but* left him just as awestruck.

The trainees began to move out of the bubble. They streamed onto the limbs that made up the million branches and filigrees of the Nest itself. There were no rooms as such, the Nest was a riot of branches; thin and fat, flexible and static that ran for miles upon miles. Barl was forced to place his feet carefully and concentrate on his balance as he negotiated several, though others were wide enough to accommodate a hundred Trainees running shoulder to shoulder in a wild charge. Transparent bubbles hung from limbs across the nest. Thousands of them. Some bubbles served as dormitories, some living quarters, some mess halls; others were places of worship, council or parliament. Approaching the centre of the Nest, the bubbles became less numerous but considerably larger. These were used for Guild Business and Aether Stages for Guild Missions. Some bubbles, he saw, were stuffed with incredible technologies he could only guess the purpose of. These were served day and night by Guild Technicians who might just as well have been priests.

The Nest was a vast, disorientating, awe-inspiring collection of wonder and mystery. Dark and stark, its branches etched blackly against the enraged purple face of Hanshavo.

"Tell me you haven't thought it too?"

Barl was looking up, marvelling at the structures around him. His face must have given away immediately the wonderment he was feeling. Gharlin floated beside Barl in his own transparent pressure-cage, his words coming through a complicated grille at the front.

"Thought what?"

Gharlin fluttered the dozen colours of amusement.

"If this is a Nest. Imagine the bird that *built* it!"

They carried on down the corridor, laughing.

Gharlin had visited Barl on his first morning in the Nest.

Barl was shocked to see his friend alive. He'd assumed the Bantoscree had been smeared along the corridors of the *Minular* with his compatriots, but no, somehow, some miracle, had saved him. Barl wanted to hug the stuffing out of the young Bantoscree, but the pressure-cage made it impossible.

He asked the only question that mattered. "I don't understand…how did you escape?"

Gharlin flushed violet with excitement, eager to tell of their trickery. "We were never really there. The Bantoscree you saw in the corridors weren't real. Just mirages."

"They *smelled* real enough."

His friend howled with laughter. "Believe me, you think I stink, but you… worse. Much worse. All of those hormones and pheromones. It's enough to drive a simple Bantoscree out of his mind."

Barl was so homesick and depressed by the whole situation this one friendly face—except Gharlin didn't really have a face as such—made a world of difference.

Barl hadn't seen Summer since they'd landed.

She'd departed with Professor Vilow and hadn't been in contact since.

Whatever ambivalence he felt towards Summer for her part in taking him from his home, she was his one anchor in this craziness. And he missed her.

Gharlin operated the controls of his pressure-cage with flickering tendrils and led Barl out of the dormitory bubble, telling him he'd been asked to help make him feel at home and show him around.

Barl hadn't stopped being astonished by the construction of the Nest. It was one third organic, a third constructed from exotic metals, and the rest made from materials and fibres Barl didn't have the first clue about identifying. Some branches pulsated with warmth underfoot as though they were living things, others felt cold and dead to the touch.

Seen through gaps and fissures in the Nest, the terrain of Pantonyle was nothing more remarkable than a scrubby desert, dotted with bushes, though he marked a distant range of mountains on the horizon, peaks draped with cloaks of snow. Strange four-winged birds fluttered around the Nest, cawing like doors with rusted hinges as they circled. Nothing on the *Liston Nine* or the *Minular* had prepared him for the sheer weirdness of Pantonyle.

As they progressed through the Nest, Gharlin explained, "You must be a very special trainee indeed for the Guild to go to all the trouble of testing you with a space-battle and your ability to weave hyperspace spells even at this early stage of your life. Remarkable."

"I don't feel that special," Barl countered.

Gharlin paused, turned in his pressure-cage, venting off clouds of steam behind the glass. "Perhaps you don't. But that doesn't mean you're not. You're the talk of the Nest. The last person they gave such an elaborate testing procedure to became one of the greatest assassins in the history of the Guild."

"And who was that?"

"You can't guess? Who did they send to bring you here?"

"Summer."

Summer didn't reappear and Barl had no way to contact her.

So, when he was called to the bubble to listen to Professor Vilow give his introductory lecture, he scanned the limbs and the intersections of the Nest, looking at every face to see if she was there. But she wasn't. It felt like another loss on top of everything else he had suffered. Everyone he came to care about left him in the end. Was that the lesson they wanted him to learn? If so, they were bastards.

The young Bantoscree led Barl into the western depths of the

Nest, past the bubble armouries, towards what he called the "Demesnes of the Armoursmiths."

Barl had no idea what that meant. Gharlin explained, "Bantoscree, due to our very fragile bodies, zero-gee nature and vulnerability to physical attack, have developed some of the finest and strongest armour there is. It isn't as though I could go into battle in a pressure-cage…"

"Bantoscree go into battle?"

"Constantly. We are a fearsome foe, believe me."

"I'll take your word for it," Barl said, trying to imagine the ball of noxious gas fighting any sort of combat.

"The Guild employ us to make the Assassin's Exoskeletons."

One more non-plussed look from Barl brought a rush of colours from Gharlin, which Barl could not decipher.

"A suit of actuated intelligent armour to protect your body in environments from hard-vacuum to being dropped into a volcano."

Barl still didn't understand what *actuated intelligent armour* might be. Oh for a few seconds of piggybacking information from Summer.

CHAPTER 23

"Stop! Stop! Stop!"

Shryke felt her hand clawing his shoulders.

Her nails dug into his skin. She yanked at his hair. He could have ignored the girl if he wanted to. All he'd need to do was concentrate on the icy dagger of agony twisting in the side of his neck and Galdar's fingernails would seem like a lover's caress.

Shryke threw down the razor-sharp triangle of pointed flint and relaxed his grip on Carlow's neck.

He took his knees off the little bastard's arms and burrowed his eyes into those of the half-dead curate.

"If you move, if you speak, if you breathe out of turn, I will finish the job the Raider's started with the nearest rock. Do we understand each other?"

Carlow, terrified, glared his assent.

Galdar let go of Shryke's shoulder and fell back. Her sobbing hadn't stopped, it had simply been interrupted by Shryke sudden explosive burst of movement as he leapt up from the stinking Raider blanket, threw a hammer-blow punch into Carlow's gut, and fell on top of him. In the silence between one heartbeat and the next the assassin had a rock in his hand, poised to smash Carlow's treacherous brains out.

Shryke was hazy on details, but he knew Carlow was, if not the enemy, then allied to them in some, making him a betrayer. He had moved without thought, intending to end the cur, but Galdar had just lost her entire people.

And Shryke knew too well what that felt like.

He stayed his hand.

He surveyed the dead Raiders. He didn't recall killing them, but the savagery and violence looked like the work of a berserker, so perhaps it was a mercy these memories were lost to him?

Shryke picked at the scab on his neck, feeling the seepage from the wound over his fingers.

He looked closely at the exudate and sniffed it gingerly.

This wasn't an honourable wound received in battle which had gone bad with infection.

This was something else.

It had the taint of codemagic on it, and the flavour of corruption.

He would need to have it dealt with by someone who knew what they were doing.

Shryke still couldn't risk drawing on his codespells to heal himself. Not that he knew the correct magic to use. If the dark magic within the wound had been cast by a Guild Assassin, it may well have its own defences built in and messing with it would only serve to make it worse. He'd seen wounds before, on other unfortunates, that had grown teeth and bitten away the fingertips of the surgeons trying to stitch them closed, and others which dumped lethal acidic poisons into the bloodstream at the first sign of the victim taking a curative potion.

Magical wounds rotted in appalling ways.

Which meant Shryke's days were numbered without the aid of a magician skilled in the darkest codespells and most potent healing ones.

He held out his hand to Galdar.

However urgent his need for assistance, there was something

they needed to do first. Galdar took his hand and Shryke pulled her up to her feet.

"Come. We have burials to perform."

Shryke and Carlow dug pits while Galdar performed last rites on the Congregation's dead. Occasionally Shryke heard her soft sobbing as he dug into the earth. Beside him, Carlow dug forcefully, too. Driven by guilt and regret? More likely he imagined every sod cleaved by his spade was Shryke's face. No matter. The pits were excavated and the blisters on the heels of Carlow's hands gave Shryke some satisfaction.

They dug in silence, only the rasp of their breath on the air as the Loop fell towards Quarternight.

When it was full dark, Shryke continued pulling the bodies Galdar had finished with into the pits and covered them as reverently as he could manage with ferns. When each pit was full, they moved the earth back to fill the graves.

Carlow lit a fire. He and Galdar cooked vegetable stew. Shryke heard them whispering occasionally and saw them look across the fire pit at him as he covered more bodies. He couldn't hear what they were saying.

As well as being concerned about the wound in his neck and the cold, rough lump beneath the skin, he was worried he was losing more of his memories and that he couldn't remember much of the last few days. That last thing he could recall was Yane making the offer to him to become the Congregation's protector, beyond that there was nothing.

A fine protector I made, Shryke thought with maudlin resignation.

But why couldn't he remember what had happened since?

Another attack on his memory?

From the same source that had left him empty before he stepped out onto the Thalladon Climbs? Shryke preferred an enemy he could smite, one that bled and wept and begged for its life, not one that hid inside his head.

Galdar hadn't told him much.

She had been steeling herself for the scene that awaited them. So much death. Not one of the Congregation had been spared. They had been opened from neck to navel and laid in rows next to each other. Reading the macabre scene, Yane had been made to watch the massacre, to increase the hurt, Shryke reasoned. Her body lay apart from the others. She hadn't been cut open. They had hung her with her own robes from a tree and set a fire beneath her.

Eventually she had fallen in to the flames.

Shryke had seen this method used by Raiders before. They called it *Ripening*. It was not an easy way to die.

Shryke felt waves of exhaustion wash over him as the Loop-moons rose over the surrounding trees.

With a weary sigh, he went back to the fire to join Galdar and Carlow.

The stew was thin but nourishing.

He felt like he hadn't eaten for a week of Quarternights and demolished three bowls before he felt even a tenth restored from his exertions.

Carlow ate hungrily with the appetite of a soul without a conscience. Galdar had a bowl in front of her, which had already gone cold by the time Shryke started eating. She just shook her head when he indicated it, then he had to bat Carlow's hand away as he reached for the untouched food when his own bowl was empty. "Don't touch it." Shryke said darkly and Carlow sat back, looking forlornly at the empty pot of stew beside the fire.

"What happened at the riverbank? I have no memory."

Galdar couldn't speak. Shryke looked to Carlow, who recounted what he had seen.

"You were unconscious. Galdar took up the battle-mace and fought the Raiders with unearthly ferocity. She met them face-to-face and fought them down, killing every last man in no more than seconds. They were helpless to her wrath. She was vengeance incarnate. At the last, a few tried to save themselves. They ran. But she chased them down and slaughtered them. She came back to where you lay, drenched in blood and gore and seemed as at ease in her blood-soaked rags as she would in fine clothes and perfumes."

Shryke took all this in with rising incredulity.

The girl had done this?

Galdar just looked into the fire and said nothing.

Her slaughter of the Raiders could only have been driven by magic. But Shryke wasn't the source; if it had been his magic the Assassins would have descended on them while he slept.

So, whose magic was it at play here?

Shryke felt darkly uncomfortable at the prospect of unknown forces being involved in his affairs.

The wound in his neck raged and pulsed.

He couldn't shake the sense that the two things were connected.

It was then that Carlow told him of the woman with the ebony skin. A woman he did not recognise who had used the battle-mace to dispatch the four Assassins who had come to the encampment first…

"The Assassins you told about me…" Shryke interrupted, feeling the bile of anger rising in his gut.

Carlow swallowed and nodded, "I didn't…" He indicated to the bodies and the pits, "…think it would come to this. I thought they would come and take you away…I just wanted you gone."

"Why?"

"Because it would hurt me," said Galdar quietly.

Carlow looked at his crossed legs and fell silent.

Shryke felt the urge again to kill the fool where he sat. But Galdar had seen more than her fair share of death this day. Much of it at her own hand. Shryke remembered the first time he had killed. How the rush had overtaken him, the rush of guilt and anguish. However much he'd been trained to kill, however deeply he believed the reasons, killing had always been a barrier that took him a long time to overcome.

Shryke rubbed his eyes.

"We have to heal the wound on your neck," said Galdar. "The woman told me it would kill you unless we attended to it."

Shryke nodded. "There is devilment in it which will take my life eventually," he agreed.

"She also said that we must travel to the Sun-Machine, whatever that is."

A boom of white burst in Shryke's skull. He felt his mind slipping, falling open like a flower. Something locked deep down inside burst out and spread through his thoughts, exploding like firecrackers and whizzing gunpowder rockets.

Shryke's head lit up.

The Sun-Machine.

Yellow light burning through an impossible sky from whirling suns. Huge leathery wings flapping. Gusts of fire and the glint of diamond studded steel.

Shryke reeled where he sat, was on the verge of vomiting up the stew he just eaten and winced as a brutal headache unfurled in his head. His vision blurred and his jaw slacked, spilling saliva.

The scab on the wound over his neck cracked open and a gush of black ichor ran down his naked shoulder. Behind the ichor, blood bubbled and spat.

In his confusion Shryke got up blindly, holding his hand over the wound as blood and black seeped through his fingers.

Galdar and Carlow pushed themselves to their feet, unsure what to do.

Shryke howled as the hard tsunami of forbidden information raged through his skull in a curling wave race of uncovered memories.

The Sun-Machine

The Dreaming Army of the Plain.

The Failsafe.

The end of *everything*.

Shryke felt consciousness ebbing away.

He grabbed for Galdar, but his hand fell on Carlow.

Blindly he pulled the boy close to him and spat, "My neck. My neck…get this thing *out* of me. Cut me open if you have to but get it out of me now!"

CHAPTER 24

The punch came out of nowhere.

Barl doubled over, and fell to his knees, gasping for breath.

Master Rhoan looked down at the boy and wiped the skin of her fist with a towel.

"Don't get complacent. Bantoscree Armour will shield you from a tactical nuke blast just out of arms reach or frustrate a flechette barrage from an air-bust above your head, but it's not good for close-up fighting. It's *absolutely* fine if you're taking out a Barsogeneral in the depths of her Autoclade with a hand-held hydrogen cannon, but when you jump through the Quantum for a single-kill, a night mission, a silent one stop in and out solo gig, you won't be clanking around under plates of Techtomesh and actuated exoskeleton. You'll be in your Blacks. Light body armour and you will be *killable*. Being killable is not a good thing. So, you must be alert to dangers all the time. Do I make myself clear?"

Barl had recovered enough to nod. "I didn't think class had started," he managed between gasps.

Master Rhoan bent down on one knee, getting her three mouths close to Barl's ear. Barl didn't look up. He hadn't yet got used to her crazy jigsaw face. It had more mouths and eyes than it needed and would reconfigure itself in to different 'identity-expressions' when the mood took her. She was a Shaper from the Articles of Zaymar. Barl didn't know what that meant beyond her being scary as hell and the leader of the least favourite period in his training day. Today her session on Close Combat had come just after breakfast and he was regretting having eaten so much.

Rhoan pulled Barl up to a standing position by the scruff of his tunic and dusted him down with her prehensile tail. "Classes never stop. Clear?" Some of the other Trainees, especially the thin faced and arrogant Maxol had a good laugh at Barl's expense. At least if Master Rhoan was sneak-hitting Barl, she wasn't sneak-hitting them.

Barl nodded, pulling his tunic down over his now exposed, and still gurgling belly.

"Good lad." Rhoan patted him on the shoulder and returned to addressing the class.

It had been six weeks on Pantonyle now, and Barl still hadn't seen Summer, or had word of her.

He was growing concerned.

None of his tutors were forthcoming when he asked, and if Gharlin knew where she was, he wasn't saying.

If it wasn't for Gharlin being in his constant orbit between classes Barl might have sacked off training and gone looking for her himself.

"Don't be an idiot," Gharlin said when he admitted as much. "You think they're not tracking you? They'd know where you were in seconds. Less."

Barl knew Gharlin was right, but there was a *God's Heart* sized ache in his guts and a Summer shaped hole in his day.

Training continued.

There were no rest days, but mornings were taken with tutorials and lectures, and the afternoons were left to the Trainees to study in the Library Bubbles near the top of the Nest. Up there the view past the far mountains and onto the gigantic bruise of Hanshavo Prime often stole his breath away, thankfully in a less painful way than Rhoan's punch.

Once lectures had finished with Rhoan, and Barl had show-ered and changed—close combat was always physically demanding and occasionally damaging—Barl made his way up through the Nest superstructure to the Library Bubbles. The ache in his being wasn't so much missing Summer now, blooms of fresh pain in his torso and face took precedence. Trainees were encouraged not to hold back with each other in close combat, and although Rhoan tried to match each student with someone of similar build and power, Barl was still the youngest and smallest of the class by far and he took a physical pounding every time he went in the ring.

Maxol had dumped him off the safety-mattresses time and again with unexpected kicks and forceful punches.

Maxol was three years older, and considerably stronger than Barl.

Rhoan promised Barl that he would catch up eventually, but that losing was "good for the soul" and that he should grow to hate it so that in later life, when on missions, Barl would really not want to lose for real. There was logic to it, and as Barl nodded at the battlemaster, he seethed inside, hating it already. Maxol was nothing more than a bully who enjoyed beating the smallest member of the class.

Gharlin was already at a terminal near the back of Library Bubble Four. It was a quiet area out of direct line of sight from the grumpy Librarian, which suited Barl just fine; he had a plan to follow through today. He was glad that Gharlin had chosen the best place for him to carry it out without him having to persuade the Bantoscree to go there, raising suspicions.

Barl was still adapting to the technological marvels he had encountered since being taken from *God's Heart*, but he was a quick learner, and had taken to the Terminals quickest of all. Not because they were easier to accept, but because of what opportu-nities they presented him in terms of escape.

Bantoscree Trainees in their pressure-cages didn't take close combat for obvious reasons and so Barl met with Gharlin after lectures.

"Is your eye supposed to be that colour?"

"No. I got elbowed in the face by Maxol."

"Interesting. One might interpret that colour as, "I feel stupid" in Bantoscree."

"Well, I feel stupid in human," Barl said, and grimaced with pain as he touched the still tender bruising.

Gharlin floated at the next terminal, his tendrils able to pass through active-airlocks to operate the keypads. The tendrils were the only muscled and cartilaginous part of his body, and could cope with the pressures outside the cage. It took effort and concentration but Gharlin said he preferred it to just using remotes—he felt less cut-off from everything.

Barl wished he had an airlock like Gharlin's to allow him to reach back to *God's Heart*. Thinking of those yellowberries he'd first tasted from Summer's plan, Barl shook his head free of the idea.

Gharlin operated his terminal, and turned back to the holo-screen, cycling though various weapon arrays that could be attached to a Bantoscree's Battle Armour. Barl looked around the library bubble to make sure no one was close.

The rows of terminals and book stations stretched pretty much as far as the eye could see in the enormous enclosed space. He saw a group of Trainees in the distance, clustered around the Librarian's desk. The grey-faced old man with his shock of white hair seemed to be barracking them.

Perfect.

Barl fired up his terminal and entered the password. Today he wasn't entering *his* password. Today he was entering Maxol's password. He'd let his sparring partner elbow him in the face on purpose. It gave him the perfect reason to go back to the Changing Bubble alone, telling Rhoan that he felt nauseous.

Once in the changing area, he'd made straight for Maxol's kitbag and taken out one of his exercise tablets. Maxol was strong and fast. But only in the body. Last week Barl had watched Maxol read his terminal password off the back of an exercise tablet. It hadn't taken much imagination to come up with his plan after that.

Barl scanned the tablet and found exactly what he was looking for; the password was etched into a piece of metal tape. He committed it to memory and returned the tablet to where he'd found it.

Now at the Library terminal, Barl logged in as Maxol.

Barl was working under the assumption that researching routes back to *God's Heart*, travel times and possible ways of making the journey, would be something the Guild's battlemasters might expect *him* to do.

But not Maxol…

The risk was that Maxol was under a similar kind of scrutiny as he was, and soon as he started searching all levels of alarms would be triggered in the Tech Bubbles bringing the wrath of the Guild's battlemasters down on him.

Making sure Gharlin was intent on his screen, Barl input a general search for *God's Heart*.

A slew of text and diagrams raced across the screen.

Barl read it all hungrily.

God's Heart had been discovered over 200,000 years ago by the space-faring races of the galaxy, long before the Guild, long before many of the alliances that had grown, decayed and been rebuilt between civilisations.

For many thousands of years, the structure of *God's Heart* had resisted study. It was postulated that it held one or two stars at its centre—gravity readings and the orbits of many outer planets in the system seemed to bear this out.

It wasn't until many years later as the use of codemagic and the skills for wielding it had advanced, that powerful Mages had been able to divine inside the sphere and see its endless lands and environments. From the inner geographical maps of *God's Heart* Barl saw he was from a vast prairie belt encircling the temperate zones to the north of the equator. There were also endless jungle regions, enormous seas, and mountainous snow-capped peaks. Barl had no idea that *God's Heart* had been so vast—the text informed him that the inner surface area of the sphere was larger than a billion continent-sized landmasses. Barl had no chance of imagining something that enormous, even though he'd lived there. Yes, he knew the horizon curved up, in direct opposition to the horizon on Pantonyle, but he had no idea of the sheer vastness the upward curve contained.

The Mages had progressed in their studies. Eventually they found ways to open small sections in the shell of the structure and had entered. There they had found simple, peaceful peoples who knew nothing of the universe outside. But what the Mages discovered too was amongst those peoples of *God's Heart* there was a much higher than average level of innate magical ability latent in the population. Some of the most powerful adepts they had ever seen, though they did nothing with their incredible power.

Barl was one of these…'simple'…people.

He wasn't sure what to think about that. He had said to Gharlin that he didn't feel special, but he didn't feel simple, either.

As the galaxy had fallen into a succession of bloody wars raging across systems, study of the *God's Heart* had stopped. It wasn't until the Guild had been set up to become The Surgeons of Peace, that their Mages returned to *God's Heart* to recruit Assassins from the peoples there.

Barl sat back.

The rush of information was washing through him, swirling in currents he wasn't sure he could keep his head above, or resist drowning beneath. He knew he had to focus. Nothing in this information could help him get home. Even if his conception of home had now changed beyond all recognition.

It took a few moments of the silver sigil blinking on and off on the holoscreen for him to realise a message was waiting for him…

Without thinking, Barl clicked on the sigil, opening the

message, then immediately regretting it. It wasn't a message for him. It was for Maxol. He was using Maxol's login.

The sigil blossomed open into two words.

HELLO BARL

Before Barl had a chance to process what it meant in its incongruity, it was replaced by a screaming skull.

Two arms, all bones and festering flesh were bursting from the holoscreen reaching to claw out his eyes.

CHAPTER 25

They reached Saint Juffour, the town at the head of the valley, by the fourth Quarternight after leaving the mounds of fresh earth and ferns covering the slaughtered.

Galdar and Carlow had been forced to finish the burial work themselves as Shryke's strength failed him. He paced the muddy ground muttering about *Sun-Machines* and *Failsafes* and when he wasn't pacing he was on his hands and knees drawing diagrams in the wet mud with his fingertips like some simpleton.

As soon as Galdar and Carlow finished the last burial, the sky, glutted with clouds, had opened and a harsh squall of rain poured down upon them like nails made of water.

Shryke still pawed at his neck and pleaded with them to remove whatever it was in there, Galdar had refused and Shryke had relented, but had withdrawn into himself, whether consciously or because of the fever raging though his body, Galdar did not know. She didn't want to contemplate what was going on with him until she had said last rites over the Congregation of the Moveable Church. Necessity might deny her a period of mourning for her people, but they would have the funeral they deserved.

Carlow explained that there was a town at the head of the valley the Congregation had passed while Galdar was away with

Shryke, so they had made their way to it. Saint Juffour, a holy settlement with a large church of its own, was their best hope of finding a Mage-Doctor to treat the pus-leaking wound on the side of Shryke's neck.

The weather remained filthy, matching Galdar's mood. She was steeped in death and it was clawing at her faith *and* her sensibilities. The God of Safehome had never felt so far away.

Shryke was able to ride, just, but he was mostly distracted, and sometimes delirious. His lips moved as if completing a vast new inventory of ideas in his head—he didn't have the wherewithal to explain what was going on in there, and Galdar could not work out if it was to do with the wound or the sudden change in him when she had mentioned The Sun-Machine. More than once, Shryke fell asleep in his saddle. If Galdar hadn't been riding alongside, he would have fallen to the ground.

On the second Halfnight after leaving the buried Congregation behind, Galdar found herself studying the liquid surface of the battle-mace. She had been in two minds as to whether to leave it buried with her people, but she felt a strong attraction between the weapon and her heart. Leaving it behind would have been as unthinkable as leaving Shryke behind to suffer. The bonds were fierce.

Saint Juffour was built at the head of the river and served as a mercantile trading post and warehousing facility for the various peoples of the Thalladon ranges. The river washed through a network of widening tributaries across a foul marsh into the dark waters of Lake Tarsh.

Lake Tarsh itself was an enormous, mist-shrouded and chill body of water prone to harsh storms. The walled town sat at its head like a big friendly face, but still the face on a body that held a sharp dagger behind its back.

Once they persuaded the Juffour Townsguard that friend Shryke wasn't carrying plague and the wound on his neck was that of an infected injury, she and the half-delirious warrior were allowed in to meet Klane, the chieftain. Carlow was made to wait outside with the horses because, as he put it, Klane, "Didn't like the look of the arsefaced-boy before and didn't like the look of him now."

Galdar was wary of leaving Carlow, not because she worried for his safety but rather because she expected him to have sold two of the horses and ridden off with the profits before they returned.

Klane met them in a small counting house on the other side of the gate. He looked with distaste at the pair, his small piggish eyes glistening with more than a little fear. "If it's not plague," he asked, "what *is* it?"

"We need a Mage-Doctor to tell us," said Galdar.

Klane held a handkerchief to his bulbous nose and took a step back. "You may see Lucillian, but Mage-Doctors aren't cheap, and as her agent in Saint Juffour..."

Galdar sighed and pushed a small leather bag of coin Shryke had passed to her in a more lucid moment this morning, across the table.

Klane opened the bag and squinted at its contents and smiled coldly. "This will have to suffice, I suppose..."

"There will be more if I am cured..." Shryke managed to whisper.

"Afford every access!" Klane called to the leader of the Towns-guard waiting outside the room wearing the most suspicious of faces. Klane was obviously more interested in the acquisition of cash than anything else and it was the way to get him to oil the wheels of assistance.

Klane got up and shooed them both out of the counting house, tossing the bag of coin into the pocket of his robe. "Off you go then. Get better and visit me at my residence before you leave, then we can work out the rest of the...business."

Galdar just sighed and helped the sagging Shryke back out onto the street.

Saint Juffour was a dark, narrow-avenued, heavily populated town with wet muddy streets. Food and human waste ran in the gutters, washed along by the fresh torrents of rain that sluiced from the pitched roofs and eves of the claustrophobic buildings.

The inhabitants were a suspicious lot.

Those who had braved the elements made no eye contact with them. The closest to human interaction they came was when someone registered how sick Shryke looked and yielded to give them right of way in a narrow passage, not wanting to get too close. Galdar had to move sideways several times with Shryke leaning heavily on her as they splashed through the ankle-deep mud.

Eventually, the two Townsguard who escorted them this far, left the pair at the steps of a small stone building on the western edge of the city. The streets were narrower still. The floating sewage filled the gutters, all of it thick and sludgy. A sign hung above the door that said *The Surgery of Mage-Doctor Lucillian Drange*. The windows were thick with grime and obviously hadn't been cleaned since the building was raised. The door creaked on rusted hinges as she pushed it open and looked inside.

The surgery, such as it was, was a dimly lit, dark cave of a room. The walls appeared to be more akin to natural rock than a man-made structure.

Galdar let Shryke fall into a dusty leather armchair that sat closest to the meagre fire, which guttered in the grate, and sank down next to him. Several times she'd been dragging him while he was falling in and out unconsciousness, unable to support his own weight. She was spent.

"Nasty," whatever the name *Mage-Doctor Lucillian Drange* had conjured up for Galdar, the reality couldn't be further from the dusty, sallow-skinned, ancient old man it sounded like. Lucillian Drange wasn't much older than Galdar, maybe a year or two. Her golden hair was tied up behind her head in a tight bun. Thin-rimmed glasses perched on the end of her nose, through which she peered at Galdar with bright inquisitiveness. Her hands were working a sweet-smelling herb in a pestle with a thick stone mortar. She had emerged from a backroom separated by thick velvet curtains. From what she saw, the room back there seemed both brighter and more welcoming.

Lucillian met Galdar's incredulous gaze. "Not what you were expecting?" The woman said. "I know. Everyone assumes I'm some crusty old coot with nostril hairs you could tie bows in," she grinned at Galdar. "That was my mother." Galdar couldn't help herself, she laughed, which pleased the woman in front of her no end. "I see your friend is dying. Shall we save his life?"

The pair took Shryke through and laid him out on clean linen on a table in the other room. They were surrounded by brightly lit candles that gave off the scent of freshly cut flowers. A much larger fire burned in the grate.

Galdar's head was spinning with Lucillian's constant babble. Streams of words washed from her mouth, not all of them making sense. She raged about Klane taking his agents cut, about hardship and misconception, about cutthroats and cutpurses and asked for the scalpel so she could cut Shryke, holding a hand out. Galdar didn't know what a scalpel was. Her hand hovered over the tray of instruments until Lucillian pointed out which one she wanted.

"Mother started the business, being a Mage and all. Dad was a Doctor. It was only natural they combine their gifts. After Dad died, Mum took on both roles with me helping and learning the trade. Magic came easy to me and I didn't fancy working in some Prince's court or shilling for Governor Klane here, so stayed on as an independent when mother passed away two years ago."

Lucillian wasn't looking at Galdar, just holding out her hand and snapping her fingers while studying Shryke's neck with a magnifying glass. She looked up and tutted.

Galdar passed the sharp looking instrument across but not before Lucillian had screamed; "Handle first!" at her.

Shryke stirred on the table, lips moving and eyelids fluttering. Lucillian felt his cheek with her palm and shook her head. "You did the right thing bringing him here. This is a magical infestation. There's something inside. I don't suppose you know how he came by the wound?"

Galdar repeated what Shryke had told her about the robed skeleton and how it had reached inside his body. She thought at the time he'd just been delirious. The only magic she was aware of was that of the tricksters she'd seen at County Fairs or had heard about second-hand; practiced in the castles the Congregation had passed along their journey. She had never seen any real magic, and to be honest she wasn't sure it wasn't all fraudulent trickery and underhand mischief anyway. The Scriptures of Safehome warned against the temptations of magic and the wielding of it; saying it would only bring "ruin to one's morals." Even Mage-Doctors...

Lucillian peered at the wound for an age longer in the glass, before deciding, "I think perhaps we should restrain your companion, just in case," she said grimly. She reached down for a pair of leather cuffs, which she used to lash Shryke to the table about his wrists, then two more for his ankles, and twin belts to tie down his chest and thighs.

Once Shryke was secured, she began the operation.

She spoke a spell quietly on her lips and a searing light emanated from her open mouth. It hung, fizzing above the wound, illuminating it as though they were in direct sunlight.

The rain outside lashed down against the window in ever forceful gusts, resenting the sunlight within.

Lucillian waved her hand above the scalpel and the blade began to glow, the heat in the metal rising until a few seconds later it was red hot. She allowed the glow to fade, and when it did Galdar saw that the blade was clean and flawless.

Lucillian approached the wound.

"I've read about wounds like this, though I must confess I have yet to encounter one, which may not be what you wanted to hear, but is very much the truth and given the seriousness of your friend's sickness, I don't think lies, no matter how reassuring or well meant, are particularly helpful." She didn't wait for Galdar to agree. "These wounds are often loaded with safeguards, which if tripped do the real damage—to him and to us—so we don't open this like we would an ordinary abscess. We take precautions."

Lucillian moved up from the wound and sliced a thin line along Shryke's jaw, the white lips of the cut opened like a corrupt smile before filling with blood.

Shryke moaned and stirred.

"Hold his head steady!" Lucillian barked.

Galdar moved around the table and placed her hands at the side of Shryke's head, holding it in place.

The Mage-Doctor wove two more spells; one which made the blood vanish in the wound, leaving the bone and muscle exposed, and another which seemed to fold the air around her left hand. As Galdar watched incredulously at her first real exposure to fresh wielded magic, Lucillian's hand shank down to a fifth of its previous size. The fingers were suddenly tiny, like bird claws, the arm thin and flexible. With it, Lucillian reached down inside Shryke's neck.

A rising stench of putrefaction and blight rose up, making Galdar retch—a thin, gritty wash of vomit pooling at the back of her throat. She swallowed it down as Lucillian's tiny arm moved inside the wound. Shryke's face bunched up in pain.

"Ah yes, very clever, ingenious even, but to be blunt not clever enough." Lucillian's face was a mask of concentration as she moved around blind, going only on touch and her knowledge of anatomy. She smiled, yanked, and then withdrew her arm. She dropped a ring of five smoking, sizzling black stones into a metal tray. They glistened with blood and small gobbets of flesh.

"What is it?"

"That's the trap. Five killspells. Five different ways for him and us to die. I shall have to dispose of them *very* carefully. One could probably wipe out half the town's wall."

"And that's what's been making him ill?"

"Oh no. That's just the *protection* set to stop us healing him." Lucillian reached back inside Shryke's neck with her thin arm. Instead of pulling something out, she appeared to be pushing something up through the infected wound.

The abscess bulged and wept; the scabbing crackled and fell away as through a gush of foul-smelling pus and rancid, old black blood, an ivory-yellow oblong of material emerged, smeared with steaming juices.

It clanked heavily into the metal tray with a solid clink.

Shryke's face and body relaxed.

The wound in his neck continued to drain of its foul contents.

Galdar looked at the piece of ivory in the dish.

As Lucillian's arm snapped back to its original size, she peered down at the tray, "I'd say your skeleton gave him the finger."

CHAPTER 26

T he skeletal fingers clawed at Barl's flesh, grasping for his
eyes.

He couldn't lean the chair back. It was rooted to the ground,
grown from the same material as the bubble walls. He tried to
push away and launch himself sideways. The grinning skull kept
coming out of the holoscreen, leaving flesh and skin on the edges
of the terminal. Behind the creature, Barl saw the blasted terrain of
The Plain. He could just make out the tiny armies fighting in the
distance and the skeleton's robe flapping in the winds of high
altitude.

Barl was too slow. He imagined with some bitterness, that his
last thought before the fingers bit into his flesh would be how
disappointed Master Rhoan would be he had not been ready for a
'sudden attack at any time.' If Barl ever got the chance to make a
mistake again he vowed that it wouldn't be this one.

His second to last thought was the Skeleton only had nine fingers.

That image registered just before both skeletal arms were
hacked off above their respective elbows.

The now armless skeleton was hurled back into the Plain by a
burgeoning cloud of red energy, which sent it spinning off into the
distance trailing a thin stream of smoke. The holoscreen blinked
off then burst into flame.

The two dismembered arms *clacked* and rattled like bone snakes on the ground, writhing for a few seconds near Barl's feet before they too dispersed into a foul-smelling smoke, like a no-longer needed spell-weapons.

Barl looked at Gharlin's pressure-cage. It was changing shape from an extruded glass blade back to its normal configuration, and the tendrils, which had woven the red rejectionspell at the Skeleton, were slithering back through the air locks.

The pressure-cage floated closer so Gharlin could observe Barl's injuries.

"You'll live," the Bantoscree said, turning off his terminal with the remote.

"How did you *do* that?"

"I listen."

"But the pressure-cage. It grew…what was that? A sword?"

"We don't just fashion armour, my young friend."

That much was clear.

They were back in Barl's dorm bubble, alone for now. It couldn't last, of course. Someone would come looking of an explanation for what had just happened. Nothing went unremarked by the Assassins and their battlemasters. But, for now at least, no one else had returned from the afternoon's recreation so they took advantage of the solitude.

Barl sat on his bed wanting to scratch at the plasters Gharlin had put on his facial wounds to hide the deep scratches across his cheek. Barl had argued that surely covering them just drew more attention to them. The Bantoscree's suggestion was a wry, "Oh, why don't you just tell people you cut yourself shaving?"

"I don't shave."

"Perhaps you should start? Though you might want to come up with a good excuse for why you blew up that terminal."

"I didn't exactly blow it up."

"Semantics, young Barl. Semantics." Gharlin flushed and rotated in his cage. "Now, how about you tell me what that thing was?"

"I don't know."

"You know more than you are saying."

"Only that it attacked me in the *Minular*'s escape capsule."

"Something or someone wants you dead. You should go to Professor Vilow."

"But what if it's Vilow who wants me dead?"

"Unlikely."

"But not impossible. There are only two people here I know I can trust. You and Summer, and I haven't seen Summer since I got here. Something isn't right."

Gharlin touched down on the bed in the cage. "Understatement. What shall we do?"

"Stick close to me, Gharlin and…"

"And?"

"I don't know… teach me how to throw energy bolts like you. I need to know how to fight this thing if it comes again."

"When."

The Plain was just as harrowing as it had been the last time Barl had set foot in that peculiar realm, but at least he wasn't alone.

Each member of the class, as well as Academician Xaxax, the Plain's Mistress, sat in couches in the bubble and projected themselves to the Plain.

It was unnerving. He *knew* that his physical body was still in a Guild Nest Training Bubble and The Plain was a construct weaved from incredible codemagics and mysticism. He *knew* that his body was unguarded back on Pantonyle, and he was vulnerable.

They were met on The Plain by a platoon of Guild soldiers in their Exo-armour, three for each student. The soldiers were there to protect them while they sensed their way into the battle to find their own Familiar.

Xaxax was a large boned humanoid woman with dark orange skin and silver eyes. She spoke without voice, her words appearing as a series of written messages across Barl's eyes. She was a Dolanian; a race who prided the written word above all others forms of communication. They had evolved to never once utter words from their atrophied larynxes. Gharlin told Barl that the Dolanian's were the master wordsmiths of the Galaxy and would probably have been its most artistically dominant species but for the fact they kept getting drawn into wars with illiterate civilisations.

Barl couldn't tell if Gharlin was joking or not but liked the idea so much he didn't try to find out.

They hadn't spoken of the attack in the Library Bubble again.

If he was being tracked, then it stood to reason the enemy could listen in on his conversations and talking was only going to betray what he was thinking.

The attack had been five days ago.

Other than having to answer a few questions from the grey-faced Librarian about the shocking amount of damage to the terminal, no one called out Barl for breaking into Maxol's account, or anything else that had happened in that Library bubble.

Knowing that he was the target of some unseen enemy, something capable of reaching him even here, in the heart of the Nest, circumventing all the defences of the Assassins, scared him. His sleep was fitful at best, disturbed by swirling nightmares, at worst —skeletons dug themselves out of the ground, codespells were cast by faceless beasts, the magic tearing through him, flensing flesh from bone. He woke time and again bathed in a sheen of sweat, gasping for breath and shivering where he'd kicked off the covers.

The scratches had healed quickly. They didn't leave a scar. Those were more mental; the memories of the two aethereal attacks wouldn't heal in a long time, if they ever did.

And travelling to the Plain for Familiar Attachment wasn't doing anything for his anxiety levels.

Words sped across Barl's eyes. It was Xaxax.

EACH OF YOU HAVE THREE BODYGUARDS.

STAND WITH THEM NOW.

They moved apart.

For the first time Gharlin was without his pressure-cage. The Bantoscree floated freely in the air. Gharlin obviously enjoyed his freedom. The colours of his chromatic flesh sang vividly. It didn't matter to him if this place was completely constructed in an unreal space.

YOU'RE HERE TODAY TO LOCATE YOUR FAMILIAR.

ALL OF YOU WILL HAVE ONE WAITING IN THE THICK OF THE BATTLE.

IT IS YOUR JOB TO FIND THEM AMONGST THE DREAMING ARMIES AND MAKE YOURSELF KNOWN.

YOU HAVE EACH BEEN BLESSED WITH THE CODE NEEDED TO EXECUTE A LOCATORSPELL. THE MAGIC CAN BE ACTIVATED ON MY COMMAND, BUT NOT BEFORE.

Barl fingered the small piece of dry parchment on which the spell was written. Activation, if he'd understood the instructions, was no more complicated that ripping it in half. Around him, the others prepared their spells, eager to weave even this simple magic. The Guild soldiers moved into a protective formation around each of them.

BEGIN.

Barl tore the parchment.

Around him, his fellow Trainees began to move toward the battle, chasing after a firefly-sized light that bobbed and weaved in front of them.

The Guild soldiers drew their weapons and moved forward with them poised to strike.

REMEMBER YOU MUST KILL COMBATANTS WHO ENGAGE. YOU CANNOT FLEE FROM THE FIELD OF BATTLE. THEIR DEATHS GIVE YOU THE ENERGY REQUIRED TO WEAVE CODEMAGIC

AWAY FROM THE PLAIN. THE SOLDIERS WILL ONLY INTERVENE IF YOU CANNOT DEFEND YOURSELVES.

GO HARD. GO FAST. FIND YOUR SOUL MATE.

Barl waited.

He held the two slivers of parchment between his fingers, willing the guiding light to appear, but it didn't.

The soldiers assigned to him started to look uncomfortable, exchanging glances, embarrassed. Academician Xaxax moved towards Barl at speed, stomping over the wet grass.

SHOW ME YOUR SPELL.

Barl was the last of the Trainees left. He held up the torn pieces of the guide spell.

TEAR IT AGAIN

Barl tore the two pieces into four.

Nothing.

Xaxax narrowed her eyes and reached into her tunic, pulling out a fresh spell. She handed it to Barl and nodded, encouraging him to try again.

Three torn spells later, Barl still hadn't managed to summon a guide light.

MOST IRREGULAR. GO BACK.

Barl's eyes snapped open in the trainee bubble. Strapped into their seats all around him were the silent bodies of his classmates.

The scene was eerie. It wasn't like they were sleeping. It was different. Their eyes fluttered open after a few minutes of him staring at bodies that didn't seem to be breathing, and then they came back towards consciousness. One by one they returned, brighter and more alive than when they'd entered The Plain. Their eyes shone. Some cried, others hugged each other. A few talked excitedly about their Familiars, describing a myriad of beings who would be their focal point in the endless battle of The Plain for the rest of their lives.

Barl felt so utterly alone, removed from them. Different. Wrong.

He watched them, not knowing what to say or think.

When Gharlin reanimated inside his pressure bubble the Bantoscree floated excitedly over, flushing a rainbow of wild colours that Barl hadn't seen from his skin before.

Gharlin twisted and laughed inside his cage, tendrils shivering as crackles of energy sparked behind the glass.

All Barl felt in that moment was a crushing sadness.

Was this another form of attack?

Had he lost all chance of wielding the codemagic that would take him away from this place?

Was it his destiny to be trapped here forever?

CHAPTER 27

G aldar followed Lucillian into the yard behind the surgery.
The Mage-Doctor carried the trap-spells out gingerly in
the tray where they lay with the finger bone squeezed from
Shryke's neck. The rain had stopped, but a squall whipped
through the bushes and sickly trees that grew in the alley's shade.

"We're going to need to be careful disposing of this. In some
ways, it might be better to leave them—but then again, they might
have a timed detonation built into the spell, or more likely have
been created to recognise when they are outside the host body...
we might only have a few moments left before..." she didn't
finish the thought.

Galdar stopped walking with Lucillian and hung back." I
think I'll just wait here until you've taken care of things..."

"Outstanding," the Mage-Doctor said, placing the tray against
the far wall. She closed her eyes and began to intone words just
beyond the range of Galdar's hearing. They'd left Shryke recovering on the table.

"Stop!"

Shryke burst out of the back door, slamming into Galdar and
sending her sprawling face down in the mud. "No! Stop! Don't..."
he screamed, but it was too late.

As Galdar lifted her head, wiping wet mud from her eyes, she saw that Lucillian had completed her spell and the bone with its five black companions were dissolving on the air into a pall of thick grey smoke.

She caught a whiff of it as she sat up, the cloying stench making her retch again.

Shryke had Lucillian by both shoulders and shook her. Hard. His neck was still an angry red, but the swelling around the stitches was already going down. Galdar hadn't seen him like this in days. Instead of happiness, his desperation frightened her.

"Hold it right there, muscles!" Lucillian said, trying to squirm out of Shryke's grasp. "I just saved your life, so calm the hell down!"

Shryke kicked the tray. It clattered against the wall. "Did you wipe all traces of my blood and flesh from the spell stones or the bone?"

"I'm a Mage-Doctor not a House-Domestic you ungrateful prick! Now *stand* down before I *put* you down." Lucillian raised her hands as if to begin weaving a counterspell.

Shryke didn't back down, and absolutely *did not* calm down.

"You've killed me, yourself and her," he pointed at Galdar, "And all because of your bloody stupidity. So no, I won't be grateful. If we don't get away from here now, you've killed everyone else in this damned city!"

At last, Shryke was getting through to Lucillian.

She dropped her hands.

"What's going on?" Galdar asked, scared.

Shryke stopped and fixed Galdar with his iron gaze. "The trap spell and the bone will still have my essence woven into them. The Guild Assassins tracking me will register their destruction as me using the magic to remove them as surely as if I'd done it myself. Right now, they will be preparing an Aether Stage to send a kill team through to end the job!" Shryke turned on Lucillian, "A little knowledge is a dangerous thing."

Lucillian boiled at the slight but didn't argue.

Shryke softened. Just a little. He shook his head. "Thank you for removing that thing. You did save my life, if only for a minute more. We have to get away from here *now*."

A Guild Assassin stepped from the air, swinging a studded battle-axe towards Shryke's head before his first foot had reached the ground of Saint Juffour. He rolled as the studded head whistled past him, too close for comfort, and shoved Galdar and Lucillian to the ground as he did so.

Regaining his feet, Shryke created a two-handed broadsword barely quick enough to parry the next blow before the Assassin could cleave his skull. The move put the other man off balance, it was only fractional, weight distribution and momentum combined with what the Assassin had hoped would be the kill stroke. It gave Shryke an opening. He didn't swing. Instead he kicked the Assassin's legs away from under him. The other man went down silently, hitting the ground hard, but even so trying to deliver another scything blow with the battle-axe even as he rolled in the dirt.

The fight lasted long enough for Shryke to stamp on the axe and then, with someone he had known most of his long life staring up at him, took the Assassin's head off cleanly.

He kicked it away.

The only sound in the yard was his raw breathing.

"We need to go. And you need to come with us."

Lucillian backed away, shaking her head, "Ohhhhh.... *No*. This is not my fight."

"It is now. Helping me is a death sentence."

Two Assassins waited in the street outside the surgery.

Shryke leapt at them with all the fury of the already damned.

Lucillian joined in, dropping one of them with a cleavespell that took out the tendons in the back of her assailant's knees. The Assassin fell backwards into the mud for Galdar to batter with the flat of the axe. Shryke finished the Assassin off after running his own foe through with the broadsword.

Somewhere in the town, the city alarm blared a shrill warning.

Bells started to ring in the spires of the churches.

Other hollers and screams filled the air from town criers: Saint Juffour was under attack.

"Galdar!"

The three turned as one to see Carlow running along the muddy street towards them holding his pack and the battle-mace. "Raiders! They've breached the main gates and are ransacking the town! What are we going to do?"

Shryke sighed. "Raiders at the gate, Assassins at every turn…"

One appeared behind Galdar, stepping out of the nothing. Shryke didn't have a choice; he shoved Galdar into him, the impact sending them both barrelling down the stone steps. Galdar rolled away from him as Shryke drew a handheld double-headed crossbow out of the aether and put both bolts into the Assassin's face.

Shryke lowered the just created weapon thinking fast. He turned on Lucillian. "There's a Governor. Important man?"

Lucillian nodded, "Klane is an idiot who loves his home comforts and his gold, and he certainly *thinks* he's important."

Shryke ran his fingers through his hair, thinking quickly. "That will do. An arrogant man will have an escape plan." Shryke heaved himself up on to a windowsill on the outside of the surgery, gaining height so that he could look further down the streets and across the town. He pointed. "The building with the spired minarets, is that his residence?"

Lucillian nodded.

Shryke jumped down. "There is magic about that building. I can smell it from here."

Lucillian led the way, Galdar followed with Carlow, but not before she had swapped the axe for the battle-mace. Galdar's connection with the weapon felt stronger and more vital than ever. Any other weapon would have been useless in her hands.

She was breathing fast, her body psyching itself for the coming battle. Galdar didn't *want* to fight, but she didn't have the luxury of a choice.

Shryke took up the rear, moving with the reloaded crossbow ready to take out any threat.

The Governor's residence was an opulent stone tower in the centre of town.

It was surrounded by a sea of mud and panicking townspeople.

A retinue of the Townsguard attempted vainly to fend off a phalanx of Raiders charging up the steps to the building.

Shryke hacked his way through the black steel of broadsword scything a path for the others to follow.

Even before he was halfway to the relative safety of the tower, an Assassin stepped out in front of him. Shryke was unbalanced from dropping two Raiders with brutal efficiency. The female Assassin delivered a punishing blow, smashing the pommel of her short blade into Shryke's ribs. He yelled in pain but didn't back down. Instead, he countered with an elbow square into the middle of the Assassin's face and as her head went back dispatched her with a dagger drawn across the throat.

"Thank the gods! Help us!" the Townsguard Captain yelled as Shryke fought his way up the stone steps to the doors of the Governor's residence.

Shryke made an apologetic face, shrugged, and tossed the Captain down the steps into the melee. It was pragmatic. He needed to get through the doors.

The others followed him inside.

The Townsguard cowered in the hallway. They didn't resist as Shryke ushered the others through. Galdar pushed the doors closed behind them. Shryke took one of the Townsguard by the throat, lifting him up onto his toes. "Where is it? The devil-door... How do we get there?"

The terrified Townsguard's eyes bulged with fear. "I can't. If I told you they'd execute me at dawn."

Shryke held the bloody dagger to the man's throat. "Enjoy those few extra hours. I can always execute you now? I will only ask one more time, where is the devil-door? I can smell it. If you don't tell me, someone else will while you're bleeding to death."

The man buckled, telling Shryke what he needed to know.

They raced up into the heights of the Governor's residence, charging up the stairs two and three at a time in a headlong flight.

Three Assassins barred their way on the fourth landing.

Their tactics were changing. Rather than stepping out of the air, hoping to take Shryke unawares, they were taking up defensive positions and waiting for him to come to *them*.

Lucillian brought down one, slicing the tendons just above their ankles with a scythe-spell. Shryke dispatched the other two; the first, with a crossbow bolt punching through his throat, the second with two black-bladed daggers he whispered into existence, not caring about subtleties or risking magic now. The final assassin fell with both blades still shivering in his heart and groin.

They ran down the corridor at full pelt, arms and legs pumping furiously.

Shryke peered at the doors on either side as he charged past them, looking for the one he wanted, but it was Carlow who found it. "Here!"

They stopped outside a wooden door alive with intricate carvings. It sported a mahogany Lion leaping at a cowering Unicorn. The Lion had a human face, a fat, shiny human face wearing a benevolent, beatific smile.

"Tasteful." Lucillian said. "Klane always was a vain bastard."

Shryke tried the ostentatious brass handle but it wouldn't turn. "Devil-Door all right." He stepped back. He closed his eyes, stood still as Galdar watched the end of the corridor, waiting for the next Assassin's attack. It was coming. She felt it. A fission in the air.

Shryke opened his eyes. He sketched out a sigil in the air in front of him and the door shimmered out of existence, leaving a blank wall where it had been.

"Well *that* helped." Carlow said bitterly.

Shryke stepped through the wall.

Galdar pushed Carlow towards the wall, and the curate disappeared too.

Lucillian followed, and while Galdar looked down the corridor again to ensure they weren't being followed by Assassins or Raiders, before stepping through the wall into an impossibility.

CHAPTER 28

Barl felt himself weakening day by day.

He was excused training after the third successive day of it. His inability to find a Familiar on the Plain had meant that he wouldn't be able to restore precious energy without feeding like a parasite from another source. That sort of piggybacking was at best a temporary solution, weakening the others to make him stronger, and until they found something more permanent, he was useless to the battlemasters. He was left to wander the Nest while conversations between Xaxax, Rhoan and Vilow sought some sort of understanding.

Even the simplest use of magic chipped away at his reserves, which were already precious little, and left him vulnerable to whatever that skeletal thing in the crimson robes had been. So, no matter that Gharlin had agreed, there was no chance of him learning to cast energy bolts even if he knew the theory and the incantation. It was pointless.

Barl still hadn't confessed to anyone about the attack in the Library Bubble. He still couldn't work out who he was supposed to trust while his world fell apart yet again.

He needed to find Summer.

Gharlin did his best to raise Barl's spirits, but he had his own studies to attend to. There were long slow ticking tracts when Barl walked alone through the Nest, forced to watch the other trainees in their various lectures, feeling more and more isolated from them, and all the more desperate to go home. But without the access to a Familiar and the magic well that promised, he knew he'd never see *God's Heart* again.

Life went on as usual around him, and that was the worst of it.

And then he heard a friendly voice.

"Hey kid, long time no see. You managed to stay out of trouble?"

Barl spun around, his smile splitting his face in two. "Summer!" He ran at her and hugged her tight. She hugged him back and somehow something so simple, human contact, kindness, made Barl feel a million times better. The warmth of her, surge of energy that passed between them, was bliss. "I thought I'd never see you again!"

She offered him a rakish grin. "You don't get rid of me *that* easy."

They walked at length into the heart of the Nest, Barl smiling for the first time in weeks.

Summer was dressed in her Assassin's blacks. Her hair had been released from the braids and moved around her head like a fuzzy black cloud. She looked older, he realised. A little more tense than before she went away.

"You've been gone ages."

"You have no idea."

She led him to a Garden Bubble near the centre of the Nest. The illumination spells were dimmed so it became a restful, peaceful place. They sat on benches beneath a tree with long thin leaves. The leaves rustled in a spell-cast breeze. They were alone. Barl felt he could speak freely.

"It tried to get me again."

Summer nodded.

"We know."

That first word hit Barl like a sledgehammer. *They* knew? Why hadn't someone said something? Were they leaving him out there like bait, something to try and hook the thing? Even if it meant he was killed? Didn't they care?

Summer put a hand on his shoulder. She saw that she'd said the wrong thing. She tried to reassure him. "When I say *we*. I don't mean the battlemasters."

"I don't understand."

"The attack on us in the escape capsule. That wasn't part of the test."

"I know."

"It shouldn't have happened. To project a presence *that* far, even a skinned one, takes energy even the most powerful Guild Assassins can't harness. So, when we got back, I knew I needed to find out what the hell was going on."

"And did you?"

"I don't know. Maybe. It's complicated."

Barl's mood sank down to subterranean depths.

"Has anyone talked to you about the history of the Guild?"

"No, but I did read some stuff about it before the terminal tried to kill me."

Barl explained what he'd read about *God's Heart* and the formation of the Guild. Summer was pleased. "It's a start," she said, "But it's far from the whole story. That involves the beings who originally built *God's Heart*."

Summer looked about to be sure no one was eavesdropping. "*God's Heart* was built by Gods. Well Gods by any definition we might understand. Beings with the power to create matter from no energy. That's the basic principle by which you measure a God. Creation from Nothing. Not matter-potential differences and fluctuations in the baseline reality of the universe, but actual creation from nothing. This is a big deal."

Barl didn't fully grasp what Summer was explaining, but the gravity and tone of voice made sure and certain he knew just how terrifying what she said next was.

"There's a thought among some of us—the 'we' I meant before, that someone or some*thing* has found a way to mimic these godlike powers, or are a God returned to carry out some foulness we don't yet understand. We think that's why you've been blocked from finding a Familiar on the Plain. Twice it's tried to kill you now and you've survived."

"But that wasn't me—that was you and Gharlin."

Summer smiled compassionately. "Trust me, without your innate energies neither I nor Balloon-Boy would have been able to do a thing to help you. Your proximity helped us in ways I'm still trying to understand. The creature…whatever it is—is trying to weaken you by proxy. No Familiar, no fresh sources of energy to draw upon. It is looking to dry you out. But even with you so reduced it's no match for you, I truly believe that, and that is why it is reverting to subterfuge and stealth attacks."

Barl tried to take all this in, but he really wasn't grasping the meat of it.

He knew instinctively what he had to do was take everything she said on trust, but that wasn't as easy as it should have been, such was the rush of vertigo in his head. "So…how did you find out all this?"

"Well we've thought something like this might happen. We'd noticed some subtle changes in the way the Guild operates, but until now there's been nothing concrete. But when the Guild Mages located you in *God's Heart*, and the levels of potential of your gift was measured, I was sent to retrieve you as quickly as we could, but without telling the Guild Authorities the truth about what you might be. Though the truth escaped, anyway. Your presence outside *God's Heart* has been noticed, Barl, and it has made someone very scared. Scared of you."

"Am I going to die?"

"Probably," she said. "But not today. And not tomorrow. And with luck, not for a lot of tomorrows." It wasn't the most encouraging answer, but she offered a wry half-smile to try and take the sting out of her words.

They left the Garden Bubble and walked back towards the accommodation areas.

"So, where have you been?"

"In terms of Nest time I've been gone, what, three months?"

Barl nodded.

"Space time, I've been gone four hundred years."

"You don't look four hundred years older."

"Flattery will get you *everywhere* kid. One of the side effects of Guild training, becoming an Assassin, is that we live a *very* long time."

"How long?"

"Essentially, until you're killed."

Barl looked at Summer more confused than ever.

"Put it this way, there isn't a Guild Assassin who ever died of old age. We don't really know how long we live. We don't age in the conventional way. Best guess, it's a property of the magic and the energy transfer with The Plain. It's not something we understand."

Being told he would live forever wasn't something he wanted to deal with any more than being told he might die tomorrow was. There were too many revelations, new truths coming thick and fast, so he went back to his original line of questioning. "But where were you? Where did you go?"

"Names and places don't matter, but I've been travelling, talking to people who might know, fighting a couple of very dull wars and falling in love. Twice. Bottom line there's a whole bunch of scared people out there who don't know what's coming but know that it is. Wars are being started all over. Chaos is coming. Fast."

"Can I go home? Will I be safe there?"

"No. This is the safest place you can be. I can protect you here; the Nest is safe. As long as you follow Rhoan's advice about being alert, you'll be ok."

"For now."

"There are no promises in this universe, kid. We need to study you; we need to find out what's inside you and how it got there. And, to put it bluntly, we can't do that on *God's Heart*."

Barl felt sad and a little angry. He didn't want to be studied. He wasn't an experiment. He felt like a worm wriggling on a fisherman's hook.

"So as long as you get what you need from me, you'll keep me alive. For now." Barl said, bitterly.

"That's *not* what I'm saying."

"That's what it sounds like."

Summer was quiet for a moment then reached into her blacks. She pulled out a small silver data-cube from her top-robe "Take this, go back to your dorm and read it. It's about *God's Heart* and more, and it's the background you need."

Barl was chilled, "Are you going away again?"

Summer smiled and touched his cheek. "I'm here for now and I'm going to do everything I can to make sure you are too."

He didn't thank her. He knew it was petulant, but he didn't feel like saying thanks given everything she'd told him. That kernel of resentment festered after they split up at the next junction. Barl walked on slowly. His thoughts on home and how it felt like whatever he did it was getting further and further away.

The data-cube felt warm in his hand. He was tempted to study it here, and wallow in images of *God's Heart* for a while.

He certainly didn't want to think about living forever or dying tomorrow.

What he realised then was that Summer hadn't told him who the 'we' actually were. Why? Was she trying to protect them or him? Didn't she know who *she* could trust?

He walked into his dorm bubble, a whirlpool of conflicting emotions; tormented by the revelations and heartened by Summer's return.

The stench hit Barl as soon as he set foot inside.

Several of the beds had been overturned and a gassy, vomit-reek pervaded the air. The last time Barl had smelled anything like it he had been in the corridor of the *Minular* when it was under attack.

The realisation hit him like a battle-mace to the side of the skull.

He raced to the first of the overturned beds, his heart sinking as he saw Gharlin's Pressure cage lying crushed and broken on the floor...

In a puddle of liquid and torn flesh, the Bantoscree lay dying, his tendrils quivering and his mouthparts screaming silently.

CHAPTER 29

Galdar couldn't move.

The immense room was fashioned from stone, with a vaulted wooden ceiling, and was easily the size of a cathedral. Her mind struggled to reconcile how it could fit under the roof above the Governor's residence.

It was impossible.

Steam rose from the centre of the impossible room.

A brass and copper engine belched into life.

Contraptions whirred and spun, men worked, feeding coal into a huge boiler and flames belched.

Above the engine was a fat, steel framed airship bumping gently against the vaulted roof. Slung underneath was a boat-like gondola, filled with crossbow wielding Townsguard and Governor Klane, sporting the same bloated sweaty red face as the mahogany carving on the devil-door. He shrieked, "*Kill them!*" at the Townsguard.

Carlow went down with a cry, taking a thick black bolt to the shoulder that spun him around, the impact enough to punch him off his feet.

Galdar threw herself behind a huge stone pillar.

Shryke pushed Lucillian out of the way as a barrage of bolts whistled towards them; the wooden shafts shivered as the steel slammed into the wall behind his back. Still bent in a crouch, he dragged the writhing Carlow to safety behind another pillar.

Gears and pulleys started to whir and clank.

One of the Townsguard cut a tethering rope with his dagger and with a deep groan that rumbled through the mechanisms, the airship started to rise. The gears and pulleys worked faster as the roof began to open like wings on a huge bird above their heads.

Shryke didn't hesitate; he ran for the airship.

Dodging bolts and firing back with his own hand held, two-shot crossbow, Shryke covered the flagstones in a blur of speed and singing death.

As he ran, the crossbow shimmered in his grip from loosed to loaded—loosed to loaded, every other half-second as he wove a codespell of replenishment around the first bolts. Each subsequent bolt he loosed took out a Townsguard, pinning the corpse up against the bulwark of gondola with a thud, an exhalation and a lung-emptying groan. Shryke struck true five times before he reached the guide rope tethered beneath the keel of the gondola. He looked up, seeing a face peering down at him, and made it six. As the corpse fell, he began to climb.

Shryke climbed quickly, hand over hand, up the side of the gondola. As he reached the top, he saw another guard loom over him, a sneer on his twisted lips as he moved to cut the rope. Shryke was faster. The man hit the ground, the meat around his bones not protecting him from the impact as he was broken by the fall.

Shryke leapt onto the deck.

Galdar and Lucillian didn't need his yelling to get them moving. Without a word exchanged, the pair nodded and in unison took one of Carlow's ankles, and dragged him bumping and protesting over the stone floor towards the sky ship. *At least if the fool's protesting, he isn't dead,* Galdar thought grimly. They covered the twenty yards to the airship in a matter of seconds.

Three more screaming bodies crashed down from the gondola

with sickening, bone snapping *thuds* as two rope ladders were unrolled over the side. The ladders were still long enough to reach the floor, but in a matter of moments the ascending airship would take them out of reach.

Galdar threaded Carlow's arms through the bottom rung of the rope ladder as it lifted, then pushed his head through between two other wooden slats so that as it went up, it would carry him with it, even if were unconscious.

The bolt from the Townsguard's crossbow was embedded deep in Carlow's shoulder. The blood seeping out around the wound was slow and thick.

Lucillian was already clambering up the other ladder. She was half-way to the gondola as Galdar, stowing the battle-mace in her belt, began to climb.

In less than a minute the airship was free of the Devil-Room.

With a gust of squall and chill stab of vertigo in Galdar's belly, it began to soar, sailing the skies over the town.

Below was chaos.

Raiders still fought Townsguard in the streets.

Buildings were ablaze.

Galdar saw Assassins swept up in a battle that had nothing to do with them.

She didn't care. Let them fight and die. She realised that the relative respite they'd had from attacks was because the Devil-Room had been fashioned by secret magic not of Shryke's making, but now they were rising from that protection there would be more come to try and succeed where the others had thus far failed.

In the streets several of the Townsguard looked up at the airship, pointing. Their shouts of anger reached up to the deck; their rage at the Governor's cowardly abandonment of them. The fight went out of them. She saw small pockets of anger, the Townsguard and citizens of Saint Juffour lowering their weapons in surrender.

The last thing Galdar saw before Lucillian's hand reached over the edge of the bulwark and yanked her off the rope ladder were four Assassins in their blacks blinking out of existence.

Galdar lay breathing heavily on the airship's heaving deck.

Through a forest of legs, she saw Shryke had Governor Klane on the point of his knife, with no resistance from the few remaining Townsguard who should have been protecting him.

"Are you Klane?" Shryke demanded.

"Pardoor Klane the Third of Saint Juffour, actually, you barbarian, and you are a dead man walking."

"Tell me something I don't know," Shryke spat. "Where is your navigator?"

Klane pointed at a weasel-faced woman who had a chart under her arm and a pencil behind her ear. "Crove. Come here."

The navigator shuffled forward. "Yes Master."

"Tell her to do as I say," Shryke said.

"Do as he says."

"I was going to anyway," Crove said, causing Klane's already flushed face to burn an even darker red.

"None of your cheek, woman, or I'll throw you off the ship myself." Klane sneered. He nodded to Shryke, telling him to do what he will. He didn't care. It was a pitiful attempt to cling onto whatever dignity he thought he still possessed.

"What course do you want me to set?"

Shryke wiped his mouth across his lips and stared up past the fuselage of the airship's balloon.

"Up," said Shryke.

Lucillian tended to Carlow, who gave good voice to his pain.

The Townsguard had drawn the ladder up to lift him up over the side as the airship continued to climb.

There was a precious hour of daylight left before Halfnight. Soon they would be above the grey heavy clouds that had brought so much rain to the town below.

Galdar couldn't make out the streets of Saint Juffour; there was just the twist of the river valley and the heaving waves of Lake Tarsh.

Overhead the Loop glittered in its own night.

Up here in the higher atmosphere without clouds and heat hazes to obscure her view, Galdar could see further along the Chain than ever before. She fancied she remembered the route the Congregation of the Moveable Church had taken across those lands when she was a girl. Imagining the route, tracing it with her finger in the air.

Carlow's latest scream of agony brought Galdar back to the present. Lucillian's hands moved over the bolt, her fingers flexing, and as Galdar watched, the bolt began to lift clear of Carlow's shoulder of its own accord, the metal tearing the wound wider as it came clear. It fell bloodily to the deck. The Townsguard looked on, shifting uncomfortably on their feet. Nine soldiers survived. They huddled together for warmth as the chill high-altitudes the airship was travelling through ate into their bones with a biting ferocity.

Lucillian began cleaning Carlow's wound and then dressed it.

"This is just an escape ship," Klane grumbled. "Short range, just enough to get us a few leagues to safety before setting down."

"I didn't ask for your opinion," Shryke told the fat man.

"It is *not* a high-altitude machine," Crove confirmed. "If you push us much higher, it's going to start to ice up. That happens, we fall out of the sky. We won't need anyone to shoot us down."

"We go up."

"It's your funeral," said Clove, "And everyone else's of course."

Shryke leapt up on the bulwark, a hawser wrapped around his grip, silhouetted against the misty face of the first rising Loop-moon. He looked up as the shadow of night began to move towards their section of link. "When the time comes, I'll deal with the ice."

"And fuel? Can you arrange that, too? We need fuel for the engine. We have about fifteen minutes of coal left."

"I'll deal with that, too," Shryke said craning his neck up, "Trust me."

He jumped down and stalked past the Governor, who sat shivering against the bulwark with cold or terror.

It was getting harder and harder to trust Shryke, but she did. With her life.

Shryke addressed the Townsguard. "You have all fought bravely, but when I use my spells to ensure the airship doesn't freeze, and to replenish the fuel and to enable the engine to push us ever faster there will be a price to pay. The Assassins who seek my death will know where I am. And they *will* come in force. They won't just kill *me*. They will kill you all. When the time comes, you have a choice to make. Fight with me, with my friends, or learn to fly. Understood?"

The nine soldiers nodded.

Shryke ordered Lucillian to leave the protesting Carlow and join him at the prow of the airship.

Lucillian stood ready to cast.

Crove looked with genuine concern at the dwindling hap of coal the firemen shovelled into the engine.

Klane cried.

Shryke closed his eyes, "I will be moments. The Plain calls."

Galdar's heart hammered in her chest with run-away anticipation, it reached an almost unbearable speed, and she thought it would surely burst clean out of her chest. After a few seconds, Shryke's eyes opened. He spoke codespells and moved his hands.

Four things happened at once.

A huge scree of new coal appeared in the hopper by the engine. The roar of the steaming pistons turning the airscrew increased tenfold, belching steam and sparks, as the airship accelerated to unheard of speeds. Black steel swords and chaos imbued shields came into the hands of the Townsguard, and lastly, *seven*

Assassins, in full Techtomesh Exo-Armour stepped from the air in front of Lucillian and Shryke.

The Assassin's hand-cannons raised up, centring over their hearts, whining desperately as they charged.

CHAPTER 30

Rhoan promised Barl it was "just a room."

Vilow didn't disagree.

It had a bed, a terminal, a place to wash and defecate. But it was unlike any other bubble in the Nest. For one thing, the walls were opaque. If the light reflecting on the outside of the bubble was bright enough, Barl could just make out the vague shadows of people walking past, but that was it. The door to the bubble could only be opened from the outside, meaning he was essentially a prisoner, with food and refreshments passed through a lensing slot next to the door.

Room? No. It was a holding cell.

The days had been a rush and a blur.

Gharlin was dead, and no amount of wishing would change that. Barl was broken. He saw the way they looked at him. He knew that he was their number one suspect. He had wept for his friend even as Vilow told him was being sealed in the opaque bubble for his own safety.

Barl felt anything but safe.

Trapped.

Alone.

Rhoan promised him as they left that, "The investigation has already begun, boy. Believe me, we do not take this invasion lightly. We will find the source, and they will be brought to justice. The security of the Nest and the Guild is paramount," and then the door had locked shut behind them, sealing with a vacuum hiss, and Barl had been left to his own thoughts.

The room was shielded against magical attack, and only accessible by highest level Guild Authority. He was simply to wait until investigations were concluded.

That had been three days ago.

At least he thought it had been three days. They had fed him nine times.

Barl had been the only one to shed a tear at the Bantoscree's murder.

He'd begged to see Summer, but Rhoan had shaken her ever reconfiguring head. Two mouths tutted and the third, sliding up her broad face told Barl that Summer was no longer in the Nest and hadn't been for months.

Barl stopped himself telling Rhoan about the meeting with her in the bubble garden.

Not that it mattered.

He could not *prove* that he'd seen her.

The data-cube she'd given him had been confiscated before he'd been able to read a single entry. The battlemasters had scanned and had taken all manner of samples from him—as Xaxax assured him, to eliminate him from their inquiries, which only heightened his sense of guilt and despair.

Barl stopped pacing and sat down heavily on the bed.

The terminal remained untouched.

He'd be too tempted to input the words *God's Heart* and after what had happened the last time, he didn't want to risk triggering any similar response from the machine.

He tried several times to use some low energy spells, nothing exciting, not even a handful of yellowberries, but the room was shielding *any* use of magic.

Barl shifted uncomfortably on the bed.

He felt a sharp pain in his thigh and rolled sideways.

There was no one else in the room. The sudden jab had seemed to come from the bed itself.

He looked at the bed.

The covers remained undisturbed.

Barl gingerly ran his hand over the sheets until his palm snagged on something.

There was an object hidden beneath them.

It hadn't been there when he'd sat down, and definitely hadn't been in the bed when he'd slept in it last night.

Barl rolled the covers back, and there on the mattress was a data-cube.

It had to be the same small silver one Summer had given him, but how had it got here? Barl didn't dare reach for it, remembering how the robed Skeleton had last come at him out of a piece of supposedly benign technology.

He stared at the thing for a good fifteen minutes, watching to see if it did something out of the ordinary. Nothing happened.

Eventually, he picked it up, holding the cube between thumb and forefinger, as he examined the tracery of intricate circuitry buried in its silver-blue surface.

There was a small switch on the side, which he assumed would activate the cube.

He'd used similar ones in class several times to research weaving particular codespells or aspects of combat.

He looked at the terminal.

Dare he use it to decode the contents of the cube?

Or was he holding another trap in his hand?

He put the cube back down on the bed and stared at it.

It sat there, inert.

Somehow it had been put there by magical means, despite the shielding and projections woven around the cell... But who had the kind of power to do that?

Barl sat, rippled with a creeping sense of unease.

'o...t...'

A voice crackled in his ear. It wasn't much. A mush of staticky nonsense, which buzzed around for a few seconds, then went silent.

The voice…

Had it been Summer?

Or was it someone trying to sound like Summer, knowing that Barl would intrinsically trust her?

Buzz.

'Do…it…eakin…up. No…pow…r.'

It *was* Summer.

Do it?

Do what?

Buzz.

'Cube…sw…tch…do…t…'

Barl picked up the cube.

He trusted her voice, as broken and distant as it was, and thumbed the switch from o to i. Instead of lighting up the terminal screen as he'd expected, light blasted directly into his eyes. The beam hit him with all the suddenness and physical force for a punch, spinning him around and dumping his arse on the bed.

"What happened?"
    'Shhh. Watch.'

Stars sped past at a crazy pace.

Galaxies flexed. A red rush. Crushed light. A planet. Golden seas. Green clouds. Down. Hands in his vision. Summer's hands. *Looking through her eyes.* Down. A continent. A mountain. A castle. A window. A room. A throne. A King. A Mage. *They don't see me. They can't see me.* They're planning. Planning a war. Planning a war against a foul warlord. They have armies to command. They have a land to protect. A people to save. A Guild Assassin. Stepping out of the air. The Mage. Killed. Beheaded. The King slaughtered. Later. The castle in ruins. The land conquered. The people enslaved. *The Guild did this.*

Stars. A planet. A different planet. A thousand-year war. Holding back the monsters. Monsters ready to burn and destroy. The war had kept them at bay. The line had held. Five huge batteries of automatic blast-guns ready to repel. In a line. A long line. A detonation. A battery blown away. Another. Another. Another. And then the last. A million monsters rushing forwards. Claws. Teeth. Murder in their eyes. *The Guild did this.*

Stars. A bridge high above a river. In mountains. An exchange of prisoners. A leader. Sent back to his people in hope that he will keep his word and end the conflict. The last hope for peace. A Guild Assassin in the uniform of the opposing forces steps forward. Guts the leader. Throws his corpse into the river. Hails victory. A war begun. *The Guild did this.*

The dorm bubble in the Nest. Gharlin waiting for Barl, happy, buzzing. Two assassins in their blacks appear behind him. Raise their swords to his pressure-cage… The Guild did this…

"Stop!"

The light extinguished.

Barl was back in the room, lying on the bed, tears running down his face.

"Why did you show me that?"

Summer sat on the bed beside him. She wiped the tears from his cheek with her warm fingers. She smoothed down his hair. "I'm sorry. It was the last piece of the puzzle. You've been looking at a fraction of my investigations. The Guild Assassins are being sent everywhere, being used to foment chaos. They are murdering good people to start wars. I've seen it everywhere. And now, it's reached the Nest. You being here has forced the hand of whoever or whatever is behind all this. It's corrupted the Guild. War is coming. The Nest is about to be attacked."

Barl didn't want to hear this; all he wanted to do was purge the image of Gharlin's last moments from his mind's eye. He couldn't shift the glint of the steel and the unsuspecting flush of colours blazing then fading and dying out in the pressure-cage.

"Barl, you're special, kid. I've known it from the start. But I didn't know *how* special. They're going to go all out to kill you. Removing Gharlin is nothing more than another first salvo in this particular war. And they're going to be coming for me, too. I'm not naïve enough to think I'm safe. They want every obstacle in their path removed. And that's Gharlin and me, most recently. We both stood against them. Without us in the picture, they have a better chance of getting to you. It doesn't matter how drained your strength is, with me around you're still safe. And they know that."

Barl sat up. "Please take me home. I can change my name. I can stop it. I will never use magic. I don't want to. I just want to be me… let me go back to how it was, before all this started. Let me be like I was… with my parents, with my family, with my friends. Just let me be a normal kid."

Summer shook her head. "Things have moved too far. I'm sorry. I truly am. I wish it could be different. I still don't understand exactly what or even who you are, not really, but I've an inkling."

Before Barl could speak, there was an explosion outside the cell.

The bubble rocked violently, and through the opaque wall Barl heard the wail of sirens and people screaming.

"It's started," Summer said, standing up. She ran her fingers through her hair. "I hadn't expected them to move this soon."

"What's happening?"

"The Guild has been compromised. The enemy…our enemy… has brought a field guard of compromised Assassins from the Outer Rim to attack the Nest. They are here to kill me, and in the process neutralize you."

Barl got off the bed, unsure what to do, but knowing he couldn't just sit on his hands. "Then what will we do? Tell me. How will we escape?"

"I need you to go to The Plain."

"Now?" He couldn't quite believe what she was suggesting. Going there left them vulnerable here.

"I'll meet you there," she promised.

Barl couldn't bring himself to shut his eyes.

"Trust me," Summer said, pulling a complex looking hand-blaster from her blacks.

Barl looked on in horror as she put the gun against her temple and pulled the trigger.

CHAPTER 31

S hryke roared and leapt towards the seven Assassins as they came towards him. He ducked into a combat roll, twisting, black blade clutched to his chest, as the seven fired. The hand-cannons ripped the deck asunder, shredding the wood. Shryke was gone. Vaporised. The smoke reeked for fire and plasma.

Galdar screamed.

The Townsguard threw down their weapons, running for the bow of the gondola, she assumed, to hurl themselves off the side and exchange one certain death for another as the Assassins turned their weapons on the rest of the crew.

Lucillian, too shocked by Shryke's demise to do anything, closed her eyes and waited for death.

Their weapons had weakened the deck below themselves; it collapsed.

They fell into the dark hold of the gondola.

A savage series of cannon blasts, several screams, and then Shryke emerged from the gaping hole in the deck, carrying one of the Techtomesh helmets in his bloodied fist.

He reached inside the helm and pulled out the Assassin's severed head like he was pulling a mollusc from its shell and tossed it over the side of the gondola with contempt.

Galdar ran across the deck to throw herself at Shryke, gripping him in a fierce embrace that he returned every bit as fiercely until he realised he was smearing blood across her and instead kissed her forehead with a smile. "Take some of our boys into the hold. Strip the armour from the dead and buckle up. Where we're going, we're going to need it."

Shryke's codemagic cast a misty pink sphere of warmth that slowly spread to envelop the gondola as it rose ever higher into the night.

Klane begged the Quantum Assassin over and over not to send the airship to greater altitudes, but Shryke dismissed the fat man's concerns. The airship shuddered and shivered, the strain on the timbers threatening to tear it apart at the seams, but his magic would protect it until they reached their destination.

Crove muttered and sighed and shook her head, but she was obviously impressed with Shryke's tampering to the steam engine. It was pushing out much more power but consuming considerably less coal. "I want to know your secret," she told Shryke. "It'll make me a fortune."

Shryke grinned.

"If we ever get back, the airship's yours." Which earned a grunt from Klane. "You're more than rich enough to buy yourself another, fat man."

"Not anymore I'm not."

"You have your health and a future in front of you. That makes you a rich man in my eyes," Shryke told him, ending any argument.

Galdar finished laying out and cleaning the seven suits of armour they had retrieved from the dead assassins. It was incredible stuff, so light and yet stronger than any material she knew. She marvelled at the tiny servos and engines arranged on the joins between plates, which made the armour move of its own accord. As she cleaned, the armour flowered open, preparing itself for her to step inside as if she were the rightful owner. The exoskeleton possessed an innate intelligence and was driven to protect those closest to it. Galdar drew some reassurance from that.

Shryke stood on the gondola's forward deck, hands lashed to ropes to steady himself.

"Where *are* we going?" She asked, coming up to join him.

They were moving towards a huge black expanse of nothing.

It curved from horizon to horizon but tinged at all four edges as if it were holding station in front of an enormous source of light.

"We travel beyond the Shadewalls," he answered, as if this was meant to explain everything. Galdar opened her palms and raised a questioning eyebrow. Shryke sighed, "We don't have time for a lesson in the mechanics of the world. Guild Assassins will locate us again, it's only a matter of time, and we have to steer the airship past the Shadewalls without getting burnt to cinders by the Sun-Machine or the dragons that protect it."

"Make time, please." Galdar said. "If I'm going to die, I'd like to know where I'm dying. And why."

"Seconded," Lucillian said with a small wave as she approached. "I don't even know why I'm here, other than I was unlucky enough to meet you. No one was trying to kill me yesterday. I have to say, between the three of us, I much preferred yesterday."

Shryke set his face towards the expanse of the Shadewalls, looking for danger.

"When I came to the Chain I came on a mission, *this* mission," he explained.

"To protect the Mage in Forthana?"

"No. Forthana was destroyed many years ago, long before I got here. I lied to you. My real memories had been…masked from me somehow… stolen. When you asked, I didn't know the truth. I needed you to trust me, so I lied. You wouldn't have followed me if you knew only half of my mind was there. That purpose, the memories of that mission, were implanted in my mind, and used to lock away my real memories."

"Who would do such a thing?" Galdar asked.

"The God-Queen. My real mission was to travel to the Sun-Machine. There I was to ensure the God-Queen failed in her attempt to re-animate the Dreaming Army. If the army are brought back to this realm, they will lay waste the entire universe."

"Slow down," Galdar said. "I'm struggling. This doesn't make any sense. You don't even believe in God."

"Not God. *Gods*."

"Are you telling me Gods are real?" said Lucillian, shaking her head.

Shryke turned on them. "Now do you understand why I didn't explain? You think I am mad."

Galdar shook her head. "I don't believe you," she said. "You are wrong. There is only one God."

Shryke looked on her with pity and compassion. "The Gods are beings. Unimaginable beings, but life forms all the same. They create universes, they create matter. They fill those creations with people for one reason and one reason alone: faith has a power. An energy all its own. When you pray, when you worship when you suffer and pay penance, that energy is transferred to the realm of the Gods. The God-King and his people want you to worship them because…it *tastes* good."

"So, there is no Safehome? The Quest was for nothing?"

"Of course, there's no Safehome, but that doesn't matter. What you believe brings you comfort and gives you purpose. It's the way of the God. It is benevolent. Mostly."

"Mostly?" said Lucillian sharply.

"When a universe breaks down into constant war and conflict, when faith is replaced by fear, then the energies transmitted to the Gods through faith become poisonous and dangerous to them. They leave a Failsafe. Once the people no longer provide the energies they require, they destroy them so they can start all over again."

"They're going to destroy everything?"

Shryke nodded. "The God-King and the God-Queen have fallen into war against each other. The God-Queen has been using the Guild to throw a cloud of chaos over the whole of creation. The universe is on the brink of triggering the Failsafe, sending it across creation to end...*everything*. My mission was to go to the Sun-Machine and protect the Dreaming Army from the God-Queen."

Galdar felt the rush of revelation running through her frame.

She wanted to take some earth and pray for the Congregation of the Moveable Church. She fell to her knees and did the next best thing, she wept. She didn't *want* to believe Shryke. He was telling her that her whole life had been a lie.

"I am sorry," he said.

"Why?" She could have meant why are you sorry, or why is this happening, why the war, why try to stand between warring factions when they are immortal beings?

Shryke said, "If the Dreaming Army leaves the Sun-Machine and destroys everything, it will leave the God-queen free to remake creation in her image. Everything we know will be gone as if it never existed. I came here to stop her."

"You can stop a God?"

Shryke nodded. "Yes. Yes, I can. That is why my memories were locked away. It was an attempt to keep them secret from her. The message you gave me from Summer was a trigger. It unlocked the codespell around my memories."

"Summer?"

"The woman who saved us. The creator of your battle-mace."

"Hold on," said Lucillian incredulously. "Why didn't this God-Queen just kill you?"

"That I can't tell you."

"Why not?"

"Because within that answer you will learn the secret of how to kill me. I'm hard to kill, but it isn't impossible. I *can* be incapacitated—I can be infected, maimed and tied in chains and so much more. Being hard to kill doesn't mean I can't be stopped. But the fact that the Guild keeps sending more of its people to die is proof they still have no idea *how* hard I am to kill."

"My head hurts," said Lucillian. She stood, arms folded as Shryke continued his incredible story.

"The Chain was built by the Gods many billions of years ago, think of it as an experimental anvil of creation. All life in the universe originates from here, from these sixteen links. The Chain is Jonderell, Mephak, Fallow-Thorn, Eden, Panthorc—whatever name you have for the Cradle of Life; the Chain is its Origin. The peoples and environments of that experiment are what were left once the Gods had finished with this universe and moved onto the next."

"Are you trying to tell us that all life is an experiment?"

"It is, and the God-Queen has decided that the experiment has failed."

"But why? Why would she do that? Why would any god destroy their creation?"

Shryke sighed. "What brings down every great house in the end? Power. Envy. Shame. Fear. A combination of all four? The God-Queen is determined to destroy everything. She seeks to save herself and punish the God-King."

The airship steamed towards the Shadewalls, leaving a trail of ice crystals from the steaming engine in its wake.

As the atmosphere thinned to nothing, the airship's speed increased, and the loop of Chain below became as distant as the loop on the far side of the sky.

They continued to accelerate.

The airship headed towards the top right corner of the Shadewalls.

Under Shryke's instruction, Crove pushed the steaming engine for all it was worth. Pistons pumped and the airscrews at the back of the ship, outside the pink haze of protection Shryke had cast, moved at impossible speeds. Crove feared that without any atmosphere, the airscrews would no longer work, having nothing to push against for thrust. Shryke told her simply, "Don't worry, they are pushing hard enough against magic to make up for the lack of atmosphere."

Which didn't exactly convince her, but after all she'd seen today, she wasn't surprised to hear they were flying through rings of magic towards the Shadewalls; the Shadewalls that brought night and day to the myriad surfaces of the Chain.

Galdar railed against the idea of there being more than one God who had created everything. She refused to accept that everything she'd believed over the years had been a lie, that they were nothing more than cattle, and every time she ate dirt, she was feeding a God with energy. This heresy hurt her deeply inside. All that death. All that pain. For this feeling of...hollowness.

Carlow, crossbow wound patched, arm in a sling, joined her on the bulwark. "Shryke is a heretic."

Galdar wasn't in the mood to argue with him.

"I don't believe him." Galdar closed her eyes. "I don't think you do, either. We know the truth; God's birthplace is in the earth. In Safehome. He comes from the earth, and we worship the earth in God's name." The light from the dawn edge of the Shadewalls reflected in Carlow's eyes as he took Galdar's hand and poured a tiny amount of dirt into her palm from a pouch he took from his belt. "Pray with me, sister."

Galdar looked at the centre of her palm, at the grains.

She thought about what they represented and what they had meant to her over the years.

She smiled at Carlow, and kissed his cheek, "I forgive you, for everything, for every ounce of anger, for your betrayals, because I knew they came from a good place, but I can't do that. Not anymore."

And with that she let the grains of dirt slip through her fingers like grains of sand, and spill away over the side of the airship, falling like stars from the point of their creation.

CHAPTER 32

The three vultures circled overhead. They had the faces of the Skull. Their wings were flapping red robes edged with tiny imperfect feathers.

The more Barl stared at them, the more they changed.

He could hear laughter above the throng of the endless battle.

A woman's voice; ageless and cruel.

It hissed across the clouds.

It echoed off the mountains.

It sank into the dead marshes.

It was the laughter of a God.

The armies broiled and fought.

Barl was in the battle's heart, on the same raised hill of bones as before, but when he looked up, it wasn't the golden-haired woman he'd seen before, it was Summer.

But not the Summer he recognised from their universe outside this blasted Plain. It was a taller, larger Summer. A more powerful Summer. An elemental Summer. A titan. Twenty feet from boot to hairline, pulling on a breastplate and securing the straps at the side.

"You killed yourself," he said, disbelieving. "You *left* me."

Summer finished buckling the final strap before she answered him. "I made a choice, my love. I sacrificed myself in that world to become something greater."

"How, how can anything be greater?"

"I will never leave you again. We are fused. Two aspects of one soul. A shared purpose. A shared power."

"I don't understand."

"I am your Familiar on The Plain. You will forever come to me for the powers needed to cast the spells that you weave in both protection and wrath. Sometimes you will project a memory of me as an extension of your will, a warrior to do battle on your behalf, an avatar to save you."

Barl stood there as the enormous woman bent, picked up a huge helm and placed it on her head, covering her face completely. She locked the catches down the side of the steel construction, each one clicking into place like nails being driven into his coffin one after the other.

Summer began sliding on mailed gloves so large they would have fitted Barl like a tunic.

He looked up at her, awestruck by the giantess.

Her voice changed when she spoke from within the helm. It was deeper, darker, charged with indefinable magicks and spells. In her hand she held a beautifully inscribed battle-mace. Barl hadn't seen her pick it up. It was just there.

"Hold out your hands," she told him.

Out of habit he pushed his elbows into his side and turned his palms face-up. Instead of a punnet of yellowberries, a battle-mace appeared across his hands. The weight felt perfect. The balance as if it had been made for him. He grasped the handle and swung it. It moved through the air with easy grace—it felt light but deadly.

"Go."

Barl knew what he had to do.

He leapt into the battle, desperate to please his Familiar.

The airship reached the Shadewalls.

Crove was instructed to keep pace with it.

The sheer magnitude of the wall was humbling. It swished silently across the sky; bringing night as world sized shadows to the links below, leaving a trail of dawn behind it. Off in the distance Galdar saw other Shadewalls at different pitches and angles, each doing the same job for the sixteen other links in the Chain.

Compared to the flying walls, the airship was smaller than a tick on a mammoth's back.

The surface of the wall was smooth and dark.

There was no visible means of propulsion; it hung in the space between the loops blocking the sunlight.

And now Shryke was going to take them all beyond it into the Sun-Machine.

Galdar had no idea if she was going to survive the day, but in a small way, she no longer cared. She had seen these wonders up close; it almost erased the loss of her purpose down on the Chain...*almost*. There was still a hum of regret around her thinking and emotions. Scripture jarred in her thoughts, but she no longer clung to it for answers. There wasn't the same strength to be found in those beatitudes.

Perhaps she would find a new purpose?

Perhaps Shryke was leading her to it beyond the Shadewalls?

Galdar was painfully aware that Carlow had been avoiding her since she had refused to pray with him. She could understand his rejection of Shryke's word and for her loss of faith. The idea that Gods... Yes. Not one God, but Gods... were real, not in some distant spiritual sense, but in a tangible physical sense as *beings*, was an idea she was still processing... but his rejection still stung.

Physical beings, so powerful they mimicked all the qualities of the Gods who had created everything. Created *her*. She no longer had to work at having a faith. The certainty of faith had been replaced by the certainty of reality. It felt like a big change inside her. It was awkward in her thoughts. It lay there strangely. An alien idea. She wanted the idea to fit. For it to continue to challenge her thoughts and her feelings until she'd worked through them. Maybe she would still come out of this process with a faith...just a different one?

Having something to believe in; something she could take back to the peoples of the Chain was planting a tiny seed of missionary zeal within her.

Perhaps the Congregation of the Moveable Church could once again travel the links of the Chain, bringing a completely new message and story?

Galdar's eyes glistened as she thought of the possible futures and hoped against hope that she would have one. A future that is.

She didn't attempt to pray for it, because she didn't know who to pray *to*, or what the energy from that prayer would feed...

Shryke and Crove were up in the wheelhouse. Galdar watched through the glass as the navigator threw her hands in the air and stormed away from Shryke.

Shryke shook his head and took the wheel with one hand, weaving a codespell with the other.

With a hiss and a clank, the steam engine was silenced.

From Klane to the Townsguard, to the fireman, to Carlow and Lucillian, everyone looked up at the wheelhouse.

But Shryke wasn't looking back down at them.

With an expression of supreme concentration, Shryke was turning the wheel.

The airship began to adjust its course, moving directly towards the featureless expanse of the Shadewalls.

Galdar had no real idea of the sense of scale, so couldn't judge how long it would be before the airship smashed into the enormous object. But, if the speed she felt within the timbers of the craft was real, it wouldn't be long.

"He's mad! Completely mad!" Crove yelled bitterly as she stomped back down the narrow stair to the deck.

That was difficult to deny.

Barl fought with the battle-mace, facing down warrior after warrior, the weapon singing in his head as he smashed bone, ripped through armour, and stoved skulls in. Swords swung at him, bending and buckling into unusable shapes against the incredible weapon.

Barl fought out his frustrations.

Barl fought out his homesickness.

Barl fought out his grief at the death of Gharlin.

Barl fought out the unbearable sadness at Summer's transformation.

Barl *fought*.

He carved a swathe of death around the hill of bones, stealing a glance through the starbursts of blood and falling bodies, up past his Familiar Summer to where the circling vultures were more feathers and beak than robe and Skulls.

The laughter had dissipated, too.

Barl felt the surge of relief within him.

He breathed hard, wiped blood from his eyes, killed two more and leapt back up onto the mound.

"Enough?" he asked Summer in her armour.

Summer's helm nodded, "For now, yes."

Barl knelt.

Thought of *God's Heart*.

Thought of his father.

Thought of his mother.

Barl *just* thought.

And waited.

The Axe came down, it sizzled and spat with heat as it were made of molten metal, it left a trail of black steam as he felt every moment of its journey through him, cleaving his body asunder.

And it was glorious.

Barl was back in the room.

Summer's body, her face gone from the blaster shot, blood seeping across the floor, lay at his feet.

Explosions raged outside.

Still the screams came.

Barl he held the battle-mace from The Plain in his first.

He took a moment to study the curlicues and carvings. The patterns moved. Twisted. Was that Summer's face he saw in there for a heartbeat? His father?

Barl bowed his head, saying goodbye to Summer, and then looked at the door.

All it took was the slightest inclination of his head and the door blew away on a gust of flame.

Outside the bubble, the Nest had become chaos.

Flames cackled and raged everywhere. He walked through a trail of dead bodies. Trainees and staff. In the distance, Barl heard a battle being fought, the distinctive sizzle and snap of energy weapons being discharged. As he stepped over the bodies, Barl looked up through the superstructure of the Nest and saw ships, tiny fighters and larger dreadnoughts, engaged in a brutal conflict across the bruised face of the Gas Giant.

It was all out war.

He headed for the armoury.

Barl reached the bubble without incident; the battle around the Nest too ferocious for anyone to worry about one person walking away from it. Assassins raced in their hundreds to defend the Nest. There was no one left in armoury to stop Barl from getting the Techtomesh armour and hand-cannon he had come looking for. He knew that if he were to survive the day, he would have to find a safe way out of the Nest and off Pantonyle.

Barl loaded a magazine of close-quarter explosive rounds into the hand-cannon, then climbed into his armour.

It closed around him, shaping itself to his body.

Slinging a bag of hand-cannon magazines over his shoulder and sliding the battle-mace into his belt, Barl left the armoury intent on waging war for everything that had been stolen from him.

The airship passed through the Shadewalls with a ripple in reality and a blast of hot white light.

The shell of warmth he had woven around the craft turned near-black with a wave of Shryke's hand, shielding them from the thirty-two suns that made up the Sun-Machine.

Nothing could have prepared Galdar for this.

"Into the armour. Now!" Shryke yelled.

The Techtomesh whirred and buzzed as it fitted around her. She didn't like the sensation of the faceplate up against her skin, moulding itself to her features.

However comfortable the suit was, she wanted that faceplate off her skin.

The faceplate swung up.

Galdar thought the opposite.

The faceplate swung down and fitted back perfectly over her face.

She raised it again, realising that the suit shaped itself to her commands, all she had to do was think it and the suit would react.

Lucillian flexed her arms, testing the limits of her own suit.

Carlow, reverting to type, refused to wear any unholy armour, arguing, "God will protect me," loudly to anyone who could hear him.

The few remaining Townsguard, Crove and Klane took refuge in the remaining armour, some being forced to share, it was uncomfortable but better than being seared alive by the intense heat of thirty-two raging suns, and a grim silence enveloped the airship as it travelled between the whirring, whirling suns.

Carlow knelt apart from them all, eating his dirt and praying.

Shryke left the wheelhouse to Crove to pilot the airship between the spiralling suns. The suns moved in circles and arcs across and around them, peeking between Shadewalls. They were held in place by a network of immense girders. Each star was much smaller than Galdar would have imagined given the size of the Shadewalls. But even behind the dark of the shell encasing their airship it was painful to look directly at them, such was the intensity of their brightness.

Shryke, in his armour now, stood at the prow of the airship, steadying himself with a rope from the rigging.

He pointed in the direction he wanted Crove to steer.

Suns on their girders slid silently past, leaving comet tails of fire which burned briefly and then dissipated.

The airship was heading deep into the centre of the cloud of tiny suns.

A golden plate spun at the heart of this magical impossibility.

Galdar couldn't make out any details of its surface, but it glowed with a beautiful light all its own.

As the airship sailed on, perspectives began to shift and change, and Galdar felt a new weight in the gravity around her. They were no longer travelling *up*. They had begun their descent.

The golden, spinning plate grew.

The edges were battlemented.

Galdar saw spires and wide roads between the golden buildings.

Shryke signalled to Crove, getting her to trim the attitude of the airship so that the bottom of the gondola was now at the direction of the travel.

The airship was coming in to land.

Galdar stole a look at Lucillian.

Lucillian shrugged and smiled. "I've had less interesting days, it has to be said."

Klane in his armour, sat hunched in the corner.

Galdar heard him gently keening through the communication grille of his suit, like a baby in the middle of the night. He had stopped acting like he had any special right to be heard and retreated into the pathetic wretch he had always been at heart.

Galdar put a comforting hand on Klane's shoulder, but he shrugged it off.

"Don't touch me," he snapped, but as she lifted her hand, he had a change of heart and reached up, pulling it back down onto his shoulder. Galdar squeezed, not sure if the armour she wore would transmit such a subtle feeling.

As the airship sank lower and lower, beneath the spiralling suns on the ends of their whirling girders, Galdar wondered what they would find down there.

Life or Death?

Before Galdar had the opportunity to explore that line of thought, the airship heaved to one side and a gust of flame erupted through the rigging, bursting a hole in the metal cage surrounding the dirigible.

The world around them lurched to the right, as Shryke leaped towards the wheelhouse shouting, "Dragons!"

CHAPTER 33

The first energy bolt hit Barl so hard it blew him off the central Nest transept and sent him crashing down through three levels of dark, twisted, crowded walkways and bubbles, into the lower reaches of the Nest.

The Techtomesh deformed around him, taking the physical brunt of the bolt, and lessening the energy burn, even so he felt the force of the impacts and the heat of the blast as he rolled into a shadow. An overhang ensured that anyone above was unable to get an easy shot.

The battle raged on overhead.

The suit's communication system and tactical display on the inside of the visor showed a swarm of hostiles and desperate defenders, but because both were Assassins in Techtomesh armour, the suit was unable to tell who would want to kill him and who was fighting to save him. All he could do was try to avoid them all.

The free-for-all shook the Nest to its very foundations.

Something exploded high above.

A rain of debris clattered down through the superstructure.

In that cloud of debris, he saw a body. It bounced off the walkways and slid lifelessly over the sides of bubbles, spinning like a Catherine Wheel into Nest branches, and *crunched* up against harsh metal rails. Shielded by Techtomesh, the figure crashed head first into a walkway just a few yards away from where Barl had rolled into cover. It lay on its back, possibly semi-conscious.

An arm waved slowly back and forward, before flopping to the floor and lying still. The emergency-evac light glittered on the left shoulder as the emergency protocols of the Bantoscree suit kicked in. It was sending coding signals to the nearest Guild Medical Team, calling out for help.

Barl went over to the body.

There were no identifying marks on it. The faceplate was dark. Whoever was inside had taken a huge hit in the blast; shrapnel was stuck in the suit's webbing, and some parts of the breastplate had cracked. Sealant seeped up from the suit's reaction layer, filling the tiny breaches in the outer skin. A hit capable of doing that to the outside of the suit like that was more than capable of breaking every bone of the body inside.

The suit's evac light blinked faster, desperate, as the life inside failed, any hope of saving reaching a critical phase.

Barl didn't have a lot of time, but a plan was coalescing in his mind.

Looking up, as the sounds of battle continued, hearing the sizzle and blast of energy weapons, the searing lightshow of war-spells being woven, fired off and countered, he knew his options were limited.

A green blinking light descended from above.

A Medical Team.

Either a Guild medics or ones from the attackers—homing in on the signal from the suit below him.

But which?

Taking a deep breath Barl activated his own critical injury alarm and sprawled across the dying body.

The phalanx of dragons rose up. Up. Up.

They surrounded the airship.

There was a moment of stillness, the fulcrum of danger hovered at some insensate mid-point, before falling rapidly to puncture the gondola's structure and ripped through it in a gout of dragon flame.

The gondola dropped like a stone.

Galdar clung to Lucillian as the massive scaly beasts, their horned heads turning, huge leathery wings slowing their beating, fanged mouths widening, banked in the air, kicking their tails back before they launched arrowlike downwards, chasing the spiralling wreckage of the airship.

The gondola twisted, the spiral tightening the faster it fell.

Carlow clung desperately onto the bulwark but there was no way he could possibly hold on long enough; Klane slipped and rolled past, clattering into the boy and sending him spinning away like a skittle.

Shryke was caught in the first syllables of a codespell.

He stood on the prow of the gondola, balanced perfectly, his arm hooked around a stanchion, as bolts of lightning crackled from his fingertips. He raised his hand, finishing the words of weaving and loosed his own fire. The elemental lightning streamed from his fingers, searing the air around the head of the first great dragon, leading the charge. From there, crackles of bluish flame rolled out across its hide, spilling over from one to the next until all seven beasts were wreathed in a complex web of power.

That power didn't just light the sky, it burned with the brightness of the Sun-Machine, searing hot.

The dragons screamed as one.

Shryke moved his fingers, the motion was so subtle Galdar almost missed it, but it was impossible not to see the connection between the sheet of magical flame and his movements as the broken dragons were hurled, spinning and flailing, far from the falling airship. The huge creatures spun away, immense bodies tumbling end over end, slamming into each other as they fell through space, speeding away with gathering momentum. They couldn't slow their wild fall. Further, faster, they fell until they were reduced to little black spots against the illuminated Shade-walls, and then they were gone, lost to sight. She had no idea if they were dead or simply banished. It didn't matter much.

Dragons?

She shook her head. She couldn't believe she could think about something as incredible as dragons in such a banal, matter-of-fact, manner, like they were some beast of burden she saw every day of her waking life. She had never seen anything approaching the mythic, majestic beasts. She wasn't even aware that they...

Oh yes.

We're *falling*.

The ground raced up at them faster than they fell, or so it appeared, and there was nothing she could do apart from cling on and hope, because prayers were beyond her, as the great gondola hit the ground and tore apart amid the impact, scattering cargo and armoured bodies in all directions.

The Techtomesh protected her from injury, but it didn't stop the impact driving the air out of her body and hurling her through the rigging and across the shattered deck. Much of the ropes and the punctured sheeting of the dirigible part of the airship had dropped onto the gondola, suffocating the wreckage. Ropes were looped everywhere, masts and stanchions smashed like balsa.

Galdar heard groans, and curses, and somehow, in the midst of it, Carlow.

He hadn't been wearing armour. How could he have survived? For a moment, half a heartbeat, she thought that his God really had protected him, but when she saw him struggling in Shryke's arms, twisting and spitting and slapping at Shryke's faceplate as he tried to escape his clutches, and she knew his salvation had been less than divine.

Shryke had used his body to shield Carlow as the airship crashed.

He put the boy down.

When he spoke, his voice was weary. His shoulders sagged. He went down on one knee, steadying himself with a hand on the ground. "You...slap...like...a...girl." Shryke said, trying to muster a smile.

"You might want to rethink sexist bullshit like that if you don't get me home in one piece," Lucillian said, reaching out to help Shryke stand. For the longest time it looked as though the warrior wasn't going to take her proffered hand, but eventually he stood.

"Thank you," he said simply but with conviction.

Carlow clambered out of the wreckage with some of the Townsguard, and for the first time Galdar took in her surroundings.

They had come down in a town square, steeped in ivy and enclosed on all sides by tall golden buildings with high windows and flat roofs.

In the near distance, spired buildings thrust up into the air over the golden plate rotating at the centre of this astonishing place.

Up above the sky was filled with suns on their impossibly long girders, revolving, dancing and spiralling through space, keeping pace with a hundred Shadewalls.

They were in the clockwork of heaven.

The skies between the suns and the city were darkened. They held the same quality as the shade Shryke had put around the airship. It had protected them then from the blazing pinpoints of whirling fire and it protected them now.

"Do I need to ask where we are?" Lucillian said to the still hard-breathing Shryke.

The warrior shook his head, chest heaving.

It's obvious, Galdar thought. *We are inside the Sun-Machine.*

Rough hands took Barl's body and threw him face down onto a flat surface.

He heard a murmur of voices around him but because of the suit's critical injury shut down protocols, most of the actual words weren't getting through.

He'd wove a small spell which he hoped would make his breathing inaudible, even through the amplification of the suit's vented breathing apparatus, and another to make the armour look as though the release mechanism was malfunctioning. Both were simple glamour's, but he hoped they would be enough trick those around him into thinking they'd need technicians to work on the suit before they could get to him.

It wasn't much of a plan.

The ground, if that's what it was, began to move beneath him, then he felt his body accelerate upwards. He didn't dare risk defogging the visor so that he could see where they were taking him; any change in the blank slate of the protective visor would necessitate turning off the injury protocols first, and that wasn't happening.

Yet.

Best guess, was being evacced by the medics, shipped away from the Nest to a designated hospital facility or mediship somewhere safe from the battle.

He listened intently, straining to hear the explosions and brutal clash of battle in the Nest, but it faded evermore distant into the deep background.

He felt more small bumps and jostles before he settled, being moved into some sort of transporter. Doors sealed around him. Silence. He had to assume he was inside a Guild Hospital Carrier, meaning he was bound for a field infirmary some miles from the Nest. He knew there to be one on the outskirts of the Pantonyle Spaceport, which was exactly what he had hoped for when the plan had formulated with feverish haste back at the Nest.

Barl released the two spells with a twist of his fingers and turned off the critical injury protocols.

The faceplate defogged.

Barl screamed.

He was miles above the surface of Pantonyle, suspended in mid-air without any visible craft to hold him.

The Nest was burning.

Vultures circled around him as the robed skull climbed into the suit to join him.

"We can't stay here."

"You're in no fit state to go anywhere."

Shryke pushed Lucillian's hand away and shook his head. He took off his helmet. The toll such powerful magic had taken on him was plain to see; his eyes were hollow, lips bloodless and a sheen of sweat glistened on his skin.

Shryke blinked and almost fell again.

"The Guild Assassins will have a fix on me. They can send an army to destroy us. I shouldn't have done that. It was stupid. I've made too dangerous a disturbance. Carry me if you have to, but we must get away from here until the shadow I've cast across the Quantum Aether has diminished enough that there isn't a target on our backs."

"Help him," Lucillian barked orders at the Townsguard, making them carry Shryke. He directed them with slow, painful gestures, making sure they knew which way to go.

Klane went next, with Crove.

They whispered frantically to each other. The fat Governor could scheme and plan to his withered little heart's content. They were weaponless, and a long way from home. The only thing that should matter to them, Galdar reasoned, was ensuring Shryke stayed alive. He was their only route home.

She tried to walk with Carlow, but he refused to be anywhere near her.

He wouldn't make eye contact.

He only said one word to her in the next hour, "Traitor."

She didn't bother arguing. She didn't want to waste a second of what was most likely her last hours like that.

The Sun-Machine was the whole city.

As they moved through narrow golden streets, they heard the constant hum of unknowable machinery behind the walls. The Sun-Girders were located over the horizon, and Galdar fancied she could hear the low rumble of gears and gimbals on which they ran. In certain areas among the buildings, as the suns moved overhead on their fifty-thousand-mile-long struts, crazy shadows swirled around corners, high building casting shadows like sundials, but sundials over which unruly suns marched and danced. Shafts of light burst through high crenulations and cool areas of shade pooled in unsuspected lees between buildings.

In a world where everything was possible, Galdar still had the capacity to feel the sheer wonder of this creation.

"Noooooooooooooooooooooooo!"

Shryke fell from the arms of the Townsguard and slumped to the ground with a sickening thud.

There was another scream of terror.

Four of the Townsguard simply liquified, and were smeared on surrounding walls; as corrupt, sickening, analogues of shadow.

Shryke lay still on the floor.

Galdar began to move towards him, but almost as soon as she took the first step, a hand fell onto her shoulder, biting into the flesh.

She gasped with pain and confusion.

The hand spun her around and shoved her into one of the golden walls, her head cracking back against the surface, dazing her. Through dizzied vision, a blackening shape swam through the tears and coalesced into…

…Carlow's black mouth moving with spit and worms.

His eyes ran with bloody tears.

His smile cracked open his face and his tongue reached out like a poisonous snake. His skin, dry as dust, and as Galdar watched with growing horror, his throat bulged and pulsated as Carlow fell to his knees, hands now claws, reaching up towards her, tugging at her clothes, the whirring suns reflected in his inflating eyes.

The last thing she saw was Carlow's wide screaming mouth and a robed skeleton, impossibly large, climbing out between his chapped and bloody lips.

CHAPTER 34

The Quarternight was chilly.

A damp mist moved through the trees.

Carlow had moved from the clearing. Yane refused to listen to him. She had rejected his pleas to banish the warrior and refused to punish Galdar for her unholy relationship with his black heart. She was a fool. She tried to convince him he was letting his personal dislike for Galdar cloud his judgement. What did she know? She wasn't party to the inner workings of his mind. Just like the others she made proclamations based on nothing and pretended at wisdom.

He needed to take time. Reassess his thoughts and consider his commitment to the Congregation and the Moveable Church.

She had threatened to divest him of his curate's trappings and cease his training in the priesthood, calling it a personal vendetta against Galdar.

She was blind.

Carlow had been sure he'd be able to convince Yane of the dishonour Galdar brought upon their people, but the reverend had merely shaken her head, and looked at him with that unbearable face of disappointment before she sent him on his way. Well, he wouldn't just shuffle back with his tail between his knees. No. He was a bigger man than that. He owed more to their God. So, yes, he left, crashing away from the encampment, stamping through the ferns, pushing back branches against tree trunks in ever-harder swings of his branch as he walked, determined not to look back.

It wasn't until the makeshift weapon in his hand finally snapped with a sharp *crack* that Carlow realised the mist had all but enveloped him. He looked up and around, and realised he had no idea where he was, or even what direction he needed to take back to camp.

He stood still, lost in more ways than one, breathing heavily; taking in great lungfuls of the cold mist that stuck in his throat. He felt the cloying dampness of the stilled air and the silence where there should have been a wealth of forest sounds in his ears.

Not silence.

He heard a low, deep throated growling of a wolf and spun on the spot to stare into the muzzle of a huge white hunter. Its red eyes bored into him, but all he could look at were the razor-sharp incisors, like arrows bared behind black lips, dripping with foaming saliva.

Behind the wolf he saw a woman dressed in red nun's robes.

Her face was wizened and pinched, but her eyes were keen.

There was nothing remotely kind or benevolent about her expression. Nothing spoke of service or prayer. Nothing promised a lifetime of devotion to God. To Carlow she appeared to be the antithesis of the robes she wore, utterly undeserving.

"Carlow," she said, stepping alongside the wolf. She ran the bony fingers of her hand through the fur on its head, scratching its ears. The wolf relaxed a little, its eyes were still locked on Carlow.

He couldn't move. His feet were rooted to the spot. It didn't matter that his body screamed: *run*. How could this woman, this stranger, know his name?

"How I know who you are is neither here nor there," she said, speaking directly in answer to his thoughts, "And there is nothing to be gained from running, believe me, my wolf friend here would take you down before you had made twenty yards. All it would need is a word from me."

"What...what do you want?"

"Now that's a much more intelligent question. Well done."

With a soft rustle of cloth, the robed woman was suddenly nose-to-nose with him. There was no moment when she had taken a step, she had been beside the wolf, and then she was in Carlow's face, her foetid breath swimming into his lungs. She cracked a smile full of rotting teeth.

Carlow couldn't back away.

His feet refused to obey his fear.

"I am going to use you, child."

"I don't understand."

"Shryke is travelling to the Sun-Machine."

The words were meaningless.

"I will travel with him."

Carlow felt his throat tighten.

"He is poisoned. I have poisoned him. But it is a mere distraction."

"It is?"

"You will help him find someone to remove the poison from his body."

"I will?"

"Yes."

"While he is concentrating on that, he will not notice or think about you."

"He won't?"

"No."

The nun's face was changing. The skin shrivelling and shifting. Wasting. Her eyes puckered, draining of liquid. Worms moved in her mouth, curling around her teeth. Carlow heard a sinewy, tearing crack as the cadaver standing before him twisted off one of her fingers and stabbed the wet bone into his belly.

The pain was excruciating but faded after a second.

Carlow gasped and fell forward onto the wet ground.

The mist had cleared.

The cadaver and the wolf were gone. The only sound in the silent forest was a whisper in his ear. "Go to the valley. Find the Assassins. Tell them about Shryke. Bring them to the encampment. Do this for me and you will be rewarded."

"Rewarded? How?" Carlow said, bringing himself breathlessly to his feet.

"With a painless death," the voice promised.

The suit bulged to accommodate both Barl and the robed thing in there with him.

As he watched, with eyes that refused to close, he saw it grow itself skin. He saw its eyes reform. Liquid flesh ran over the bones, as though the skeleton had arrived here first, the flesh only now beginning to catch up.

As its eyes grew, Barl was close enough to see the veins in them begin moving, pulsing once more with grey, lumpen blood.

Now skeleton had the means through which it could look more closely at the boy.

Barl couldn't move.

The suit had him trapped. It clamped ever tighter around both of their bodies. Words stalled in his throat. The skull's face was almost complete, a wizened, pinched faced of a woman, somehow a contradiction, both ageless and yet full of years. Her mouth was black and deep inside he saw bloated fat-bodied worms writhing and coiling around coffin-nail teeth. She couldn't be alive and yet wasn't dead.

She had lips so the skull's rictus grimace became a smile.

Past the head of the thing in the suit with him, beyond the wings of the vultures, out to the huge columns of smoke, full of red explosions, punching up like fists, Barl saw the ruin of the Nest.

Battles still raged around it, different factions of Assassins fighting to the death and in some cases beyond.

The war was far from over.

"This war will *never* be over," the stinking woman answered his thoughts, "I have been fighting it forever, in your terms. It will continue to the end of time itself. Chaos will reign. Everywhere."

"Who are you?" Barl finally found his voice. It was dry and brittle in his mouth.

"Have you truly forgotten me?"

Barl had no idea what she meant. "I am Barl. Barl from *God's Heart*. How can I have forgotten someone I do not know?"

The woman smiled sadly and Barl felt her bony arms encircle him in a deathly cold embrace. She put her forehead on his shoulder, hugging him tight. "Sweet summer child, you know that I must end you," she said simply. Barl felt the bones of her hands begin to burrow into the flesh of his back. No suit of armour could protect you from an enemy if they were in there with you.

Barl closed his eyes.

The suit crashed to the ground in the midst of the battle.

But not the battle for Pantonyle.

The forces on the plain fell upon it, hacking with their swords and axes, ferocious, desperate, brutal. The Techtomesh resisted as long as it could, but the onslaught was relentless. Cracks began to appear in the material. Fissures opened and at last, bones were exposed.

Summer in her armour, twenty feet tall, brandishing her black double-headed battle-axe cut a path through the ravening hoards. Bodies were battered aside. Severed limbs flew in every direction, heads spun in the mud, ribcages torn asunder, guts exposed and trailing, spines ripped from torsos.

Summer cleared a circle of baying combatants, holding them at bay with nothing more a look from behind her shining mask.

She reached into the broken armour.

With one giant hand, she pulled Barl from it and left a pile of bones behind.

She hoisted the terrified boy up and took him through the widening path of warriors back to her mound of spines.

Barl's eyes snapped open.

He was looking up at Summer.

But a new Summer. A different Summer. Not his dead friend. This was the Summer of the Plain. His Familiar.

"What happened?"

"I repaid my debt."

He sat up, struggling to understand. But then he knew. "I'm still in the suit, aren't I? With that thing."

Summer nodded, "Yes. And you only have one route to escape."

Summer told him what to do, and then she killed him.

Galdar fell back from the cadaver climbing out of Carlow's mouth.

Lucillian struggled desperately to shake Shryke awake, but he was still insensate. The last three Townsguard had scattered, running for their lives. Klane pulled the navigator, Crove, to him and held her like a shield.

"*Help!*" he screamed frantically to the walls.

The cadaver, robes wet with Carlow's spit and blood, stepped away from the dead boy's ruined body and shook itself, drawing life into its dead limbs.

Galdar stood transfixed, unable to run or speak.

Flesh began to run over its bones, up over the thing's face and hands, filling the carcass in with corrupt life.

Muscles formed and built up. Veins curled and twisted. Skin shivered like a shroud, swelling behind, rolling down the limbs and up over the skull.

A woman.

Her face was deeply lined and furrowed with years.

Her eyes settling on Shryke.

Shryke, vulnerable. Barely conscious.

Shryke, his face a mask of agony.

The thing in the robes stalked towards him.

Then…

Barl burst from the shoulder of the cowled woman.

The boy ripped out through her robes with a black steel sword he'd woven as he emerged. Blood and torn muscle covered his thin frame. He rammed the blade up, into her, digging his way out through the meat of her newly created body, his other hand gripping the mailed fist of the creature who followed him.

The robed cadaver shredded, disintegrating into wisps of grey smoke as the twenty-foot-high armoured behemoth, clanked an immense steel foot down on the surface of the Sun-Machine.

The robe lay on the floor empty.

Summer bent, lifted it to her mouth, and sniffed at the cloth.

"It's not over," she said, and turned to regard Shryke.

Barl was breathing heavily, covered in blood and flesh from the demolished cadaver. As well as blood and gore, he wore tattered bits of wrecked Techtomesh. He looked up at the whirring suns on their dazzling stalks—at the golden city of the Sun-Machine and the Shadewalls spinning through near-space. Beyond the Shadewalls, loops of the Chainworld hung serenely, twisting their blue, green and brown surfaces up at the magical suns which warmed them. And for a brief second Barl could see beyond the loops of the chain. Out many millions of miles.

Before a Shadewalls obscured his vision, he saw enough to know that he was home.

The Sun-Machine, the Chainworld and everything else was hung at the centre of *God's Heart*, just as Summer had promised it would.

CHAPTER 35

"They are the Dreaming Armies of the Plain."
Row upon row of warriors, of every race, every hue.
Weapons at the ready.

Frozen in time as well as place.

Rank after rank after rank.

Shryke held onto Galdar for support.

Lucillian had given him some herbs from a pouch inside her jerkin, but it was a long way from healing what was wrong with him. Still, he took the herbs for her.

Summer, the Familiar of both Shryke and the strange boy, whose name Shryke couldn't recall, had led them through the city at pace. The giantess's enormous strides were impossible to match even when Shryke was at full strength. Depleted as he was, it nearly killed him.

They arrived at a set of huge black iron gates. Summer placed her shoulder against the huge constructions and with a clanking of armour and supreme effort, opened the gates on screeching, millennia-stilled hinges.

Beyond, stretching as far as Shryke could see, were ranks of warriors.

They disappeared into the hazy distance, over the horizon of the Sun-Machine. Crazy shadows danced among them as the suns whirled overhead. A speeded-up shadow-day around their feet. The engines of the universe twisting around their feet.

Shryke took his arm from around Galdar's shoulders. He needed to stand on his own two feet. The boy hadn't muttered two words in all the time since he had climbed out of the body of the robed skull. "I'm home." That was it. The boy troubled Shryke in a way that he couldn't fully articulate.

There was something about him Shryke recognised; but at the same time felt unknowable.

There were more pressing matters to deal with now than ponder the child's strange nature.

He had a mission to complete, one that had been unlocked in his mind from behind the codespell.

He remembered fully why he had come to *God's Heart* and the Chainworld circling the Sun-Machine at its heart.

He had come to protect the Failsafe: The Dreaming Armies of the Plain.

Barl was unhappy that the whirling suns and Shadewalls kept him from seeing beyond the Chainworld out across the endless surface of *God's Heart*.

He had been only given a glimpse of the true nature of the world in which he had been born, raised, ripped from and then returned.

He had no idea if he would be able to escape the Sun-Machine and travel back to the surface of the enclosing *God's Heart*, his town, his friends and his family. It didn't matter that they were millions upon millions of miles away, he *felt* as though he could just reach out and touch them.

There was even the faint aroma of yellowberries in his nostrils.

When Summer had killed him on The Plain, he had returned to the suit hanging above Pantonyle with the energy of a thousand suns burning within him. He didn't know how she had done it. He was on *fire*. The robed woman's fingers melted from his back as he reached into her chest. He had torn a thousand agonies from her corrupt lips and spoken the Spell of Travelling that Summer had taught him on the mound.

Barl had been dragged *into* her body by the spell.

Inside the warm, wet darkness he felt the icy chill of her black, calcified heart beating slowly against his face.

And it was there that Summer met him.

Then the screaming blue of the Quantum Aether had bloomed around them.

Summer yelled at him to make a sword. He needed a weapon where they were going.

The journey had taken both an instant and thirty-five thousand years to complete followed in between two blinks of his eyes.

Barl's body coursed with new energies.

Energies drained from the years, sucked from all that time into his burgeoning body... then with a detonation of flesh and brittle bone, he was bursting out of the woman's flesh, cutting her apart with the black steel sword in his hand even as he reached back to pull Summer out behind him.

Once he realised where he was, the rush of vertigo threatened to drown him in joy.

Summer revived the fallen warrior, calling him Shryke, and told the others that they were still not safe from the forces ranged against them. The God-Queen was abroad and would do everything in her power to unleash the forces of the Dreaming Armies on an unsuspecting creation.

It was imperative they made time now to travel across the city to defend the Failsafe where they would fight the final battle.

It must be protected at all costs.

Shryke's eyes met Barl's a single time on their flight across the city, but the force of that meeting had sent the boy reeling, it was so much more brutal than any physical blow. Who was this warrior? He looked maybe a decade older than Barl, but his eyes held a sad wisdom that was much, much older.

Barl also truly felt as if he'd known this Shryke his entire life, but also that he didn't know him at all.

It was a strange and unwelcome feeling.

"The Dreaming Armies of the Plain." Summer repeated, leading the party down the gap between two ranks of frozen, but still living, warriors.

Barl recognised the armour and even the faces of some of them. He was sure he'd knew them from their endless battle and had killed his fair share in search for energy on the Plain.

These warriors, though, weren't covered in the gore and mud of battle, like those toiling eternally in that hellish place. They were pristine. Their armour new, their weapons sharp, the feathers in their helms fresh-plucked from a menagerie of exotic birds, and their faces, unmoving, frozen and yet so very alive.

"When the Gods created this place, the Chainworld, and the Heart around it to serve as the anvil of creation, they built into that system a Failsafe. Should life in this universe displease them or become unworthy, this army was fashioned to break out of *God's Heart*, to sally forth among the endless tracts of the galaxies and bring an end to all life."

Barl looked up at the nearest, fearsome warrior.

She stood poised, ready to kill.

Another beside her was ready to leap from his awful sleep and do battle.

As Barl looked around him it became clear that the warriors were all ready.

A second from battle.

It chilled him to the very core.

"The Gods left this universe and went off to create others. It's the way of the Gods. As we make children, they make universes. They never thought to return here to us. Save one."

Shryke nodded. "The God-Queen."

Summer took off her helm, and looked down on the tiny travellers below her, "Yes. The God-Queen. Cast out and jealous of the God-King's creation here, she vowed to take revenge. She would come here in disguise so as not to arouse his suspicions and manipulate those susceptible to her power. She would create the conditions which would trigger the Failsafe.

"In the Guild she found the perfect weapon to bring chaos to the universe. To unbalance everything. And when she had achieved her aim—a trillion worlds at war, bringing untold misery to the peoples of the universe, she needed to come here and release the army."

"And you brought her here!" Klane mewled. The fat man hid behind Crove. He pointed a trembling finger at Shryke, Barl and Summer, "You've destroyed us all."

Shryke bowed his head.

Summer replaced her helm and looked up to the whirling suns.

Barl felt the full force of Klane's accusation.

It was true.

They had brought catastrophe to the heart of creation.

They moved on, down the rows, crossing ranks, the stream of warriors never ending, each so incredibly different from the last.

It was painfully obvious that Shryke was suffering, both physically, and from the sting of Klane's bitter taunting. She wanted to go to him, to offer some form of comfort, but more than anything she wanted to shut the fat bastard up once and for good. But she knew Shryke would not countenance it. He was still a good man. Better than many she had met. He lived by a code that was stricter in nature than many a holy man. Galdar comforted herself by staring daggers at the corpulent governor and wishing fervently that looks could just this once kill.

The battle-mace *thrummed* with energy in her hand. It would have been so easy to end the governor's wailing on the spot.

Klane looked at her then as though he could read these darker thoughts and made sure Crove stood between them. "What I can't understand is how you think a moron child, and a thick-headed barbarian can take on a Goddess, even with the help of a giant woman? What could possibly make you think you have a chance? You're dead. All of you. Dead. And you've dragged *us* into your stupidity. What did we do to deserve that?"

"Without him you would be dead already," Lucillian spat at the fat man. "The walls were breached. The Raiders were swarming the streets. You'd be hanging from a flag-pole, food for the carrion eaters by now without Shryke."

"Which is beside the point," Klane argued. "I didn't die there. And now I don't want to die *here*!"

"Just shut up!" Barl barked at Klane. The younger man raised his black steel sword, and in that moment, it looked like the boy would have happily gutted the fat man. That shut him up. Klane's face blanched, and with a nimble sidestep for such a fat man put Crove between him and the boy's blade.

"Do you mind?" The navigator shoved Klane back into Barl's path. "I'm not your bloody bodyguard! You might remember them, they're the ones smeared on the walls back there. You remember, the ones that fled, abandoning you."

"You still work for me," Klane said. "And don't you forget it."

"Well that's easily fixed. I resign. Effective immediately."

Crove jogged ahead to catch up with the fast striding Summer. "Hey, Junkyard. Wait up." Summer stopped and looked down at Crove. "Tell me you've got a plan. Because you wouldn't come all this way without a plan, right?"

Summer came down on her haunches.

She was still easily four feet taller that even Shryke.

"My plan is no longer possible. I had intended for Shryke to come here many years ago. I sent him, as his Familiar to wait here for the God-Queen. When she arrived, I was to cast the travel-spell, leave the Plain and come here to defeat her. But when she discovered Shryke's purpose in the Shrine in the Thalladon climbs, she discovered my plans, and began her attacks on Barl and the Guild Nest to distract me. I was forced to divert my energies there."

Barl raised his hand as if he were in school.

Galdar saw the boy was suddenly overcome with a sudden embarrassment, so dropped his hand. "I don't understand," he said. "You've only just become my Familiar. How could you have done this…to yourself…so many years ago?"

Summer looked down on Barl with genuine grief in her expression as she moved to comfort him. "I'm sorry, Barl. I have been economical with your truths. The travel-spell I shared with you on the Plain not only moved us in space, but also in time. We are thirty-five thousand years in your future. The Nest attack and the subverting of the Guild's real mission to protect peace in the universe has born all the fruit the God-Queen desired. Beyond *God's Heart*, the universe is at war with itself. It is tearing itself apart; the war to end all wars. And we must find a way to prevent the Failsafe from being triggered, or we usher in the end of everything. And to do that we must find the God-Queen."

"So, where is she?" Galdar could no longer keep silent, the battle-mace bucked in her hand, fizzing with energy; felt almost *too hot* to hold.

Summer looked deep into Galdar's eyes and said quietly, "You want to drop the mace, don't you?"

Galdar looked down at the weapon. "Yes. It feels like it wants to escape my grasp. Like it is a living thing. It's *burning*."

"That's because it's trying to flee from the presence of the God-Queen," Summer said.

Galdar felt sickness sweep through her guts. "Escape? But… how… where is the God-Queen now?"

"Inside you." Summer told Galdar.

CHAPTER 36

S hryke gripped Galdar by the shoulders.

She couldn't move.

Summer's huge fingers plucked the battle-mace from her tiny hands and tossed it to Barl, who caught it clumsily.

Fear surged like cold fire through Galdar's body.

Her eyes swam, and her ears sang.

It couldn't be true.

That thing… a God… couldn't be inside her.

No.

She saw Klane and Crove backing away, and behind them the soldiers of the Dreaming Army loomed large, like they were looking at her expectantly, duty in their bitter eyes.

"Put her down," Summer boomed.

Galdar's world upended. And then came agony. Her back smashed into the floor. Shryke knelt on her shoulders. Searing pain shot through her bones.

Summer bent over, blotting out the suns, her enormous eyes squinting with both enquiry and wariness.

"Stop!" Galdar screamed, begged, struggling against Shryke's weight, but she couldn't possibly fight him. He was too strong. She had nowhere near the strength she needed to shift him.

Summer placed one huge hand over Galdar's ankles to still her kicking legs, and leaned in intently, examining her face.

The scrutiny was unbearable. Galdar felt the surge of panic rise to the very top of her mind, drowning all else. What did they mean? How could they even think that that thing, that vile monstrous skeletal thing that had killed Carlow was *inside* her? And then she knew she was going to die here, in this strange place, in the shadow of the dreaming army, because the only way to get it out of her was to rip her body to shreds.

The dirt.

Drifting from her hands over the bulwark of the airship, Carlow's look of disgust.

Her faith in the God's Safehome lost on the winds of new Gods.

New Faiths and the loss of her own.

Was that when she'd let this devil in?

Was that when she'd lost herself to evil?

As Summer bent closer, Galdar tried to find something, a reserve of calm in the churning ocean of terror in which she was drowning.

This was what happened when faith was lost.

This was punishment.

Summer's palm was bigger than Galdar's whole head. It came down over Galdar's face and everything went dark.

"We travel," was the last thing she heard Summer say before...

Shryke opened his eyes to the Plain.

The shock of cold air and freshening wind, gusting hard over the marshy ground, made him shiver.

He looked down.

He was no longer pinning Galdar down.

He knelt.

The wetness seeped up into his skin. He felt the ache of rheumatism stiffen the joints of his limbs. He got up carefully, gingerly. Summer stood, back in full armour, helm down. She moved immense battle-axe from hand to hand as she looked out to the horizons.

The boy stood beside her.

He was nervous.

The battle-mace hung limp in his grip.

Shryke still couldn't bring himself to look at the boy. There was something about him that was just *wrong*. He couldn't place the start or endpoint of it. It was just there, as if it were a crack in his emotions. Uncomfortable and unsettling. *Wrong.*

He had to look away.

"Why are we here, Summer?" Shryke heard the boy ask.

"We must battle the God-Queen on The Plain. She is in the girl. When you and I arrived and she became smoke, she seeped into the girl's bones as a means of escape. She thought to hide there from us. Her magic is strong, but here we have a chance to send her back to the realm of the Gods."

Shryke didn't like the idea of sending this enemy back anywhere.

He had a better solution "Why can't we just kill her?"

"Because Gods never die," Summer said, patiently. "We just stop believing in them."

Summer stalked off across The Plain. Shryke and the boy followed in silence.

Galdar didn't know where she was.

It was cold as death.

It was wet.

She lay in dew-damp grass.

She sat up and looked around.

Not a field; a blasted marsh under a swollen sky.

She could make out the peaks of mountains in the far distance one way and in the opposite direction, almost at the limits of her vision, she saw the endless streams of beetle-like warriors hacking and killing each other. Their armour black with blood or mud or both.

NOOOOOOOOOOOOOOOOOOOO!

Inside. A voice. It wasn't Galdar's, not the voice of her own thoughts, but it was inside her head.

She ground the heels of his hands into her temples trying to force it out, but it had taken root. It was in her.

More words. Words in a language she did not understand. But she sensed the intent.

A codespell.

The surge of magic seared against her ribs.

The words skittered around inside Galdar.

She felt them, sharp and shivery in her guts. She felt them crawling up into her skull. She felt them echoing through her.

But the spell did not ignite.

An anguished cry tore through Galdar's skull. Something gripped her heart. Bone-cold fingers closed around it. Not bone. Smoke. Smoke encircled the wildly beating organ.

It was trying to squeeze the life out of her...

"Stop! Please, stop!" Galdar clawed at her chest, but it wasn't as though she could reach inside and make a vent for the smoke to disperse.

The vile choking black smoke of bones squeezed.

And squeezed.

She felt the ripples of shock around her heart.

Images flashed blazing bright through her mind. Was it true, her life would return to her in those last seconds, fever fresh? Last thoughts. Shryke. Yane. Her parents. The desert of the loop. The Moveable Church. Dirt drifting away from her palm. Carlow's bloodied and broken body, the vile bones clambering out through his impossibly dislocated mouth.

The grip around her heart released, howling another desperate scream of frustration, and beneath it all, anger.

The smoke drifted away inside. Galdar felt it curling and curdling in her belly. Like a sickness. An infection.

It pulsed inside her blood, down into her legs, turning her, making her walk towards the fighting armies. She fought against it with all her strength, but there was nothing she could do against the will of a God.

Her feet plunged on, into the sucking mud on the marsh land. She sank into the cloying mud up to her knees, and still clawed and fought her way desperately forward, muscles burning in protest, as the thing took her to the battle.

CARRY ME.

"No…"

CARRY ME.

The voice was so loud inside her surely its demand had to carry all the way across the Plain, louder than the clash of battle she was being drawn toward.

"What are you?"

I AM YOUR GOD

"I have no God," Galdar said. "I don't believe in anything…" It sounded pitiful now she said it. It wasn't some fierce roar of defiance.

AND THAT IS WHY I AM GOING TO KILL YOU, GIRL. A LOSS OF FAITH MEANS A LOSS OF LIFE.

"So, kill me. I don't care anymore. Do it. Or can't you? Is that it? I can feel you inside me. You are smoke. I felt you try to squeeze the life out of my heart, it's still beating. You can't kill me, can you? You're trapped inside me. Summer did this to you. She trapped you."

YES. I AM TRAPPED. BUT I POSSESS ETERNITY. ONCE YOU REACH THE ARMIES OF THE PLAIN I SHALL BE RELEASED.

Galdar looked to the distant armies locked in wild battle. She saw the arrows streaking across the blood red sky in flocks. She saw the banners fluttering on the tops of spears, the dull glints of black steel blades cleaving and cutting up arterial sprays of blood.

And still she walked on, inexorably forward, towards her what she realised was her doom.

Barl struggled to match the punishing pace of Shryke and Summer.

He knew he could trust his Familiar, but Shryke...he had no idea who this man was, but there was no denying his mere presence made Barl decidedly vulnerable and unsettled. Moreover, he really couldn't buy the idea he had somehow stepped out over 35,000 years into his future. What did that even mean? He was in the Sun-Machine inside *God's Heart*, home, at least, but everyone he had ever known, everyone who had ever cared for him wasn't just dead they were ash reborn in the land, in trees and grass and everything else?

He had heard incredible things in recent months, and even grown used to terrible wonders and the sense of dangerous awe that the Assassins inspired, but this? He didn't dare ask Summer if it was possible for a spell to take him *back*—if not to where he had departed Pantonyle, but somewhere close, because he was terrified the answer would be *no*.

They marched on, striding powerfully through the wet marshy land, eyes fixed on the battle before them.

On the edges of hearing, Barl could just barely make out the screams and roars of total war, of a million and a million more warriors fighting to the last. Their numbers never diminishing, their dead never outnumbering the living, as if every time one died in battle, another was spawned somewhere else in the throng to give the eternals a never-ending supply of fresh death and destruction.

Barl hated the infinite nature of it, the pointlessness of it. All that pain and suffering, just to create the charge to power magic in the real world.

It was both cruel and torturous.

It spoke of the true evil at the centre of the mind capable of creating such a mechanism.

Barl wanted no part of it.

The power of becoming a Guild Assassin, however much good it was supposed to bring to the Universe, was corrupted beyond bearing. The thought of being shaped into a surgeon of hope, his blade being used to cut out that cancer of wickedness had been utterly corrupted by this God-Queen…

He stopped. Dropped the battle-mace in a damp grass.

The wind slapped his wet hair against his forehead and blew away the tears that welled in the corners of his eyes.

"Enough," he said to the fast-receding backs of his companions.

Shryke and Summer stopped and turned.

"What is it, Barl?" Summer asked lifting her faceplate so that Barl could see the concern chiselled into her immense features.

"I don't want this. I don't want to fight any more. This isn't right. This isn't what it should be." He held out his empty hands, palms up. "Look at me, Summer. I've lost *everything*. I've lost my home, my family anything that was ever important to me. And now you tell me I've lost myself in 35,000 years of nothing. I don't *want* to be an Assassin. I don't want to have to kill. Surely you can understand that murder isn't noble. Killing is vile. It shouldn't even be a last resort. My father knew a better life. He grew crops, not corpses."

Summer knelt in the grass. "I'm sorry, kid. I truly am, but it is the truth, Shryke and I cannot do this alone."

"You'll have to." Barl grunted, then lashed out with a booted foot, sending the mace rolling away. "I'm not picking it up."

"He's just a child. Leave him." Shryke bent and picked up the battle-mace. Then dropped it with a sudden howl of pain and stared down at the steam rising from his scorched palm.

"That's not you weapon, Shryke. It's Barl's," Summer told him.

"I just want this to stop."

"Look kid," Shryke said, not unkindly, but trying to speak to the boy the way his Familiar had. "The universe is at war with itself. We didn't do that. But we can end it. The three of us. If there's going to be a chance for peace, we need to stand against the God-Queen." He looked to Summer. "Back me up here."

The Familiar smiled sadly. "I may look the strongest, but it is nothing more than a perception filter. An illusion. I am nothing without you. I am your Familiar. Without you at my side, I have no strength, just as you have no power without me. If you won't stand Barl, then we *all* fall."

Barl looked into Summer's eyes. There was a warmth and a truth there that moved him.

"I don't want to die."

"Look at me, Barl. I need you to look at my eyes when I tell you this, so you can see I'm not lying." He did as he was told. "If you *don't* fight, you *will* die. And so will everyone else. The God-Queen will unleash the Failsafe and from that moment everyone and everything is doomed. If the Dreaming Armies awake it is the end of everything."

"How can you be sure we'll defeat her?"

"Oh, my sweet dear friend, I'm not. I have no idea if we will have the strength to win. But I know that without you, we have no hope."

Summer picked up the battle-mace between her thumb and forefinger and placed the heavy weapon back on Barl's upturned hands.

"There is still so much for you to find out about yourself. Both of you know so very little of your true natures. But there is no time for revelations now. Now we fight the greatest evil any of us have ever faced. You cannot go home, Barl, but what you can do is give it a future."

Barl looked down at the battle-mace.

It was wet with the water from the marsh; the breeze moved the droplets across the carved surfaces. He saw the patterns weave away beneath the water, in constant motion. It was a face, wasn't it? His mother? His father?

Or was this merely another trick?

"It's not a trick," Summer answered his thoughts aloud. "You see what you *need* to see. You see what will give you the strength to do what has to be done."

Barl looked up at Summer.

Beyond her in the sky, enormous black wings that seemed to stretch from edge to horizon's edge beat at the air like drums: the dragons returning.

He looked to the battle.

The warriors were no longer fighting themselves. All heads turned towards the mythical beasts. All swords raised, black steel glittering and shimmering with bloody glee. All axes brandished, spears forward, bows cocked with arrows.

Their war cries burst from their blackened, hateful mouths.

Barl was no longer moving towards battle.

The battle had come for him.

CHAPTER 37

Three stood against the multitude.

Summer, impossibly tall, armour slick with blood and gore, swinging her axe through sweeping arcs. Each swing brought more pain and suffering to the onrushing army. She must have decapitated a thousand bodies and more, her face lit with fury and focus. Her axe smoked. Its blade cut the air with a song of defiance.

Shryke launched volley after volley of arrows, the black steel tip streaking through the sky as they flew at dragons. Arrowheads speared them through their flaming mouths. Arrowheads pierced scales and armoured plates, punching deep into their flesh. Arrowheads embedded in glassy eyes. Arrowheads send beast after beast falling away, wings stilled, onto the warriors below.

He kicked out his mailed boots at eternal combatants who got too close. He drove his boots into ribcages, breaking bones. He hammered them through legs, snapping bones. He lashed out, tearing jaws from faces. Every kick sent stalagmite spumes of blood into the air.

They froze for a second, long enough for the fighter behind to be given a sense of the future that awaited them in a grim premonition of their demise.

Another deadly arrow speared a dragon in the eye.

Barl ran tiny between the onrushing bodies, swinging the battle-mace, each one crippling a foe who stood staring up at Summer. He battled bones. Broke the hinges of knees. Thrust up and tore out guts. And hated every single death he wrought. But there was nothing he could do but kill.

How long could they last like this?

How long before they drowned in this endless tide of war?

Summer began wading forward. She was taking the fight to the army. A thousand dead, screaming filled the air. She crushed more skulls, using them like writhing cannonballs. She brought slaughter to the battlefield.

And as death's energies swept towards them Summer began to grow.

Taller.

Wider.

Wilder.

The sheer wild magic of death swelled the Familiar. She *grew*. Huger now. Every footstep she took flattened a dozen warriors beneath her boot, crushing the life of out them.

The boom of her steps punctuated the screams of death.

Beside her, Shryke felt the fire in his muscles as they grew. Every tendon was aflame. But the power pent up inside him needed release. He felt his legs grow ever stronger, his accuracy with the arrowheads unerring. Every arrow flew true.

Where once there had been a black cloud of wings in the sky, lit by dragon fire, now there was a ragged flock, reeling from losses suffered to Shryke's arrows.

The *twang* of this bowstring was constant; there was no gap between firing and reloading. Arrows turned the sky to black steel. The great winged serpents banked and rolled, rose and fell, twisting and squirming in the air as they desperately tried to evade his rain of death, only to crash down in huge gusts of flame, burning soldiers into cinders where they fell.

Barl moved faster.

He didn't have to think, he cut swathes through warriors. His

Shryke saw Galdar, giant now.

Twice as tall as Summer. Feasting on dreaming warriors.

Her chin black and wet with their blood.

Eyes red with mania.

Running towards their position. The ground trembled beneath her feet.

Each ripple and buck through the plates of the world sought to unbalance them, but they kept their feet.

The earth heaved.

Still, the dreaming armies came at the boy and the warrior. More fought Summer's axe and the ferocious Assassins of the Guild.

Shryke wove a shorter blade, and shield for his free arm, and stepped out to face Galdar.

Warriors went down, crushed.

He and the boy held their own, fighting side-by-side.

He was granted a glimpse of the future: once the two giants engaged, there would be less protection for him and the boy, Barl, and however well they fought, supported by their own magic, Assassins and Summer's influence, they would be overrun. It was inevitable. The Dreaming Armies would win by sheer force of numbers alone.

Shryke stared down at the ruined faces of two warriors he had brought down, then called up to Summer. "Should we retreat, Familiar? We cannot win this fight."

WE CANNOT. IF WE LOSE THE DREAMING ARMY WAKES. WE FIGHT.

"And we die!" Shryke yelled.

THEN WE DIE. BUT WE DIE FIGHTING!

"So be it," Shryke said, and launched another blistering attack.

Barl saw the shadow of the girl before he saw her giant frame.

It fell across the heads of the warriors attacking them, turning the sky dark.

Galdar eclipsed the sun.

Warriors behind the ranks of those attacking screamed, trying to flee as Galdar came into view. The black blade of her impossible sword seemed to stretch on forever. Barl's gut lurched as he witnessed her feeding. Even from here, he saw the anguish etched onto her face as she crunched down on the dying warriors. Aguish and revulsion. She wasn't doing this. This slaughter and wholesale death wasn't her doing. The God-Queen had grown her, and used her as a weapon, just like a battle-mace or black sword.

Barl's heart went out to the girl.

But it could only reach so far.

Another wave of attackers came for him, swarming between Summer's feet, ignored by the Familiar as she readied her axe to meet Galdar's attack.

STAND! Summer screamed, raising her axe a mile to meet the black sword as it crashed down...

CHAPTER 39

Their eyes opened.

Shryke lay with Barl and Galdar.

Both were breathing and both were uninjured.

They were back in the square on the Sun-Machine.

The Dreaming Armies of the Plain stood motionless. The Fail-safe had not been woken. The eternal warriors were not about to break away and destroy all life across all of creation.

They had won.

Shryke looked down at the hand that had been joined to Barl's.

It looked no different from how it had on any other day in his life save for the fact that there was now a five-fingered scar on his wrist. It was shaped like the small hand of a child.

Barl held up his arm to Shryke, on the forearm was a five-fingered scar from the hand of a man.

Both their arms looked as though they had healed after burning in a terrible fire.

Shryke held out his hand for Barl.

They shook wrist to wrist.

Shryke no longer felt uncomfortable looking into the eyes of the boy.

Shryke reached down to pick up Galdar.

She wiped her mouth and chin on her sleeve. He didn't need

to be a mind reader to know she was trying to purge herself of that terrible taste. Shryke stilled her hand, "It's gone," he promised her. "And it's been gone for centuries. What happened back there, in that other place, that was a *long* time ago and so very far away. You're free of it now. I promise."

Galdar hugged Shryke then, and he pulled Barl into the hug too.

The three stood there. Silent.

The shadows moved crazily around them and the heart of the clockwork of creation.

As the suns came out again overhead, Lucillian, the navigator Crove and the fat man, Klane, made their way through the ranks of the Dreaming Armies to greet them.

Shryke looked up at the still turning suns and dancing Shadewalls.

He was sure they were safe for now.

But while the Dreaming Armies of the Plains existed there would always be a threat. No, a promise, because it *would* come.

Galdar hugged Shryke tight, not daring to close her eyes in case she was dragged back to that hellish place.

She blinked back the tears, seeing the scars on his neck and the wounds written across his body from battle.

She heard his heart beating through his chest.

As she listened, she seemed able to make out a strange double echo to his heartbeat, one she hadn't noticed before when she had been this close.

She listened, trying to make sense of what that echo meant, only it wasn't from Shryke—it emanated below Shryke's heart. It was Barl's heart. But it was beating in the same rhythm as Shryke's, matching it beat for beat. Just as strong and just as loud. The heartbeats rose in volume as the embrace continued, as if both Barl and Shryke were enveloping Galdar in their love.

Barl hugged the two of them as tight as he could. Tighter. He couldn't let go.

There were no words for the emotions flooding through him. He was free of that place and that battle.

He vowed silently never to return to that hell, knowing even as he did that he was lying to himself. He would have to return. And return again. Summer was there.

The heartbeats of all three, his, Shryke's and Galdar's, seemed to reverberate around his head. It felt good. Right. Like he belonged here.

He watched the Shadewalls, the whirling suns on their fifty thousand-mile stalks, and through the crack in the sky, he could see down once again to *God's Heart*.

It wasn't his home any more, but it would always be part of him, however much time had passed.

And he knew he never wanted this feeling of belonging to leave him.

Lucillian reached them first. She waited patiently for the three to stop hugging, as did Crove, but Klane couldn't help himself. The fat man waddled forward and stabbed a thick index finger into Shryke's back.

Shryke broke from the embrace and stood arm in arm with Galdar and Barl. He looked down on Klane with a raised eyebrow.

"You can give me all the dirty looks you want, barbarian. But I have three very important questions. And you will answer me."

Shryke waited.

"One: Are we safe? Two: How are we getting home, and Three: What the hell happened today?"

Shryke smiled. "In answer: Yes. I don't know and as to the third question..."

"Yes?"

"That's a story for another time..." said Summer, stepping out from behind them.

EPILOGUE

"Forgive me Mother for I have sinned."

"How long has it been since your last confession?"

"Thirty-five thousand, four hundred and ninety-six years," he said. There were days and months in there, but he thought such accuracy was irrelevant.

"This is going to take some time, I assume?"

"I have much to confess," he agreed.

"Start at the beginning."

"Difficult."

"Start where you are comfortable starting then."

"Thank you. I'll start *before* the beginning."

The Mother Superior, who was really the God-Queen, placed her bony fingers around Shryke's heart and squeezed.

Through the window, Shryke could see the Overloop and the cloud bridge. The codespell was cracking open in his head, the true nature of his mission to the Sun-Machine revealed bright and fresh in the middle of his memory.

The God-Queen revelled in the knowledge, her face illuminated with corrupt glee. She saw everything. And yet...

Suddenly the fingers unclasped. The arm slithered from the top of Shryke's head and the God-Queen fell back, tumbling over a stone pew and clattering to the ground.

Something else had uncloaked in Shryke's mind. Something that not even he knew before and certainly was in no position to understand; the ghost-scar from a future battle shimmered on his forearm. Before it disappeared completely, he made out the faint outline of a boy's hand.

The God-Queen gathered herself up, pulling the red habit around her. She backed down the sacristy with a face full of confusion and not a little fear. She didn't make it more than five steps away from the Warrior.

With a crackle of energy, Galdar stepped from the Quantum Aether, and with one almighty swing, smashed the battle-mace through the old woman's bones, felling her. She collapsed in pieces. Broken. The skull rolled away like a child's ball. Cogs and wheels, servos and gears clattered and wheezed amid the bones. There was nothing mortal about the God-Queen. The machinery that kept her alive struggled, failing.

Summer nodded with satisfaction as she herself stepped out of Aether and surveyed the aftermath of the violence.

"Who...who *are* you?" Shryke said, rising, both hands clutching at his temples. The rush of memories clamoured madly through his mind. The force of them made him stumble. He was forced to hold a hand out to stop himself from falling.

Summer went to Shryke. She cast a new and deeper codespell across his memory. Shryke fell unconscious and Summer picked him up as if he weighed nothing. She threw him over her shoulder. "Let's take him down to where he rescues you from the Raiders." Summer said as she brushed past Galdar.

Galdar looked at the pile of mechanical bones. "Have we killed her?"

Summer stopped and looked around, "The God-Queen? No, we still have to go there to get here. It's the way of things. But the God-Queen won't remember who Shryke or Barl are, or rather that they are one and the same, and that's the important thing. That's the secret that must never be told."

Galdar followed Summer from the Sacristy as the Overloop above the Shrine turned and sparkled in swathes of golden light cast the Sun-Machine high above, a glittering chain, a beautiful illuminated helix…

The story continues in The Science of Magic.

CPSIA information can be obtained
at www.ICGtesting.com
Printed in the USA
BVHW031409110619
550711BV00001B/42/P

9 781949 890327